BURNING
EDEN

BURNING EDEN

An Eden County Mystery

SARAH BEWLEY

LEVEL
BEST BOOKS

For Pat Payne — The love of my life.

Praise for Burning Eden

"In *Burning Eden*, Sarah Bewley creates a wonderful cast of characters, skillfully depicting life—and crime—in small-town Florida. *Burning Eden* is one hot debut!"—Alan Orloff, Anthony, Agatha, and two-time Thriller Award-winning author

"We tend to associate the Sunshine State with the glitz of Miami and the whirlwind of colorful theme parks that is Orlando. But *Burning Eden*, Sarah Bewley's strong debut, is a gritty procedural set in the drought—and brushfire-stricken swamps of northern Florida. Complex, sympathetic characters and a well-plotted mystery make for a compelling introduction to this author. Just don't start it until you have plenty of time to read. It's hard to put down."—Loretta Ross, author of the Auction Block Mysteries

"From its first descriptions of the burning swamps of north Florida to its slam-bang ending, I couldn't put down Sarah Bewley's debut, *Burning Eden*. Part Southern Gothic, part contemporary Florida man, it's filled with vivid characters and richly described settings. Sure to be on my Best of 2023 list."—Neil S. Plakcy, author of the Angus Green FBI thrillers

Chapter One

'EDEN IS BURNING! Is this the "fire next time?"' Just what Jim needed. Sheila Ward, talking about the apocalypse in the newspaper. The goddamn swamp was on fire, yes. Wildfires burned out of control all over the state, yes. But it was Florida, and the rest of the world seemed to be doing fine. The problem was, Eden County was 804 square miles of scrub and swamp. The drought had dried up even the muck. The fires drove the gators and the snakes out to look for water. The smoke from the burning peat kept the county under a grey haze, blocking the sun and filling everyone's lungs.

Jim hacked and spit out the stink of burning dirt. The Seminoles had called this area Cahoketa, which meant "gobbling up." Then some delusional white man had come along and renamed it Eden. Jim had to admit that there were some damn dumb white men among the ancestors of people in Eden.

Jim walked his usual running route, carefully keeping to the shoulder. Instead of morning fog, the smoke hid him from oncoming cars. It hugged the ground and hung in the tree canopy like Spanish moss gone out of control.

His lungs burned not from exertion but from the pollution in the air. He finally gave up, turned around, and headed back to his house. Michael would be getting up soon anyway, and if he was lucky, he might get breakfast with his son before he disappeared for the day.

When Jim opened the back door, he could hear the shower running. Michael was up. Jim went to the kitchen sink and turned on the cold water for a moment. He could hear the shout all the way into the kitchen, but at least it would get the kid out of the shower before all the hot water was used up.

He heard the shower cut off, the bathroom door slam open, and a moment later, a dripping Michael stood at the door to the hall.

"I wasn't in there that long, Dad!"

"Want some breakfast?"

He watched the sixteen-year-old wrestle with his desire to remain angry and the offer of someone making him a full meal. Michael's stomach won. "Yeah."

"Great. I'll grab a quick shower, and by then, you should be dressed and have that hair of yours done. Bacon and eggs?"

"Scrambled. None of that brown crusty stuff."

Michael turned on his heel and headed back down the hall. Jim could see the wet footprints that tracked from the bathroom to the kitchen door and then back to Michael's bedroom. He heard the blow dryer turn on.

He had time to take a leisurely shower. Michael took forever with his hair, which was a mystery to Jim as great as any in the universe. He could not figure out how it took someone so long to create a bad case of bedhead, much less why anyone would do it on purpose.

Jim had showered, shaved, dressed, and was in the kitchen scrambling eggs by the time the blow dryer turned off for the last time. Michael walked into the kitchen and dropped heavily into a chair at the table.

"What's on your agenda for the day?" Jim asked.

Michael shrugged. "Biology quiz, baseball practice after school."

Jim nodded. He'd played football and baseball at the same high school, and it had led to a free ride to college on a football scholarship. Michael had a shot at the same thing in baseball if he kept his grades up.

He spooned scrambled eggs, with "no crusty brown stuff," onto Michael's plate, and the phone rang. He grabbed the receiver off the wall and held it between his shoulder and ear as he finished dishing out breakfast to himself.

"Sheriff Sheppard," he said.

"Sheriff, this is Junior. We got a call on a missing preacher, and Dee and Waylon are out on an accident on 27, and Bobby's picking bales off the beach again, so I got no one to send to talk to the wife."

Junior's voice was always an oddly high whine, but he was in full squeak mode this morning. "Who is it?" asked Jim.

"Donald Hatcher. He's the preacher over at the Holy Fire of God Pentecostal church on Lee Road."

Lee Road was in the opposite direction of the Sheriff's station and his office, but if he took the call himself, it would save time and manpower. "All right. Give me the address. I'll take it. How long's he been missing?"

"Disappeared sometime during the night. Naked."

"Fine. I'll head out there as soon as I can." Michael reached out to take more of the bacon, and Jim snapped his fingers. Michael grinned and picked up a piece of toast instead.

"Yes, sir."

Jim made a quick note of the names and the address. It wouldn't be hard to find. Warren was a town of 5,000 and the largest incorporated part of Eden County. There were a handful of churches inside the city limits, and the Holy Fire of God was one that he was vaguely familiar with. The preacher before Hatcher had gotten it into his head to become a snake handler and ended up nearly killing himself with a water moccasin during a service.

The new minister had been there a couple of years and seemed to be generally a pretty decent guy. He'd had his group focusing on hosting some AA meetings and holding food drives. Jim had appreciated the change.

"So, what's on your agenda for today?" asked Michael around a mouthful of toast.

Jim smiled. Michael always treated his career formally. He remembered doing the same with his father. "A missing preacher."

"Anyone I know?"

"Hatcher from Holy Fire."

"Don't know him." Michael jumped up, put his plate in the sink, and drank his orange juice as he stood there. He put the glass in the sink and turned to Jim. "How's the smoke?"

"Bad. Coach making you run drills in this?"

Michael shook his head. "He's had us in the gym. We're playing over in

Bradford County Friday, but Coach says they may cancel if the fires are bad over that way."

"I'd rather you did cancel. I hate to think of the bus traveling at night with this kind of visibility."

"You could always give us a police escort?"

Jim snorted. "Yeah, right. That's going to happen."

Michael laughed and headed back to the bathroom.

Jim finished his breakfast quickly, then poured his coffee into a travel mug. Michael headed out the front door at the same time he did.

"I'll see you tonight," Michael said. He got into his ancient Datsun and drove toward the high school.

Jim opened the door to his department-issued sedan. It creaked, and the suspension groaned when he got in. The car was nearly ten years old, and with the rough roads he covered in the county, he was surprised it hadn't collapsed in on itself. There simply wasn't money in the budget for many new vehicles, and he was not the one out chasing speeders and drunks, so he made do with the car he'd been issued when he'd first been elected. At least he had a car. His Great-Grandfather had to use a horse when he was Sheriff in Eden County.

Chapter Two

Ryan Edwards stood in the doorway to his motel room. He'd thought he would go out for a short run before he headed in to his first day at Doc's office. The thickness of the smoke was giving him second thoughts. He liked keeping his lungs intact. Since the attack two years ago, he'd taken a new approach to being healthy. He wanted to be strong. Hacking up a lung would not help.

He'd have to find out if there was a gym in the area. He needed weights, and maybe there would be a treadmill.

The morning light was dim through the grey haze, and the smell permeated everything. Though he'd showered last night and put on clean clothes this morning, he'd smelled smoke in his t-shirt as he'd pulled it over his head.

Ryan turned back to his room. When he stepped in Bonehead didn't even raise his head. The dog's disinterest in life and Ryan radiated outward like a wave of leaden pain. Danielle would have known what to do. But if Danielle were still alive, he and Bonehead wouldn't be here.

"I'm going to McDonalds. Want me to bring you something?"

The dog rolled his eyes toward Ryan and snorted.

"How about I take you for a walk after breakfast?"

Bonehead closed his eyes and remained silent and unmoving.

Ryan picked up his wallet and left the room. If Danielle said the word walk the dog would go crazy leaping and bounding around.

With Ryan, he allowed himself to be leashed and taken out.

They were uneasy companions, left behind with no choice but to co-exist and with little or no understanding of each other. Ryan's work had kept him away from the dog a lot when Danielle was alive. Once she was gone, they had both seemed adrift. But now that Ryan was well enough to work again, even though it was in a different world than the high-intensity of the George Washington ER, he'd committed himself to trying to make a home for them both.

So far, Bonehead had not shown any enthusiasm for the project.

"Suck it up, dog," Ryan said as he headed outside. "We're in this together."

Mcdonald's looked like a beacon of normalcy to Ryan. Everything else about the town, the surrounding countryside, and even the state left him feeling like he walked in a weird dream. The one familiar thing had been lots of black faces, but they spoke a different language than he did. The white faces weren't much better.

The young woman at the counter offered a cheery, "Morning! What'll you have?"

As an intern, Ryan had practically lived on McDonald's. Not because he had to, but because other interns did, and someone always made a McDonald's run.

"Good morning. I'll have two egg McMuffins, one sausage McMuffin, two hash browns, and the biggest coffee you can make me."

"Darryl! Get off your butt and make this man his breakfast!" the woman yelled over her shoulder. "Anything else?"

"That will do it."

She rang us his total, and he handed over his cash. "You're new in town. I seen you coming from over at the Bambi."

"I just moved here."

"Why the hell you do something like that? Where you from?"

"Connecticut."

She gave him a thoughtful look. "Darryl! Where the hell's Connecticut?"

"Northeast somewheres," yelled a male voice from behind the machines.

"East of New York," Ryan answered.

"Oh! That's way up there." The McMuffins slid down to a spot under the heat lamps. The young woman quickly bagged his breakfast and filled his

6

large coffee. "So, what are you doing here?"

"I'm Doctor Markham's new partner. I'm Ryan Edwards."

Her eyes widened. "Darryl! He's the new doc! Get your butt out here!"

She looked at Ryan, "Don't go nowhere." A moment later, a tall, thin white man came through the door from the back. He had a towel wrapped around one hand. "Darryl managed to burn himself bad this morning, the dumbshit. Can you look at it?"

Ryan nodded. "Sure."

Darryl came to the counter, and Ryan carefully unwrapped the towel. Underneath he could see the nasty blisters on the back of the man's hand. The angry red skin was already beginning to peel. "Did you run this under cold water?"

Darryl nodded. "Did that first thing. Hurt so bad the cold water felt good."

"Do you have a ... kit?"

The woman ran into the back and came back with a standard first aid box. "We got this."

Ryan opened it and found antibiotic cream. "I need gloves to do this," he said. He was quickly handed plastic food-handling gloves. They would do. He spread the antibiotic cream across the skin then wrapped it loosely in gauze. "You keep this covered while you're working. I can look at it again this evening if you want." Having worked in DC and seen more than his share of working poor, he had a feeling that Darryl didn't have insurance.

Darryl nodded, "I get off before Doc's closes. I could come in, if it's not going to be too much money."

"Don't worry about money. You can't let this go. I'll take care of it, and we'll work it out."

The woman elbowed Darryl. "He's going to be as big a pushover as Doc."

"Doc's a pushover?"

"Oh yeah, half the town owes him."

Once Darryl's hand was wrapped, Ryan picked up his breakfast. "Nice to meet you both, Darryl, and ..."

The young woman laughed, "Dorrie Mae."

"Dorrie Mae."

Ryan made his way back to the room, where he found Bonehead still lying on the bed. "I brought you something," Ryan said. He pulled out the sausage biscuit and unwrapped it. The dog raised his head and sniffed. "Yeah, I know. She wouldn't approve. But it's just you and me now, and I think an occasional treat is okay. Don't you?"

The big dog's head came up, and he looked at Ryan directly. He sniffed the biscuit again, and then he leaned forward and delicately took it from Ryan's hand. It was gone in two bites.

"I don't suppose that earns me any brownie points with you, does it?"

The dog eyed his McMuffins.

Ryan shook his head and unwrapped one, and split it in half. "God, I'm such a sucker."

The dog was not quite as delicate this time. After he'd swallowed, he burped.

"You have no manners, Bonehead." He ate the other half of the McMuffin, then he let out a loud belch. The dog flinched. Ryan laughed. Danielle would have been horrified by both of them. But Danielle wasn't here anymore, and it was just the guys. Belching was allowed.

Ryan reached over and ran his hand over the dog's big head, tugging on each ear for a moment. He'd seen Danielle do it hundreds of times. He knew Bonehead liked it.

The dog sighed.

Chapter Three

The drive to the preacher's home felt wrong. It was too quiet for this time of morning. Jim knew a lot of people were keeping off the roads as much as they could. Fortunately, in Eden, they really hadn't had many homes threatened—yet. The big problem here was the smoke. It was flat killing livestock.

In Central Florida they'd lost entire neighborhoods to the fires, and in Alachua County, they'd had to evacuate one of the small towns. But so far, the worst of it was all to the east of Eden County.

Jim prayed they would get some rain before the end of the month when the summer heat really set in. If the smoke stayed heavy like this, they were going to start losing the elderly and children, and he didn't know what the hell he could do about it.

Jim hadn't gotten out of his car before Mrs. Hatcher was out of the front door and headed for him.

"Did you find him?" she asked.

She was a small woman, thin and plain, and her eyes were red and swollen from crying.

"I'm sorry, Mrs. Hatcher, we haven't found your husband. I'm here to get more information."

She seemed to sway for a moment. Jim caught her by her arm and held her steady. "Why don't we go inside?"

She nodded, and they went silently into the house together. She automatically headed straight for the kitchen, and Jim followed. She was clearly distressed enough that he didn't want to interrupt whatever behavior made her feel normal. She sat at the table, and her hands circled around a cup of coffee.

Jim soundlessly pulled a chair out from the small table and sat down across from her. "Mrs. Hatcher?"

She looked at him and appeared surprised that he sat across from her. "Yes?"

"When did you discover your husband missing?"

"When I got up. He wasn't in the bed. I thought he'd be in here, but he wasn't. He wasn't anywhere."

"Do you know when he might have disappeared? Approximately?"

"We went to bed at eleven. We always go to bed at eleven. I got up at six, like always, and he was gone."

"So sometime between eleven last night and six this morning?"

"No, later. I was awake for a while. I have trouble getting to sleep sometimes. I remember looking at the clock around 12:15, but not after that."

"Did he take anything with him?"

"Like what?"

"Did he pack something?"

"Didn't that deputy tell you? He was naked. He didn't take anything. Not even his Bible. He never goes anywhere without taking his Bible. But it's on the bedside table. Just where he put it last night."

"Are you sure he didn't take anything? Maybe he got up and dressed...."

"I know he wasn't dressed! His clothes are all here!"

She got up from the table quickly and went into the hallway. Jim followed her. In the bedroom, she threw open the closet door, and there hung five white shirts, one pair of black pants over a hanger, and one pair of shoes on the floor of the closet. She opened a hamper that stood next to the bed, pulling out a white shirt and a pair of khaki pants. "This is everything. He has six white shirts, two pairs of pants, one pair of shoes. It's all here!"

Her voice broke, and she began to cry. Jim took the hamper top out of her hands and led her back to the kitchen. "I believe you."

She snuffled and went to the kitchen counter, where she grabbed a napkin

10

and blew her nose.

"Did you hear anything? Or has someone contacted Reverend Hatcher recently, who was new to the church?"

She shook her head.

"Is there someone who can come stay with you? I don't want you to be alone right now."

She shrugged, and Jim tried to think who might know Hatcher's congregation. He got her to sit, and her hands went back to grasping her coffee cup as though it was the one thing that would save her. "I'll be back in just a minute, Mrs. Hatcher."

Jim stepped out the back door and looked into the woods that bordered the home to the north. He radioed Junior. "Can you try to raise Elsie Sanborne for me, Junior? I need to find someone to come stay with the preacher's wife."

"Sure can, Sheriff. Need anything else?"

"Yeah, call over to the Florida Department of Law Enforcement and see when they can send us a tech. This is looking like it might be something serious."

"Sure thing, Sheriff."

Jim looked around the yard and stood near the woods, looking at the house. There was a light fixture next to the back door, but no bulb in it. He walked back to the house and saw that there was glass on the ground and the base of a bulb screwed into the socket.

He looked closely at the back door, but couldn't see any sign it'd been forced. Of course, people in Warren didn't lock their doors half the time. Hell, he didn't lock his door.

He walked back to the woods and saw that there were boot prints in the loose dirt. He carefully followed them, and they came out on the other side of the narrow- wooded area onto a lime-rock road. There was an oil slick on the lime rock that was still wet.

He stopped and turned around. He could just make out the house through the trees. It wouldn't be hard at all to walk up to the back of the house. If the light had been broken, no one would be able to see whoever might take it into their head to check out the preacher's home.

"Huh."

"Sheriff?"

Jim clicked on his radio, "Yeah, Junior."

"Miss Elsie's going to come right over to the Hatcher's place. And there's a tech should be at the house within the next hour. You going to stay there?"

"Yeah, Junior. Anyone needs me, just give a yell."

"Yes, sir, Sheriff."

* * *

Bud Peterson got out of his van carrying his eternal travel mug of sweet iced tea. The ice rattled against the plastic as he walked. He stopped and took a long drink from his mug, sighed, and continued until he was in front of Jim.

"Hey, Jimbo. How you holding up?" Bud rasped. He always sounded like his throat was raw, but today he sounded even worse.

"I'm fine. You sound like hell."

"Fucking smoke," Bud said. He took another drink from his tea. "I'm up to almost two gallons a day of tea. I piss every fifteen minutes. It's starting to really tick me off."

Jim grinned.

"So, what we got here?"

"I'm not sure. I've got a missing preacher, and I don't think he went on his own."

Bud nodded. "Point of entry?"

"Back door. There's boot prints go from there out to a lime rock road that runs behind the houses. Broken porch light which the wife says it was fine last night when they went to bed. Front light is good."

"She going to have a conniption if I start dusting?"

Jim shook his head. "She wants him found."

Bud turned around to the tech carrying their gear up from the back of the van. "Dust all the doors, and keep your eyes open for any kind of foot prints. Got some glass out back needs to be picked up, and look around for what mighta smashed it."

The kid nodded his head and hurried inside.

"I'll give her a good going over. Let you know what I find."

"Thanks, Bud."

Jim watched the man saunter inside. He turned to look up the road. What he needed was for Elsie Sanborne to show up. Mrs. Hatcher was holding it together, but he'd feel better leaving once he knew someone was with her. Elsie made it her personal mission to take care of anyone who didn't have anyone. Probably because she didn't have anyone herself.

When Jim's dad had been Sheriff, Elsie's husband had been a deputy. They'd been newlyweds, and two months in, Danny Sanborne had pulled over a drunk driver on 27 and they'd both been killed by an 86-year-old tourist from Ohio who'd fallen asleep at the wheel. The tourist's wife had been killed as well, but the old man had been uninjured.

Elsie had, from that point on, become the unofficial official caregiver to all victims when the Sheriff's department needed her.

A few minutes later Jim spotted her car coming down the road. She was hard to miss. She drove a 1971 Plymouth Duster. It had been Danny's pride and joy, and Elsie had spent a fortune keeping it in pristine condition over the years. She'd even kept the original orange paint in perfect condition.

She pulled up along the street so as to not block either Jim or the FDLE van from getting out. She got out of the car and stormed up the drive.

"What we got, Jim?" she asked anxiously. She was a tall woman, and lean, and her graying hair stayed pulled back in a ponytail at all times.

"Preacher Hatcher's missing. His wife's pretty scared."

"She got no people?"

"No. Least not around here."

Elsie nodded. "I'll take care of her." Elsie headed for the house at a fast clip.

"Elsie?"

She stopped and turned around.

"I'm heading into the office. Bud Peterson's in there."

13

Elsie nodded again. "I'll keep her out of his way." She hustled inside and Jim headed for his car. The smell of burning was heavy in the air and he felt a headache coming on.

The drive to his office was short. There was little traffic on the road. He had barely gotten into the building before Junior was telling him he had a call. The big man's dark face creased with concern as he told Jim that Doc Markham was on the line for him about Michael.

"Hell's bells," Jim said. "I'll take it in my office, Junior."

He closed the door and grabbed up the handset and heard the gruff wheeze of Doc Markham.

"Afore you go and get yourself in a swivet, Michael's fine," Doc said, "but he's got a hell of a goose egg on his noggin and he's going to be hot about what I had to do to his hair."

"What?"

"Some damn thing fell on his head at the high school. So he's here in my office. Took about six stitches to close it up, and he's got a concussion. Other than that, he's good."

Jim felt his heartbeat race. "Michael's hurt?"

"Hell, Jim, catch up. Yeah. Got a knot on his head and a pretty good gash, but he's just got a mild concussion. Headache more than anything else. You want to come see him afore I send him home?"

"I'll be right there."

Jim did manage to remember to tell Junior where he was going as he left, but beyond that, he didn't even remember the walk to the doctor's office. He stopped at the desk and before he could say anything, Claire said, "Doc is with him in exam room three. Do you need a drink of water? You look pale, Sheriff."

Jim shook his head and let Claire lead him down the hall to the exam room. She opened the door and Jim stepped in. Doc Markham sat in a chair next to Michael who held an ice pack against the top of his head.

"What the hell happened?" Jim asked softly, in deference to the headache he knew Michael must have.

Michael opened one eye. "Jason and Squirt knocked a bookshelf off the

14

wall onto my head."

"How did they do that?"

Michael shrugged ineffectually, the paper from the examination table crinkling underneath him. "Being dumbshits."

"As usual," said Jim. Jason and Squirt, the quarterback and team manager respectively, didn't have one good brain between them on a particularly bright day. "Is he going to be all right?"

Doc Markham laughed. "Yeah, he'll be fine. He's got that Sheppard thick skull. We did an x-ray. Nothing's broken."

A man taller than Jim stepped into the doorway. Jim didn't know him and stepped back to keep his distance.

"Oh, sorry, I just wanted to let Dr. Markham know I took care of Mrs. Williams," the man said.

"How's her sugar?" Doc asked.

"It was good. She's lost weight since her last visit."

"Good. Glad to hear it. Let me introduce you to the Sheriff of Eden County. This is Jim Sheppard. Jim, this is Ryan Edwards. He's my new partner."

Jim held out his hand. He guessed the man to be in his mid-thirties. He was easily six four and muscular in the way of a thin man who worked out a lot. His hair rivaled Michael's for terminal bed head, and a scar peeked out of his hairline on the left side.

"Nice to meet you, Dr. Edwards."

"Ryan. No sense in being …." he started and paused.

"Yeah, no sense in being formal," said Doc. "Call him Jim. Everyone does, even the people he arrests."

Ryan looked relieved and shook Jim's hand. "It's good to meet you."

"I didn't know Doc was taking on a partner."

Doc laughed. "It's all part of my master plan. I'm going to retire one of these days, and I figured if I roped some young'un into a partnership, I was more likely to be able to actually do it without being bugged to death by everyone in the county."

Ryan grinned. Apparently he was aware of the doc's master plan and didn't have any issues with it.

"I'd better get this guy home. Do I need someone to stay with him?" Jim asked.

"Nah. Just give him a call every couple of hours and make sure he can answer the phone. Long as he wakes up and is coherent, it's fine," said Doc.

Michael groaned and sat up. "Got any sunglasses, Dad?" he asked.

"Not enough sun visible out there to worry about," said Jim.

Doc handed Michael the ice pack. "Hey, Jim, your dad's apartment still empty?"

Jim felt surprised. "Yeah...," he said cautiously.

Doc nodded at Ryan. "He's going to need a place to live at least for a few months to give him time to look at houses and find something he wants. You willing to rent it out on a month to month?"

Jim nodded, relieved. "Sure." Ryan Edwards was better than Jim expected. Doc had a soft spot for people, and Jim always braced for the worst when Doc asked a question.

"How 'bout I send Ryan by this evening? He's staying over to the Bambi and Lord knows, he isn't going to get a decent night's sleep there."

Jim smiled. The Bambi was one of two motels in the county, the other one being quite a ways east of town. The Bambi housed migrant workers, the occasional drug dealer, and had one room that everyone knew was rented out on an hourly basis, and not to pros. It was kept plenty busy with the traffic of locals who were getting a little on the side. "We'll see you this evening, then, Ryan."

Ryan nodded. "Thanks. I'll ... see you then."

Jim and Michael walked out to the car. Michael blinked and winced at even the filtered sunlight.

"If I take you home, you going to be okay?" Jim asked.

"All I want to do is lie down in the dark and not move."

They walked down the block to the Sheriff's office and Michael eased his way into the car, trying to not jar his head any more than necessary. Jim reached over and patted his leg gently. "You'll be fine. After all, you've got the thick Sheppard skull."

"Yeah, right," muttered Michael. He closed his eyes and leaned his head back against the seat.

Jim pulled out and headed for the house.

Chapter Four

Once Jim made sure Michael had settled into his own bed, he headed back to the office. He needed to get to the members of Hatcher's congregation and do some interviewing, but he also needed to check into his office and make sure that everything was copacetic there before he did that.

The problem in Eden County was there was never enough of anything to do all that needed to be done. He didn't have enough manpower, or equipment, or expertise. Junior handled the office well, and fortunately, the county shared 911 dispatch services with local state law enforcement.

With the fires, there had been a lot of accidents on the main highway that went north/south through the county, and it played hell with his ability to cover other things.

He could be damn sure that the locals were taking advantage of the situation. The coke machine at the Chevron station had been broken into, and there'd been a series of car burglaries in one of the nicer neighborhoods. Right now, all he could do about it was take reports and try to find time for someone to follow up.

Deputy Bobby Dale had gotten back to the office. Two bales of marijuana sat on the floor next to his desk, and the thin, blond man was squinting at his computer screen, trying to write up his report.

"Hey, Jim," Bobby said. "I covered the whole beachfront but only found two bales."

"Can you get them over to the state police today?"

"No problem. Just filling out an evidence form so I can have them sign for the transfer."

"Thanks. After you get that done, how about relieving Dee out on 27. I want her to follow up on that peeping tom report."

"You got it."

Junior handed Jim a handful of telephone messages. "I called Holy Fire and Hatcher's secretary is going to meet you at the church office at noon."

Jim nodded. "Thanks. Good work." He flipped through the messages. A retired Air Force Colonel who'd had his Jeep broken into had called three times. Jim dropped the notes on his desk. The last two messages were from one of the County Commissioners. Jim didn't even want to think about returning that call. The woman called him at least six times a week, wanting him to do something for one of her friends. It could be anything from tearing up a ticket to having someone come talk to a particularly difficult child. Those got tossed on his desk, too.

At least today, he had a good reason to not return calls. A missing person took priority, and not even retired Colonels or County Commissioners could argue about that. Jim found his camera and headed out to the church. He'd check Hatcher's office, and hopefully, the preacher's secretary would turn out to be one of those women who knew everything that was going on.

* * *

As it turned out, the secretary was the kind of woman who knew everything that went on in the church. She also kept impeccable records. The problem was that none of it helped answer any of the questions Jim had.

The pressboard desk had two drawers, neither of which had jack in them. He'd found a budget file, a record of the offering the church was receiving week to week, a list of sick members to be prayed for, and twenty-two neatly printed sermons. Hatcher's calendar showed meetings with a couple of church committees, visits to members in the hospital, and a handful of counseling sessions with couples in the church.

The church secretary kept a log of phone calls, and they had caller ID on the telephone, so he'd pulled off all the numbers that had called in the past couple of weeks. There was little to be had beyond that.

Walking to his car from the church office he heard her voice before he saw her.

"Sheriff?"

Jim turned and found himself face-to-face with Sheila Ward of the Eden Morning Star. Oh, God help me, he thought, groaning internally. "Yeah?"

"I heard about Reverend Hatcher. What can you tell me?"

"That he's missing?" Jim smiled.

"Come on, Sheriff."

"Seriously, Sheila, I don't have anything at the moment. Donald Hatcher is missing. We know he disappeared sometime during the night. That's it."

Sheila had her sunglasses pushed up on top of her head, making her short dark hair spike up like the collar of a ruffled lizard. Her pinched face and hunched posture didn't do anything to erase the image from Jim's mind. "Well, can I print that he's missing?"

"Yes, you can."

Sheila looked at him suspiciously, the furrow between her thick, dark eyebrows deepening. "What do you mean by that?"

Jim's head dropped back slightly, and he swore silently. "Sheila, you asked me if you could print that he's missing. I said yes. That's all it means. Donald Hatcher is missing."

"Can I talk to the wife?"

"Give her a break, Sheila. She's pretty upset." Jim was also afraid that she might mention that, apparently, the good Reverend was naked when he disappeared. God only knew what kind of mileage Sheila would get out of that piece of information. "You know, Sheila, two bales of marijuana washed up on the beach this morning."

"This is Florida. Big fucking deal." Sheila pulled her glasses back down on her face and turned to leave.

"Sheila, if you come across anything or someone contacts you, you will let me know, right?"

She shrugged as she walked back to her car. Jim wanted to slap the back of her head as she left. That woman made his butt work buttonholes.

Jim got into his car just as Junior called him on the radio.

"Sheriff, Miss Elsie just called and said you need to get over to the Hatcher's place right away."

"Any reason given?"

"I could hear Bud in the background telling her to tell me to light a fire under your ass to get you there pronto."

"I'm on my way."

He'd barely pulled up to the house when Bud came out of the house and waved him to come in. "We got something!"

Inside the house Elsie, Bud, and Mrs. Hatcher stood in the living room. They pointed to a large family-style Bible that lay on a stand against one wall.

Jim walked up to it and saw a slip of paper that had been inserted between two pages. What appeared to be a drop of blood was smeared across a verse in Ezekiel.

"Is that blood?" he asked Bud.

"Sure as hell is," replied Bud. "Read it."

"Behold, all souls are Mine; as the soul of the father, so also the soul of the son is Mine; the soul that sinneth, it shall die."

Jim looked at Mrs. Hatcher, "Does this mean anything to you?"

She shook her head. "No. And Don would never do that to a Bible. That Bible belonged to his mother. It's got all his family listed in it, going way back past his Great-Great Granddaddy."

Bud nodded to Elsie, who took Mrs. Hatcher's arm and gently led her back into the kitchen. "I'd lay odds that it's the preacher's blood. I'll need to take it to the lab, but I'm betting we find diddly, just like we have in the house. Other than the tire treads back in the woods, we're dealing with a ghost here. Well, a ghost with size 12 feet, but still a ghost."

"Nothing?"

"Nothing."

Jim took a deep breath. "You think FDLE will help?"

"I think I'm about as far as they'll go right now."

Jim walked into the kitchen. "Mrs. Hatcher, I think it would be better for you to stay somewhere else for a while. It might not be safe here."

Elsie took the woman's hand. "She can come stay with me. Come on, let's get you a bag packed."

The two women left the room, and Bud came in. He put one hand on Jim's shoulder. "You go on. I'll close up the place and seal it when I leave. I'll call you soon as I have something you can work with."

Jim shook his head. "I don't even know where to start with this, Bud."

Bud squeezed his shoulder and then went back to his work.

Chapter Five

Ryan leaned against the wall in an examination room as Doc Markham worked with a patient. The older woman was substantially overweight, her breathing labored as she simply moved from the chair to the table.

"Edna, I've told you to stop smoking. I bet your blood pressure's up around one-sixty at least," Doc's tone was patient, in spite of his words to the contrary.

"It ain't the smoking, Doc. It's that damn boy. The smoking calms me down."

"Bullshit." Doc efficiently strapped the blood pressure cuff to her right arm and pumped it up. "One-sixty-five over ninety-eight. Edna, you're going to die if you don't stop that damn smoking and get your blood pressure down."

"Doc, the smoking's the only thing keeping me from killing the boy." Edna's heavy jowls trembled, and her eyes appeared to tear up.

"Ah…hell, Edna." Doc leaned back and looked at the woman for a moment. "How much are you smoking?"

"Pack a day, most times."

Doc nodded. "Okay. I'm going to increase your medication. Put you up five more milligrams. But I want you down to less than a pack a day. You don't smoke unless you're fixing to kill that son of yours. Got me?"

Edna nodded. "Promise, Doc. You're a good man. If I have to quit the cigarettes, I'm going to kill him for sure."

Doc nodded and patted her knee absently. "Edna, this is my new partner, Ryan Edwards. Dr. Edwards, this is Edna Bass. She and her son run a bar just outside of town."

"Nice to meet you, Ms. Bass."

Edna eyed him seriously, cocking her head to one side, narrowing her eyes. "Where you from?"

"Originally? Connecticut."

"Huh."

Doc grinned. "Yep. Going to have a Yankee doc here. Think you can stand it, Edna?"

"He any good?"

Ryan smiled. He could tell Edna's question was dead serious.

"He's real good. You don't think I'd let just anyone come in here and treat my patients, do you?"

Edna shook her head, setting the rolls of fat shaking that began at her chin and didn't stop until the juncture of her legs. "No. You wouldn't. You're a good man, Doc."

Markham handed her the prescription and motioned for Ryan to leave the room. Ryan heard Doc speaking to her softly, then he came out, closing the door behind him. "It'll take her a minute to get off the table and get out of there."

Ryan nodded and followed Markham down the hall to his office. "I... there's no way she'd...lose weight or change...diet."

Doc laughed. "What Edna needs is to quit worrying about that son of hers. That'd do more for her than losing a hundred pounds."

They stepped into the office, and Ryan closed the door behind him. Doc dropped heavily into the chair at his desk. "I am getting too old to do this all day."

"I think I'm starting to get a feel for how you do things."

Doc raised an eyebrow. "You are, huh?"

Ryan nodded. He sat in the chair in front of Markham's desk. "Like with Edna Bass. There's a limit as to what you can ....do with her. She'll make small steps, but probably doesn't even hold to those. So you do what you can to keep her healthy. But you don't make her... unhappy by demanding...," Ryan paused.

24

"I don't demand change."

"Yeah."

"That's pretty much it. Some patients will change. You've got to do what you can with each individual. Edna's son is going to get himself shot long before Edna ever dies. I've had to patch him together a half dozen times in the past year alone. He runs the bar, and he has a bad habit of pissing off mean drunks. Probably because he's one, too."

"You think after he's….gone, she'll do better?"

Doc shrugged. "I doubt it. But her stress level will go down." He finished making a note in Edna's file and tossed it into the box on the corner of his desk. "So, what do you think? Really."

Ryan scrubbed one hand through his thick hair. "I… it's just a matter of them getting…." The pause lasted a moment. "Getting…to know me."

"You're right about that. And they'll like you fine, once they do get to know you. Well, I'm heading over to Gainesville to see some patients I've got in the hospital. Why don't you check out Sheppard's apartment? See about getting yourself out of that motel."

Ryan realized he was still touching the scar on his forehead. He self-consciously brought his hand to his lap. "Sheppard and his son seem…. " Ryan stopped and took a deep breath. "Sorry."

"Relax. Take your time. You're still tired from the trip." Doc leaned back in his chair and propped one foot up on the trash can next to his desk. "You're right. Jim and Michael are good people." Markham wrote a phone number onto a Post-it and handed it to Ryan. "This is the number at the house. Claire's got your cell phone number in case there's an emergency. Shouldn't be. People know I go to the hospital every week about this time, so they get more careful."

Doc stood up and came around the desk. He stopped next to Ryan and laid a hand on his shoulder. "You're going to do good here, Ryan. Once everyone gets to know you, it'll be fine. Just take it easy. I'm not going anywhere for a while."

Ryan nodded. "Thanks."

Ryan looked at the number in his hand. He needed to plan what he wanted to say. He hated starting a sentence and not being able to find the word he needed. He didn't think he'd ever get used to this. He'd always been a smart-ass. Glib. Quick to comment. Well. That was then, as they say. He took a piece of scrap paper and wrote out several sentences, taking his time, thinking through different possible scenarios. Then he took a deep breath and reached for the phone.

The voice that answered the call was deep, but sounded sleepy. Ryan decided it must be Michael Sheppard. "Hi, Michael. This is Ryan Edwards. Is your dad there?"

There was a long silence on the other end of the line. Too long, Ryan thought. "Ah...we met at Dr. Markham's office? I'm his...." The word disappeared. Crap. Ryan hadn't expected to have to explain who he was.

"Oh! The new doctor! Sorry. I'm kinda fuzzy," Michael's voice warmed considerably on the other end of the line.

Ryan took a deep breath.

"Dad's not here. Did you want to come by and see the apartment?"

"If you feel... okay." Ryan gritted his teeth. He sounded like a damn moron.

"Sure. I'm up, and Dad's called me like every twenty seconds all afternoon. Might as well do something useful." Michael laughed. "Do you know how to get here?"

"Ah...no. No, I don't." Ryan made quick notes as Michael gave him directions. Warren was small enough that Ryan didn't think it would be possible to get too lost, but then, what the hell did he know about driving in a town this small? Not a damn thing. So he wrote the directions down carefully. He set up to be at the house in thirty minutes. That would give him time to go by the motel and pick up Bonehead. The dog would need to approve of the space they were going to live in. One of the things he'd learned in the past two years was that Bonehead was damn picky about where he made his home. He'd been unhappy since they'd left the apartment off DuPont Circle, and an unhappy big dog was a major pain in the ass.

Thirty minutes later, Ryan pulled into the driveway of a frame house nestled beneath many large trees. He had no idea what kind of trees they were, but they were all huge. Bonehead pawed anxiously at the passenger window, wanting out.

"Hey, you!" Ryan parked the car and grabbed at Bonehead's collar, pulling the dog's broad head to face him. What was with the dog? "You are going to behave, you hear me? No jumping, no barking, no pissing on anything. And no taking a crap. Got it?"

The dog licked his face. Crap. Crap. Crap. Crap. What was going on? He'd gone from a morose lump of hair to excited, and Bonehead hadn't been excited in two years. It certainly wasn't in response to a sausage biscuit. Though he'd eat any treat offered, the dog remained as unhappy as ever.

"Behave. I mean it, Bonehead."

Ryan clipped the leash onto the dog's collar and opened the driver-side door. The dog leaped across him, hitting the car horn and stepping on Ryan's crotch, crushing his testicles, and jumped out the door, dragging Ryan out with him. Ryan crashed to the ground, his feet still in the car.

"You....crap! Crap! Stupid...shit!" Bonehead strained against the leash.

Ryan heard a screen door slam, and then he saw feet. Bonehead began to jump, dancing on his hind legs and stretching up to meet whoever owned the feet. What the hell? Ryan turned on his back and looked up into Michael's laughing face.

"Cool dog. What's his name?"

"Bonehead."

"Need some help?"

"Yeah." Ryan handed up the leash, then untangled his legs from the car and stood up. He brushed dust and leaves off himself, and closed the car door. His testicles ached, and he leaned against the car to cover up for the fact that he still couldn't stand up straight.

"So, how come you named him Bonehead?"

"You see what he did...."

Michael laughed and nodded. "Yeah, it was pretty funny. So you named him Bonehead for being one?"

"Not on purpose! Just made the mistake of calling him that too much when he was a puppy. He took to it."

"I like him."

"Great." Ryan could stand up straight now. He moved away from the car and pointed toward the garage. He could see that it had a second floor, with stairs that went up the side of the building. "That the...place?"

"Yeah. Come on. It's not locked."

The yard in back of the house was as shaded as the front and fenced in. There was a gate through the fence at the bottom of the stairs. That would be nice for the dog. Give him someplace to run and hang out.

The dog walked beside Michael sedately, happily turning his head from side to side, surveying the new surroundings. When Michael stopped and opened the gate, Bonehead sat, waiting patiently for him to do it. Ryan was amazed. Bonehead was acting like he used to with Danielle. He stopped, took a deep breath. That thought physically hurt. He rubbed a spot in the middle of his chest.

Michael was already halfway up the stairs, with Bonehead right beside him. Could Michael smell like Danielle? Ryan practically smacked himself for that one. He doubted seriously that a teenage boy smelled the same as she had. The dog's reaction just didn't make sense.

They were already inside by the time Ryan got to the top of the steps and the door. Michael had pulled up the blinds, turned on a lamp. The apartment was open and airy, furnished simply with a couch, a couple of chairs, a small dining area. The main room had a countertop dividing the kitchen from the living space.

"The bedroom's back here." Michael opened a door into a large bedroom. Past the bed, one entire wall was a sliding glass door that opened up onto a deck.

"May I?" Ryan asked, pointing to the deck.

"Sure."

Ryan opened the door and stepped out onto the screened-in deck. It was shaded and would probably be cool if there was a breeze. Right now, the haze of smoke hung in the trees like fog. The land behind the garage was heavily wooded. Ryan hoped like hell the fire didn't get close, because there was nothing between this place and the trees.

Ryan stepped back into the bedroom. Bonehead had settled down on the bare mattress, his chin resting on his front paws. His eyes were closed, and he was breathing slowly. Ryan shook his head. "I'm sorry, he's got no manners."

Michael nodded. "Don't sweat it. Do you have furniture?"

"No. No, I don't. I...got rid of everything. I used to have...stuff. Now I've just got clothes and him."

"So, you want the place?"

"Ah...sure. Yeah, I guess."

Michael nodded. "I can bring you some sheets. The air conditioner works good. You keep the doors closed, and it'll help keep some of the smoke smell out."

"When my plane landed, I thought we were going through clouds, but it was smoke," Ryan said.

Michael plopped on the bed next to the dog and began to pet him. "Yeah, it's been burning since the beginning of May. So far, we're just getting a lot of smoke. The swamp east of us is burning like crazy. People've been finding gators, deer, even bears in their back yards."

Bonehead stirred and rolled over onto his back. He'd realized he had someone who was willing to scratch him and was taking full advantage of the situation. Michael began to stroke the dog's stomach. "You want to move in today?

Ryan stood up, sticking his hands in his pockets. "Yeah, I like it."

"Okay. Great. I'll get you a key. You can work out the other stuff with Dad either tonight or tomorrow."

Michael took off back through the apartment. Ryan could hear his feet on the wooden stairway as he headed down to the yard.

Bonehead looked up at him, his head turned slightly.

"Yeah, we're staying. Are you happy?"

The dog settled back down and closed his eyes. The bed was a king, which was good. The bathroom was small, the window in it looking out onto the back yard of the Sheppard house. When Michael came out of the house, and back to the garage, Ryan could clearly see the bare spot on the top of his head where Doc Markham had shaved the hair away.

A bright red bird landed on the window sill in front of Ryan's face, startling him, and he startled the bird when he gasped. It jumped, but didn't fly away. The bird was beautiful. Absolutely solid red, with a little peak on its head. It looked at him curiously.

"Hey," Ryan said softly.

The bird fluffed its wings, chirruped, then flew away. Ryan heard Michael's thumping up the steps. He leaned his head against the glass of the window and looked up, trying to see the sky through the trees, but it was impossible through the haze.

"I got you a key. Listen, if you want to leave Bonehead here while you get your things, I can watch him."

Ryan turned around. Michael's face looked flushed. "You shouldn't be running. You've got a...." Ryan stopped, closed his eyes, and muttered a fuck under his breath. "You've got a head injury."

"Concussion."

"Yeah."

Ryan took the key.

"You've got that talking thing, aphasia."

Ryan's heart hammered in his chest. Crap. "How...?"

"My Grandma had it for a year before she died. She had a stroke. She couldn't remember the words she wanted to use. She talked around the words she couldn't remember. They said it was aphasia. You've got something like that, don't you?"

Ryan nodded.

"But you're not old."

"Brain injury. I got hit in the head." Ryan's hand automatically went to the scar, touching it, feeling it beneath his fingertips. "It's just word retrieval. I can't find the words I...need. Sometimes. Most of the time."

"No biggie," Michael said, shrugging. "I just knew because of Grandma. I don't think it's that noticeable."

Ryan smiled and nodded. "Yeah, right."

Michael smiled. "Hey, I got a cop for a dad. I notice shit. Okay?"

"Okay."

"So, you want me to watch Bonehead?"

"Yeah. I'll be back as soon as I can get my stuff and check out of….that place."

"Does he like to Frisbee?"

"Tennis balls. He loves tennis balls. I've got…..in the car."

Michael followed him down to the car where Ryan found three tennis balls under the seat. He handed them to Michael. "Do me a favor, wear his butt out. Okay?"

Michael laughed. "Be glad to."

"But take it easy. Let him do the running. And you should be drinking lots of fluids. It's hot out here."

"Yes, sir, doctor, sir."

"Ryan. Call me Ryan."

"You got it."

Ryan got into the car. He watched Michael walk back to the gate. Bonehead had come down the steps. The minute he saw the tennis balls, he leaped off the steps into the yard, heading for Michael as hard as he could run. Thank God the kid's big, Ryan thought. The dog hit him full in the chest, but Michael only rocked back a little.

Ryan started the car and backed out of the driveway. Maybe the damn dog wouldn't drive him so crazy now. Maybe he'd stop waiting by the door like he was expecting her. Ryan's hand went right for the scar again, but he caught it, stopping before he touched his forehead.

"Stop it!" Ryan said out loud. He put both hands back on the steering wheel, gripping it too tightly. He and the dog both had to stop waiting for her.

Chapter Six

Jim closed the front door behind him and heard voices coming from the bathroom. He headed into the hall and saw a bushy dog's tail hanging out of the bathroom door wagging.

What the hell?

One of the voices was definitely Michael.

As he got closer, he could hear Michael swearing. When he stepped into the doorway, straddling the dog's tail, he saw Michael angling a secondhand mirror to examine the damage Doc Markham had done to his hair. Ryan Edwards was standing next to him, trying to calm him down.

"It's not that bad."

"Are you kidding me? The bastard butchered me!"

"It'll grow."

Michael snorted in disgust.

Ryan pulled out his wallet and handed Michael his driver's license. "See that? They shaved my head."

"Holy shit. You had long hair."

"Yeah."

"How long did it take to grow back?"

"A few months, but I didn't want it…..like that anymore. New me, new hair."

Jim could see the scar on Ryan's forehead in the mirror. It must have been a serious injury if they shaved his head. Jim saw Michael catch his reflection.

"Dad, Doc has ruined me!"

Jim laughed. "Nah, just your hair. You'll survive."

Ryan quickly put his wallet away and looked embarrassed. "Hey, Sheriff."

"Ryan."

The dog between Jim's legs looked up at him and seemed to smile. "And who is this?"

"Ah, sorry. He's mine. I.….brought him inside," Ryan moved to grab the dog's collar.

"He's fine. What's his name?"

Michael cackled. Ryan blushed and said, "Bonehead."

Jim reached down and gave the big dog a couple of friendly thumps on his side. "Nice to meet you, Bonehead. I take it this means you took the apartment?"

"Yes, thank you. I need to work out the rent with you."

Jim shrugged. "We can talk about it over dinner, if you have time."

Ryan smiled and nodded.

"Sloppy Joes?" Michael asked.

"Lousy for my cholesterol," Jim replied.

"But I got my hair fu…screwed up by Doc and have a concussion."

Jim rolled his eyes and headed for the kitchen, "Yeah, yeah, yeah. You're such a poor, put-upon child."

* * *

They finished a dinner of sloppy joes and steamed broccoli, and Michael went to his room to study. Jim started clearing the table, and Ryan offered to do the dishes.

"You wash, I'll dry," said Jim.

Bonehead slept in front of the back door, and the two men worked together amiably. There wasn't much to clean up. Jim's cooking abilities were pretty much limited to a skillet and the microwave.

"Thanks for the…food," Ryan said as he rinsed off another dish and handed it to Jim.

"It certainly wasn't anything special," Jim said. He dried the plate and set it up in the cabinet. "So, about the rent, what do you think about two hundred."

"Two hundred? That's crazy."

"That includes utilities," Jim added.

Ryan laughed. "No, I mean, it's crazy cheap. I have never paid that little for a place to live."

Jim shrugged. "It's only two rooms."

"I paid twenty-five hundred for a one-bedroom in D.C."

Jim shook his head. "That's crazy."

"Yes, two hundred is great. Thank you."

They finished the dishes and Ryan nudged Bonehead in the butt with his shoe. "Come on, big dog, time to head home." The dog raised his eyebrows and cut his eyes to look at Ryan but made no move to rise.

"He minds you real well," Jim noted.

Ryan shook his head. "Yeah, we've always had a sort of...tenuous relationship." He leaned down and rubbed the dog's ears. "Seriously now, move it."

Bonehead slowly got to his feet, stretched, hind quarters high in the air and his head and front feet low to the floor. Ryan opened the door, and the dog wandered slowly out. Ryan nodded his thanks again, and the two walked across the yard to the garage.

Jim closed the door behind them and watched until they were inside. However, those two had come to be living together, it was clearly not because either had chosen it. They had the air of step-relations and not the kind that loved each other.

Chapter Seven

Jim sat at his desk, trying to focus on setting up the schedule for the next month. At least it would give him one damn thing accomplished for the day. He'd canvassed neighbors all around the Hatcher home and found no one who'd heard or seen anything. One woman had complained that her neighbor's dog had started barking around 4 am, but that could or could not mean anything, as she also said the dog often barked during the night.

He finished up with the schedule and tossed it in his outbox for Junior to put into the computer.

He had half a mind to head home when Junior stuck his head in the door, "Bud Peterson's on line one for you, Sheriff."

Jim sighed, waved thanks to Junior, and picked up his phone. He'd caught Bud in mid-drink because he could hear the ice against the cup. "Hey, Bud."

There was a moment and the thump of the travel mug being set down and the shuffle of paper. "I got an interesting piece of information for you, Jim. The blood on the Bible isn't the Reverend's."

Jim was surprised. "How do you know?"

"Got it typed, and it's O+. Not his type. I called Elsie's place and asked the wife if she knew his blood type. Turns out he's rare. AB-. She knew that because he donates regularly on account of being a rare type."

"So, whose blood is it?"

"I'd say your kidnapper's. We'll send it off for DNA, but that's going to take a while. They're backed up at the State lab. Probably going to be six months before I can get an answer, so that won't be much help to you right

35

now."

Jim rubbed his forehead. "Might not be any help at all if the guy's not in a database somewhere."

"True enough."

Jim paused, and then he thought of something. "Bud, how rare is AB-?"

"Very rare. One percent of the white population, less of other groups."

"Thanks, Bud. That might actually help."

"You thinking someone wanted the preacher for his blood?" Bud's tea swirled and clunked. "We've both known worse motives."

"We sure have," said Jim.

They broke the connection, and Jim decided he would ask about that. Sitting at his desk wasn't getting him anything except a numb ass.

He picked up his hat and headed out into the office.

"You heading home?" Junior asked.

"No, I think I'll head over and talk to Doc. Anything I need to do before I leave?"

"Did you sign the two purchase orders?"

"Yes."

"Did you call the Commissioner back?"

Jim shuddered. "Yes."

Junior smiled broadly. "Then I guess you can go."

"I finished next month's schedule. It's in the box," Jim indicated with his thumb over his shoulder.

"You know, Sheriff, someday you're going to have to learn how to use the new computer program."

Jim looked at Junior, "You planning on quitting?"

"Nope."

Jim grinned. "Then I don't need to learn the program."

Junior's laugh followed him out the door.

* * *

Jim caught Doc as he was leaving his office. He saw Jim and raised one eyebrow in question.

"I need your expertise," Jim said.

Doc snorted. "About what?"

"Rare blood types."

That definitely surprised Markham. He motioned over at McDonald's across the street. "Buy me coffee, and I'll talk to you."

Jim laughed. There were two fast food places and one actual restaurant in Warren, and Mcdonald's had the prime location right in the middle of town. "All right."

They found a table in one corner near the windows. There weren't many people in the place. It was too early for working families who would just be getting off work, and too late for anyone to be grabbing lunch.

"What do you need to know?" asked Doc as he stirred four sugars into his coffee.

Jim stared at the mix. "Like a little coffee with your sugar there, Doc?"

Doc grinned. "You know how it is. Do as I say, not as I do." He took a long sip of the hot liquid and smacked his lips.

"I've got a man who's disappeared from his home during the night."

"Preacher. Yeah, I heard."

"He's got AB- blood."

"Huh." Doc sipped at his coffee a bit more. "You're thinking maybe someone took him for his blood?"

"Would it make sense?"

"Possibly. You take a little at a time, you could have a good source for a while. You take it all, with an average adult male, maybe 16 pints, or more. Depends."

Jim hadn't even taken the top off his coffee. He felt like something might be connecting. This could be a lead to who would want the preacher. "Anyone you can think of that has that blood type?"

Doc shook his head. "Not in my practice. It's really rare. But, you start talking about this region, add in places like Alachua County, you might hit the jackpot."

"Is there a way to find out?"

Doc thought about it for a few moments then he said, "I've got some contacts. I can make some calls. If your preacher was in the American Rare Donor program, it's very possible that we could find your connection."

"Would you do it, please?"

Doc nodded. "I'll make some calls and get back to you as soon as I have something. It'll take a bit of time."

"I don't know how much time I have."

"I'll hurry it all I can."

"Thanks." Jim got up from the table. He left his coffee. Doc looked at it. "You going to drink that?"

Jim shook his head. Doc pulled it over to himself. "I'll drink it."

Chapter Eight

"I should have ordered the sandwich," Ryan said.

Doc grinned. "Want the other half?"

Ryan shook his head. "No, I really should eat the salad. The food down here is going to kill me."

Doc laughed. Filly and Claire and a few patients had taken it upon themselves to feed Ryan Edwards in the week since he'd started working. Fried chicken, banana pudding, chicken fried steak, sweet potato fluff, pecan pie, and mash potatoes rich with butter had flowed in to the office like a cafeteria conveyor belt. He thought it was both that Ryan was tall and slender and that he was handsome that had all the ladies in a tizzy.

"How are you and Jim getting along?" Doc asked.

Ryan paused and thought about it a moment. "I like him. He's...kind."

Doc's head nodded. "That's a good word for him."

Ryan pushed his salad onto the desk and sat forward. "I don't want to pry, but what can you tell me about him?"

"Jim and Linda were high school sweethearts. Got married when he was in graduate school over to UF. She was on her way to see her mother and must have fallen asleep. She died."

Ryan took the information in. "That explains why he and Michael are so close."

"Maybe. Jim Sheppard is kind of a local mystery, despite being from here. After his wife died, he dropped out of grad school and moved home with Michael. Took a job as a deputy with his Dad. We all knew it wasn't what he wanted to do. He'd been clear about that all his life. Guess he felt like he had to, once he was alone with a child."

"What did he want to do?"

Doc laughed. "Teach. He wanted to teach high school history. I remember Bob complaining about it. He wanted him to just quit, come home and go through the police academy over in Alachua County. Figured that was all he needed to become a deputy. But Jim stuck it out.

"When Bob retired, Jim had been a deputy for nearly twelve years. Bob put him in for sheriff, and Jim was elected. He didn't even campaign. So he's been sheriff since his dad retired."

Ryan thought about the man he'd met. He certainly didn't seem like a hard-charging, ambitious man. "No one runs against him?"

Doc laughed hard. "I don't think it's occurred to anyone to want to. Sheppards been sheriffs here for the last ninety-some years." Doc quieted. "I've known Jim Sheppard since he was in high school, and everything I can tell you about him is superficial. He played football because his father wanted him to. He went to UF on a football scholarship. He was a defensive back. Good player, but didn't have any interest in the pros. I don't think he gave a damn about playing the game. He liked baseball, but he didn't get offered a scholarship for that. I think his daddy saw to that. Bob wanted Jim to be a football hero with a sweet wife and a family. Wanted him to be sheriff like he was. And that's exactly what Jim did."

"He's not like that with Michael."

"No. He's not."

Doc pushed the other half of his sandwich toward Ryan. "Go on and eat that. You're looking at that salad like it killed your dog."

Ryan laughed and took the sandwich. He took a bite, and the flavor of fresh tomato, crisp lettuce, and rich smoked bacon filled his mouth. "Oh my God, this is…the best sandwich."

"Listen, Jim is a good man. I don't have any doubt about that. Like you said, he's kind. He loves his son. He's a good boss. The deputies like working for him. But I don't think that there's a person in this town that can tell you what goes on in Jim Sheppard's head. He's always been like that."

Ryan swallowed his bite of food. "Private."

"Yeah. And in a small town, that's damned hard to be. Especially when you're in the public eye like he is."

Doc picked up his bag of chips and tossed a couple into his mouth. "You two ought to get along just fine, seeing as how you're pretty private, too."

Ryan's hand went to the scar on his forehead automatically. He felt the rough edges of it under his fingertips. He had many reasons for being private. He wondered what Jim Sheppard's were.

Chapter Nine

Jim sat in the atrium of Shands Hospital in Gainesville. He had an over-priced coffee in his hand, wore his uniform, and sat in a chair in the bright, open area watching people go by him. The teaching hospital complex was huge, so he was glad he'd only had to find this part of it.

Finally a man wearing a white coat who looked to be near Doc Markham's age stopped in front of him. "Sheriff Sheppard?" he asked.

Jim stood up, "Yes. Dr. Renaldi?"

"Yes, good to meet you, Sheriff."

"If your young preacher was taken because of his blood type, I think the chances are that it was not for his blood specifically, it would be more likely be about an organ transplant..."

Jim's stomach churned. If someone had taken Hatcher so they could take his heart....

"But, I think that it's a slim possibility at best. First of all, the woman's still on the list. If he'd been taken for his heart, I would think she would have had herself taken off the list. Also, she doesn't have the resources for this. There's insurance, but insurance wouldn't pay for a black market operation. This kind of thing takes big money."

"How do we check?"

Renaldi shrugged. "I'm going to make some calls. I'll also see if anyone on the kidney or liver list has been removed suddenly. Of course, this far north in the state, it could be someone in Georgia, maybe even Alabama who's in need of an organ."

Jim groaned. "I don't even know where to start."

Renaldi smiled. "I'll start. I'll send you whatever information I get, and anything that looks unusual so you can follow it up."

"Thanks."

Renaldi stood up and held his hand out to Jim. They shook, and he laughed. "Tell Ben I said he owes me that fishing trip he's been promising me for the last two years."

"I will. And if he doesn't pay up, I'll arrange one myself."

* * *

The drive back to Warren let Jim worry over the information he'd gotten. There were all kinds of urban myths about people being taken for their organs. He knew jack about the system, the lists, or how it all worked. Thank God, he'd never had to know.

He hated having to rely on someone else to do his information gathering, but Doc had warned him the lists weren't public, and the only way to get the information would be through Renaldi. He had access.

It didn't sit right having to wait, but he'd run down every possible lead or hint he could think of in Eden County and come up with nothing. He was going to have to grin and bear it, waiting for Doc's friends to come up with the possible leads.

He'd turned off County Road 26 onto State Road 98 heading back to Warren when the smoke hanging over the road got heavier. The two-lane narrowed after it crossed the Suwannee River, and just inside Eden County, Jim saw what little traffic existed slowed as it disappeared into the curtain of smoke that crossed the road.

Jim turned on his headlights and slowed, and within a quarter mile he saw orange flames on both sides of the road. His heartbeat sped up, and he realized that the fire coming from the east had just jumped the road, catching the tall dry grasses on the west side. He could see heat waves distorting the air above the road.

"Hell's bells," he whispered to himself. Traffic slowed more, and two cars ahead of Jim, he saw a tanker truck with bright red flammable signs on it trying to make its way past the open flames.

Jim flipped on his lights and siren and pulled around the traffic. He pulled up next to the cars ahead of the tanker. He could see the terrified face of the driver in the first car. It was a middle-aged man in a shirt and tie. The man didn't seem to realize that the real danger drove behind him. He turned on his speaker and shouted to him, "Keep driving, get up to speed, move, move!"

The car in the lead had slowed to nearly 15 mph, and at this rate, the tanker would be near the flames far too long. He stopped his car to prevent the cars heading south from getting in the way and got out, and waved the cars on.

"MOVE! MOVE! GET UP TO SPEED!"

Finally, the driver in the lead began to increase his speed, and in a few minutes, everyone, including the tanker, managed to get past the flames and into an area that was more open.

Jim could feel the sweat soaking his shirt from the heat from the flames on the west side of the road, but once everyone was through, he got back into his car, pulled out of the opposing lane, and followed north.

A mile up the road, the tanker had pulled over. He waved from Jim to stop. He pulled up behind the semi, and the man ran to his window.

"Thanks, man. I thought he was going to stop."

Jim nodded, "Me, too. Thanks for not panicking. If you'd pulled into the southbound lane, it could have gotten uglier really fast."

The man shook his hand and headed back to his truck. Jim got on the radio and called Junior arranging for the two deputies on patrol to head this way until they could get some firefighters into the area.

His heartbeat didn't return to normal until Dee Jackson and Bobby Dale had pulled their cars up on either side of the road. Jim gave them quick directions, and Bobby Dale headed south to stop cars south of the flames. He had them both turning traffic back to alternate routes until the flames had either moved on or the firefighters got there.

He headed back into town, hoping that both of his deputies would be safe. Dee had the good sense to run if things got bad, but Bobby Dale would likely try to stay long past safe. By the time he got to the office, he felt like he needed a long nap and something cool to rest his head on. He walked into the office and found Junior on the phone. That wasn't unusual. What was unusual was that Junior wasn't saying anything other than an occasional "Uh-huh."

Jim stopped and watched. Junior rolled his eyes and wrote on a piece of paper, and pushed it toward Jim. He picked it up and saw 'Colonel Mann' written on the paper. He set it down and practically tip-toed past Junior. The Colonel had to be on some new rampage, and Junior had caught it. Jim, being both a wise man, and having a strong survival instinct, had no intention of getting involved if he didn't have to.

One of the best things about Junior was his willingness to step into the line of fire when it came to those who were Jim's main pains in the ass. Junior's sense of duty nearly compared to that of Bobby Dale.

The minute Jim sat down at his desk, he called Sweet Ella's Barbeque and ordered Junior's favorite meal, and asked them to drop it by the office.

Ella laughed at his call. "What did you do this time, Sheriff?"

Junior was still on the phone with the Colonel when the delivery arrived. He put the phone on speaker and began eating his lunch. He turned toward Jim's office and gave him a thumb's up. The Colonel's voice continued in his litany of complaints.

Jim felt retroactive pity for anyone who'd had to serve under that man. He went back to his desk and gratefully began to complete some of his paperwork.

Chapter Ten

The phone rang just as Jim headed out his front door. He turned around and answered it, thinking probably Junior had something he needed Jim to do. Instead, he heard the voice of Dr. Renaldi on the other end of the line.

"I've got someone you should talk to. How soon could you get to Savannah?" Renaldi asked.

Jim took a deep breath. "I can drive there today. Be there early this afternoon."

"Good. Go. You need to be at the Liver Transplant Center in Savannah and talk to a Dr. Clinton. She'll give you the information. I've talked with her, and she's willing to see you."

"Is this…?" Jim couldn't finish his question.

"Maybe. There's an irregularity there. Talk to her today."

"Thank you," Jim said. He hung up the phone and then dialed Junior. "I'm going to be out of town today, Junior. I've got something I need to check into in Savannah."

Junior paused, which was unusual. "Savannah? Georgia?"

Jim would have laughed if it wasn't so damn serious. "Yeah. I'll be gone all day. Back this evening. You won't be able to reach me, so I'll call in to you. If something goes pear-shaped, talk to Dee."

"You got it, Sheriff," Junior responded.

Jim went into the kitchen to leave a note for Michael. He didn't want him worrying. If he called the office, Junior would let him know what was going on.

He grabbed a map of Georgia out of a drawer in the kitchen and went out to his sedan. Savannah was about five hours away, but doable. He'd have driven to New York City, though, if Renaldi said it might be a lead. Hatcher's disappearance weighed on his mind. Jim didn't think he was a great investigator. Never had a reason to be one before now. That alone scared him worse than anything else about the case.

He'd talked to an agent in the Gainesville FBI office and been told unless they had some solid evidence that Hatcher's disappearance was a kidnapping, they could not get involved. The evidence of the van and a male with size 12 feet and O+ blood didn't rule out that Hatcher had left of his own accord. There had been no ransom request, no indication that his disappearance had been violent in any way.

It felt like Hatcher's life lay in his hands, and he did not know what to do with that feeling.

* * *

Jim stopped every two hours and found a pay phone so he could call Junior and check in. Fortunately, things were pretty quiet. Since the fires had jumped US98 the day before, a whole section of forest in the southern part of the county had burned, but other than threatening a hunting camp that was near the gulf, it hadn't been too dangerous.

A timber company from Levy County had come up and bulldozed firebreaks east of the hunting camp. Fire fighters had managed to save two small homes and a frame church on the north side of the fires.

During the fires, Jim had come to be glad that a large portion of the county was swampland. The swamps burned, but they mostly created smoke. The smoke created more than its share of hazards, but it burned slow. The real danger came when the fires hit patches of timber.

Finally, he pulled into Savannah. The hospital was on Waters Street. A guy in a gas station pointed him in the right direction. Then once again, Jim found himself sitting in a waiting area of a hospital. This time with a truly lousy cup of coffee in his hand. Overpriced or not, the coffee at Shands was better.

He was surprised when a lovely woman, who had to be in her late thirties at the most, walked up to him and introduced herself.

"You must be Sheriff Sheppard. Margaret Clinton."

"Thanks for seeing me, Dr. Clinton."

She guided him to her office and closed the door behind them. "Since this is very unofficial, I want to be sure that no one hears what we're talking about."

Jim nodded. "I understand. Dr. Renaldi said there was an irregularity?"

Clinton took a deep breath. "Dr. Renaldi and I have known each other for a few years. He put out a note to several of us asking to let him know if something unusual happened with any patient with AB- blood. I've had something happen."

She wrote a name and address on a piece of note paper and handed it to Jim.

"This patient has been on the liver transplant list for about three years. Suddenly last week, he notified me he was removing himself from the list. When I asked him why, he said he didn't want to talk about it. He just wanted off the list."

"And he's AB—?"

"Yes."

"Thank you."

She shrugged. "It could have nothing to do with your question, but it's odd timing. Also, I know this patient has some resources at his disposal. If he really wanted to do something like this, he could. He doesn't seem like the type of man to do that, but you never know when you're dealing with life and death."

Jim read the name. Reynold Stendal. The address was in Valdosta. He looked at Dr. Clinton. "He's dying?"

Dr. Clinton smiled sadly. "All my patients are dying. Some more rapidly than others. He's on the fast track."

Jim stood up, and she held out her hand. "I wish you luck with finding your man."

48

"Thank you. I appreciate you providing me with the information."

***

Technically Jim could have driven to Valdosta on his way back from Savannah. However, he thought that more information would serve him better. If he showed up, half-cocked, looking for answers, all he'd do would be to tip the man off.

So, Jim called Junior, gave him the man's name and address, and had him pull as much background information on him as he could.

At a little before 6 pm, Jim pulled up in front of his office. He could see Junior at his desk. Junior looked up and saw him as he walked up to the door.

"I'm heading out. No, I don't have the information you want. Yes, I will have it, probably no later than noon tomorrow, and you should go home and have some dinner. Nothing is going on that needs you right this minute," said Junior in his high, thin voice.

Jim stopped, lowered his head, and tried not to laugh. "All right."

He turned around and headed back out.

"'Night, Sheriff," Junior called after him.

Chapter Eleven

Bonehead pulled on the leash, apparently wanting Ryan to move faster. Ryan had no intention of trying to run in this heat and smoke. He hadn't survived a brain injury and come out stupid. He intended to continue living a healthy life, no matter what the dog wanted. Right now. that meant walking rather than running, no matter what the dog wanted.

They came up on a lovely open area with a few big trees, surrounded by a low brick wall. It wasn't until Bonehead turned into it that Ryan realized it was a cemetery. He'd spent very little time in cemeteries in his life. Both of his parents came from wealthy families that had large above ground vaults where everyone's ashes were interred. There had never been any visiting of graves on a regular basis. Even when his grandparents had died, both his parents had gone together to the funerals and left him at home, or school, since he was in college when the last died.

These were graves. Most were marked with plates at ground level, a few with large concrete covers that carried names and dates. He could see a handful of crosses and headstones, but generally, it was very flat and subdued.

On his honeymoon, they had gone to Paris, and she had insisted on going to Pere LeChaise cemetery. Danielle had loved the magnificent tombs and statuary that marked the graves. He'd never seen anything like it, but had let her drag him along and show him her favorites. For him she had translated all the epitaphs, led him from one area to another, noting the famous, the wealthy, and finally, the Jewish and Muslim grave enclosures.

Bonehead sniffed the ground, but seemed more interested in the squirrels that took off like a shot for the trees than the actual graves. He nearly pulled Ryan off his feet trying to go after one that raced across a large open patch trying to get to a tree ahead of the dog.

"Hey!" Bonehead stopped. "Thank you. What were you going to do…if you caught…? You hit fur, you'd …. you'd stop."

He'd been in a coma when Danielle's parents buried her. Though his parents had offered her a place in either of the family vaults, her parents had decided to bury her in a graveyard outside of D.C. They had put up a stone with her name and the words beloved wife and daughter beneath. Ryan had only gone there once. The stone was beautiful. Next to it was a bare spot of grass. Her parents had bought the plot next to her in case Ryan did not come out of his coma. They had already arranged with his family to bury him next to her.

He'd surprised everyone by surviving. Then he'd spent the next year learning to walk and talk again. He'd refused to go to see her grave until he could walk to it alone, not wanting anyone there with him when he saw it.

At the last minute, he'd decided to take Bonehead with him. Though he and the dog were not companions in any real sense, he felt that Bonehead deserved to see where she had been laid to rest.

The dog settled at his feet here. At Danielle's grave, Bonehead had lain down directly in front of the headstone, resting his head on the ground toward it. He had sat down next to the dog and cried as he read her name, speaking it softly.

The squirrel chittered at Bonehead from a lower branch of the tree. Bonehead began to growl. Ryan found himself laughing. "That…squirrel? It's faster than you…and it can climb trees."

A pine cone sailed out of the tree and landed in front of them. Ryan looked up at the squirrel, and it began to chitter at him. "I didn't chase you!" Ryan shouted. Bonehead barked, and the squirrel skittered up the tree.

"C'mon, you won," said Ryan. Bonehead growled once more, then walked away with his tail wagging.

Chapter Twelve

Four days. Four days since Reverend Hatcher had disappeared. Jim had a name and an address in Valdosta, Georgia, but until he had more information than that, he had to sit on his thumbs and wait. What he did have was more smoke, which was causing accidents all over the damn county because people still drove too fast to get where they were going, ignoring the limited visibility. He had a string of burglaries of summer houses out near the beach and thought they might be related to the car burglaries that had suddenly stopped happening in town. He had an increase in domestic violence, drunk and disorderlies, and just general orneriness.

Jim leaned against his car door and watched the traffic moving through town. It was noon, but the haze in the sky was so thick the sun looked red and minimal light was getting through to the ground. He hadn't even tried to run that morning.

Jim's stomach growled. No matter what happened in the world, things went on. The body got hungry and thirsty. People worked and slept.

His radio clicked, and Junior's voice buzzed, "Sheriff?"

"Yeah, Junior."

"Bobby found himself a body."

Jim felt his stomach clench and roll. "Where?"

"Off Baden-Powell Road, just south of Libby's dairy. The wildfire went through there last night."

"You called FDLE for a tech?"

"Yes, sir. They're on their way."

Jim looked back at the traffic. Everything kept moving, like nothing had happened. He sent up a little prayer that it wasn't his missing preacher that had been found.

* * *

The ground was still smoldering where the body lay. The smell of burning wood mixed heavily with the smell of cooking bacon. The body was huge, which immediately eased Jim's apprehension. It wasn't the preacher. Hatcher was only 5'9" and slender.

About one hundred yards in from the road, Jim saw firemen working to contain the fire that had swept through here a short time ago. Heavy bulldozers pushed dirt and debris against the flames trying to contain the blaze. They had discovered the body and called it in. Bobby had come to contain the scene while the fire fighters moved on.

"Hey, Sheriff," called Bobby. He'd tried to string crime scene tape around the body, but it was melting and falling into pieces around the pine tree trunks. There were only oaks and pines left standing. The oaks had burned to blackened shadows of themselves.

"Don't waste any more tape, Bobby. Get some traffic cones and put them around instead."

Bobby nodded and took what was left of his roll of tape back to his car, where he began to unload some small orange traffic cones.

Jim could feel the heat rising from the ground, making the soles of his boots feel sticky. He walked to within a couple of feet of the body but didn't get any closer. Whatever might be left of the scene, he didn't want to contaminate it. He was pretty sure the figure was male because of the smoking boots on the feet, but other than that, he couldn't tell much. Any clothing was gone, along with the skin and hair. "Wonder what the hell someone was doing on foot out here?"

Bobby walked back to stand next to Jim. "I don't think this guy was walking out here," said Bobby. He motioned for Jim to follow him, and they carefully stepped around the cones to the other side of the corpse. The head of the corpse was twisted violently to the left.

"What the hell?" said Jim softly.

"I think that pretty much rules out this being an accident," said Bobby.

"No shit." Jim made a circuit of the body. When he looked closely, he could see where the spine twisted and broke. While the rest of the body looked like a typical burning death, necks, and heads didn't twist like that from the heat of fire. "The head is nearly twisted off!"

"It's not the preacher. I checked the info on him when I found it. This one's way too big to be him."

Jim walked back out to the road. The fire hadn't jumped the road, and the dairy had a wide firebreak plowed on the north side of the fire. There were signs of scorching of the grass on the other side of the road. "You talk to anyone at Libby's, yet? Someone had to be out here watching the fire."

"Haven't had time."

Jim nodded. "I'll go and check with them. You stay here and wait for the techs. If you need me, yell."

He got back into his sedan and drove down a mile to the entrance of the dairy farm. The office was a low concrete block building set about fifty yards away from the barns. The only other building near it was the garage that held the vans Libby's workers used. Beyond the barns were wide, open fields on one side, and to the east stood the Libby house. When Jim got out of his car, Richard Libby was already charging out of the office.

"Jim, you here about that damn fire?" Richard Libby was a big man, with a huge square head and a face that always made Jim think of a bull. He snorted angry bursts of air through his lumpy nose and spit words out between gritted teeth. "I had my boys plow that firebreak a couple of weeks ago, and we still had to go out there and dowse some trees and beat out the grass that was lighting up on our side of the break. If we hadn't caught it early, it could have been up here to my barns in no time."

Every conversation with Richard Libby was a frontal assault. Jim bit back the words that first came to his lips, because they wouldn't do a thing to calm Libby down. He took a breath. "Who was out on the fireline?"

"Why?"

"Cause we got a body just on the other side of it."

For once, Richard Libby didn't seem to know what to say. Jim enjoyed the moment, because he knew it wouldn't last, and it might be the only time he'd ever seen Libby speechless.

"You think it's the fire bug?"

"Doubt it. Looks like the fire may have been used to cover up his murder."

"I'll round up the boys that were out there."

Libby wheeled around and headed back into the office. Jim went back to his car to get a notepad. If anyone remembered anything, he wanted to have it written down so it wouldn't just be his memory he had to rely on for the report.

Chapter Thirteen

Doc Markham had taken the day off, and Ryan had gotten through the first half of the day without any problems. Filly Ellis, the only nurse in the practice, had smoothly swooped in with the right term whenever he couldn't find it. He was going to have to buy her flowers or something, because she helped his medical competence shine even when his vocabulary failed him.

He finished his notes on his current patient and was dropping the chart off at the desk when the front door burst open, and Edna Bass threw herself through it into the waiting room. The handful of people there watched with fascination as she staggered toward the desk.

Ryan met her halfway. She was trembling so hard that her body shook in waves moving up and down.

"What's wrong?" Ryan asked.

"He ain't come home. He ain't closed the bar, and he ain't come home. I...I...I...." she gasped and then began to sob.

Ryan led her to a chair, and she fell into it. Filly came from the hallway. She had a bottle of water in her hand, and she handed it to Ryan. He opened it and had Edna sip it slowly. She finally seemed to get her wind again.

"Your...boy?" Ryan asked. "You're talking about him?"

Edna nodded. "I thought maybe he'd got into a fight and was here getting patched up. Junior at the Sheriff's office says he's not there. I've called everyone and looked everywhere, and he ain't nowhere."

She grasped Ryan's hand tightly, and he was surprised at the strength she had. "Tell me he's here."

Ryan shook his head, "I'm sorry, Ms. Bass, he's not here."

Filly put a hand on Edna's shoulder. "Doc's down at Cedar Key fishing today, Ms. Bass. Why don't you let me take you back where you can lie down for a little bit?"

Edna cried softly. "I know he's a bad boy, but I love him."

She let Filly and Ryan help her up from the chair. Filly looked at Ryan, "I'll put her in the ped's room. She'll be able to lie down in there."

Ryan nodded and watched as she led Edna back to the examination room for children. The lower table in that room would allow Edna to lie down without having to heft herself up to the regular examination table height.

He revised his gift to Filly. He was going to have to give her a gift certificate to a really good restaurant. Flowers just wouldn't be enough.

He looked around the room and smiled, trying to ease the tension of everyone watching. Then he made a quick exit to the private office. He'd left D.C. and the emergency room because he knew he couldn't handle the pressure. The words he needed were too elusive, and the pace there too demanding. He'd thought a small-town practice would be just right.

Even Doc Markham had assured him that there would be less pressure. But there was a difference he hadn't counted on, and that was in a small town, he'd know his patients. They would look to him to understand their lives, their families, and their fears.

This was a whole new level of medicine. Yes, he still needed to know what the hell he was doing with their health, but now he needed to know them.

What the hell had he gotten himself into?

There was a tap at the door, and Filly opened it to look in. "Ms. Bass is lying down, and I've got your next patient in an exam room."

Ryan nodded, but didn't make a move to get up.

Filly stepped in and closed the door behind her. She was a tall woman with short hair, big dark eyes, and skin the color of caramel. She gave him a crooked grin. "You're doing well, you know."

"Really? I'm not so sure."

"Doc, you remembered what Edna's main problem is."

He flashed on the visit with Edna Bass a few days earlier. He had remembered. "I also got her name right," he said, grinning.

Filly laughed. "See. You're doing great. Now come on. Dil Reilly's in the exam room, and if we don't get in there soon, he'll start playing with all the buttons on the table. He likes to do that."

Ryan got up and followed her out into the hall. He was going to have to talk to Markham about giving Filly a raise. The woman was worth her weight in gold.

Chapter Fourteen

Good to his word, Richard Libby had let Jim talk to everyone who'd been working the fireline, including a couple of men he knew were illegals. He had bigger problems at the moment, and unless one of them had sneaked off to kill a man and come back to fight the fire, he really didn't give a damn about their immigration status.

It was clear from the interviews that all the men had been in sight of someone else before the fire, and that none of them had snuck off during it. They had fought it along the property line until it had turned and moved away, and then they'd gone back to their jobs at the dairy.

No one had seen anything, but then, none of them had been near the area of the fire until after it had started. Richard's son had seen the fire first when he'd come out of one of the milking barns.

Jim thanked them all, tossed his notes in the car, and headed back to Bobby and the body.

Once again, Bud Peterson had drawn the short straw and been sent to the site. He had two technicians and an ambulance with him this time.

"These damn fires are driving the populace bug-shit crazy, Jim."

"I won't argue with you."

Bud waved out at the corpse and the techs. "There isn't jack in the way of evidence. Everything burned the hell up. And that body? You know how hard it is to break someone's neck like that? Takes a goddamn strong person."

Jim shuddered.

"We'll get him over to the medical examiners, but I can tell you right now, they're backed up there, so it's going to be at least two, three days before we get anything on this. Even I know this guy didn't die in the fire. No one would survive that type of break." "You want me to have Bobby stay here until you're done?"

Bud shook his head. "No reason to. We'll take it from here."

"Thanks." Jim went over and told Bobby to go on. He got back into his car and headed back into town.

He hadn't even gotten the door closed behind him at the office when Junior told him to stop and turn around. He was going to be heading right back out.

"Where?"

"Doc's. Edna Bass is over there. Made a big to-do in the waiting room."

"Edna?"

"She was here before that. Buddy's gone missing."

"Ah, shit," Jim muttered. Buddy Bass was one of his regular pains in the ass. "Was he at Doc's?"

"Nope. No one's seen him. Edna found the bar wide open and no sign of Buddy when she went down there this morning. She's been all over looking for him. I think she called half the drunks in town."

Jim shook his head.

"So you need to get over to Doc's. Though Doc isn't there. It's that new guy. Filly Ellis had the girl at the desk call me and told me to have you come right over when you got back."

"Great." Jim turned around, put his hat back on, and walked over to the doctor's office. If Filly Ellis thought he was needed then it was pretty damn sure he was. Despite the silly-ass name her mama and daddy had saddled her with, she was smart. She'd been an ally in several cases of child abuse and more than one domestic violence case. Patients talked to her who wouldn't talk to him or Doc Markham.

The young woman at the front desk rose up from her seat when she saw him come in the door. "I'll go get Filly," she said as she disappeared down the hall.

A moment later, she came back and told him that Filly was waiting in

Doc's office.

The door was open, and Filly was waiting for him. "You need to talk to Edna Bass."

"I heard."

"Buddy's an asshole, but he wouldn't leave the bar open like that. Even bleeding, he'd lock those damn doors."

Suddenly Jim flashed on the burned body. It was big, like Buddy Bass. "Ah shit," Jim whispered.

"He's dead," Filly said without flinching.

"Might be."

"How?"

"There's a body, out near Libby's. Burned up in a fire."

"But you're not sure it's Buddy."

"Could be. Right size. Big guy. At least, I think it's a guy. Whoever it is, he was killed, and the killer tried to use the fire to cover it up."

"Don't you be telling Ms. Bass that."

"I won't. We'll have to wait to confirm it anyway. No way to recognize the body except probably dental records."

Filly huffed. "Like Buddy ever wasted a nickel on a dentist."

"If it's DNA, it's going to be months for an ID."

"I'll take you to her. You better figure out what you're going to say 'cause I do not want that woman having a stroke in this office. You hear me?"

"Yes, ma'am."

She led him back to the examination room where Edna Bass sat on the low pediatrics table, her back against the wall. Her face was red and wet with tears. Jim's stomach knotted, but he took a chair next to her and sat down.

"Ms. Bass, do you want to tell me what happened this morning?" he asked her.

She nodded and took a wheezy breath. "I go down to the bar this morning like I always do. I do the deposits for Buddy and write the checks for the bills. When I got there, the door ain't locked. That's never happened before. Buddy's never up in the mornings. By the time he closes up, it's near 4 am, so he just puts everything in the office. I come in and take care of it. This morning, the door's unlocked, and when I go inside the lights are still on. The money was in the register. I know Buddy wouldn't leave the money like that." She sobbed softly. "Something's happened to him. I know it. He ain't at his house, and he ain't with anybody I know."

Jim took her hand and held it gently. "This is what we're going to do. I'm going to take you home, and then I'll go and check the bar myself. I'll probably need to get someone in there to look around to see if we can figure out what happened. While I do that, I want you to just go home and try to rest. Do you need someone to stay with you?"

Edna shook her head. "I can give you my keys. I didn't take nothing, just left it all like it was. I just looked for him, you know."

"I know. I know you're scared, too, but you have my word that as soon as I know anything for sure, I'll come and tell you myself. If I find Buddy, I'll bring him with me."

Edna nodded. "Thank you, Sheriff. I know he's been trouble to you, too, but he's my boy."

"I understand," Jim said. "We love our children, no matter what."

Jim stood up and helped Edna to her feet. Filly touched his shoulder and nodded approvingly. Jim suppressed his grin. He always felt stupidly proud when Filly Ellis approved of his actions.

Chapter Fifteen

Sergeant Dee Jackson met Jim at the Cedars Lounge. It was a one-story concrete block building with a gravel parking lot that sat on the edge of town. Four tall cedar trees backed up the place, which had no windows and only two doors. Edna's father had built the place in the late 1940s, and Edna had run it until Buddy was old enough to be inside it legally.

Jim unlocked the doors, and they walked inside together. The smell of stale beer and body odor was overwhelming.

"Christ Almighty!" said Dee, and she propped the front door open.

"You ever been here?" Jim asked.

Dee gave him her patented 'You stupid?' look. Bigger men than Jim had quailed at that face.

Jim realized how stupid his question was. Dee Jackson stood about 5'8" with a slender but muscled body. She'd been a track star at the local high school, joined the Marines, and been Military Police during Desert Storm. Then come back and gone on to get a Bachelor's Degree in Criminal Justice from the University of Florida. She was halfway through her Master's program. She'd taken the job with his department strictly because Jim was willing to work her schedule so she could go to school. She had neither the time nor the inclination to be in a place like the Cedars. Not to mention the fact that color lines were pretty much still recognized at the local bars. Though Jim never thought about any of his deputies by race, his momentary lapse about the rest of the county's attitude made him want to smack his own forehead.

"Sorry," he said.

Dee smiled at him. "I don't doubt that you spent some time in here during your reckless youth."

Jim blushed. "Surprisingly, no."

Dee laughed. "That's right. Your daddy was the sheriff. I don't imagine you were any more welcome in here than I would have been."

As Edna had said, the lights were on. Jim went to the bar and checked the register. The money was still in the drawer. The trash cans were empty, but the floor was a mess. None of the tables had been cleaned, and the chairs were scattered all around the floor as they would have been after a night of customers.

Jim pointed Dee to the office, and he went to check on the restrooms. They were filthy and stunk to the high heavens. He came out of the men's room coughing and trying not to gag. The women's restroom wasn't any better. But both were empty.

Dee came out of the office. "Doesn't look like anyone ever cleans this place. There's a shit-ton of nasty old girly mags stacked up all around that desk."

They went to the back door together, and it was unlocked and slightly open. Jim pushed it, and it hit something and drifted back to nearly closed. He tried to push it open, but whatever was on the other side was heavy.

"Here, let me," said Dee, and she slipped through the narrow opening. He heard a metal-on-concrete scraping sound, and then the door opened.

When Jim stepped out, he saw what she'd moved. There was a big metal bin full of bottles, cans, and flattened cardboard.

"Watch where you step, Sheriff," she said and held him back as he started to step around the bin. "There's blood over there."

There was. A tacky puddle covered one whole side of the concrete stoop on the other side of the bin. When Jim stepped around, he could see there was blood on the side of the bin as well.

"You want me to call for an FDLE team?" she asked.

"Bud Peterson's probably still out at the body site near Libby's. See if Junior can get him to swing by here before he heads back to his office."

"Will do." Dee walked around the side of the bar toward the parking lot. She'd radio from her patrol car.

Jim squatted down and looked more closely at the stains. The bin leaked, which explained why the blood on the concrete wasn't dry. The drips on the side of the bin were dry. The whole concrete pad under and around the bin smelled of beer and booze.

It looked more and more likely that his body out at Libby's might indeed be Buddy Bass. Thing was, with Buddy, the list of who might want him dead was pretty long. But that list got considerably shorter when you added, 'killed Buddy and didn't take the money out of the register.' Most of those who wanted Buddy dead would have taken the money, too.

Dee came back around the side of the bar. "Bud's going to be headed this way. He said to tell you he's sending the body on to the medical examiner, then he'll bring his team on over."

Jim stood up. "You want to wait here for him, or you want me to take it?"

"Oh hell, no, I'm not talking to Buddy's mama."

"Here, take the keys," he said, resigned to his duty. "I'll let her know that she shouldn't plan on opening up tonight. There's a key on there to Buddy's house. Call Junior and get the address and take Bud and his team there after they finish here."

Dee nodded. "Yes, sir."

* * *

Jim had just managed to get out of his car when Sheila Ward ambushed him.

"What happened to Buddy Bass?"

"I don't have any idea what you're talking about," Jim responded.

Sheila bristled more than normal. She pushed her sunglasses up on her head and motioned for a big man standing a short distance away to move closer. "Carl, take a picture of the Sheriff standing in front of Edna Bass' house. The caption will be 'Sheriff goes to talk to Edna Bass about nothing.'"

Jim snorted. "Don't waste my time, Sheila." He started walking up to the house.

"There's two men missing now," said Sheila. "Hatcher and Bass. What are you doing about it?"

Jim stopped. It took everything in him not to walk back and just take Sheila's head off, at least metaphorically. He turned around. "I'm doing everything I can. I'm following procedure. Searching for witnesses and evidence. What else can I do?"

"So Bass is missing."

Jim sighed. "All I know is he's not where he should be."

"Will Edna Bass talk to me?"

"About what?"

"About Buddy being missing?"

Lord, the woman never gave it a rest. "I think you should leave her alone."

Sheila rolled her eyes. "Like you thought I should leave the preacher's wife alone? If it was up to you, I'd never write about anything newsworthy. What are you going to tell her?"

Jim shook his head and turned back around. It made no sense to try to talk to Sheila. No matter what he said, she'd want more, or find some way to twist it to make her story more interesting. She called after him, but he just kept walking.

Edna stood in the doorway by the time he reached it. "Did you find him?"

"Let's go inside," he said.

Edna stepped back and let him in. She struggled over to an easy chair and settled herself into it. It had ruts where her body had rested against its fabric and stuffing. It fit her like a glove.

Jim sat down on the green Herculon couch. "I went by the bar and checked it out. Like you said, it was open, and the money still there. I left a deputy there to meet a team to go over the place and see if we could find any evidence of what might have happened."

"What's that reporter want?"

Jim winced. "She wants to talk to you. She's got a photographer with her. You may have heard that there's a young preacher missing."

Edna shook her head. "I didn't. You think it's got something to do with Buddy being gone?"

"No, I don't," Jim said. "I think that she's just looking for something to write about."

Edna nodded. "Then she can just sit out there 'til she rots. I got nothing to say to her."

Jim wanted to grin at that. Edna Bass had handled too many drunks in her life to be intimidated by one short, woman reporter. "We may have found some blood out in back of the bar," Jim said gently. "We can't be sure about it until we get it checked."

Edna nodded. "Buddy's always getting into something with somebody. Might not be his, and that might be why he's gone."

Jim was grateful that Edna's mind went to that possibility.

"You'll tell me if you find out something?" she asked.

Jim reached over and touched the back of Edna's plump hand. "Yes, ma'am. I'll come myself."

"All right then," she said. She settled back into her chair.

Chapter Sixteen

Jim got a call from Bud once he got back to his office.

"I hate to break the news to you, but I think you got something nasty going on."

Jim sighed. "Okay, hit me with it."

"Your corpse had blunt trauma on the skull, which would be consistent with the amount of blood we found at that bar, and his neck was broken. That's what killed him. Coroner says, from the looks of the break, your murderer is at least as tall as the dead man, but probably bigger. The head was twisted to the left, so probably a left-handed man. Though I've seen some big women that might be able to do it, with the struggle, I'm figuring it's another man."

Shit. "Wouldn't surprise me. Buddy Bass had a habit of making enemies."

The tea in Bud's eternal mug swirled as he took a drink. "We also found a message."

"Oh, hell's bells, Bud," Jim said.

"Found it on one of the tables. Had a couple of beer bottles holding it down, but no fingerprints on anything. You want to guess what it said?"

"No." Jim wanted to put is head on his desk and just closed his eyes.

"Behold, all souls are Mine; as the soul of the father, so also the soul of the son is Mine; the soul that sinneth, it shall die."

Jim swallowed the bile that rose in his throat. "How was it written?"

"Not written. Page torn out of a Bible, the words highlighted in blood."

"O+ again?"

"Yep. King James version." Jim set his mug down with a soft thump. "I

68

think you got yourself a serial killer."

"Don't say that, Bud, I …."

"Hey, I'm not the one with a missing preacher," Bud interrupted. "You ever find out who named Eden, you need to go piss on his grave."

Jim almost laughed. Depend on Bud to bring that up. It'd been a running joke with him for years that naming a county that was so poverty-ridden and mostly swamp took a madman.

"Seriously though, I do think it may be your bar owner. That bleed was pretty consistent with a head wound. Seen my share of those in this business."

"Thanks, Bud. I'll wait for a definitive identification before I notify his mother. Just in case."

Bud snorted. "You're a soft heart, Jim Sheppard. Going to get your ass killed for it someday."

"I'll make note of that, Bud."

Chapter Seventeen

The day had been routine pediatric and sick adult examinations. Doc Markham had already headed over to Gainesville to see the hospitalized patients. Everything had moved along quickly, and Ryan found himself making notes in his last chart as Filly Ellis gathered her things together to go home.

"You seem to be getting the hang of this small-town doctoring thing," Filly said, leaning toward him and speaking softly.

Ryan smiled. "Yeah, I think so."

"You have yourself a good evening."

She grabbed up her bag and disappeared out the back door. The young woman who worked the front desk had left as soon as the last patient checked out. Ryan heard the click of the door locking behind him and focused on finishing his notes.

He put the folder in the tray of things to be filed and began shutting off the last of the lights. He let himself out the front door and turned to walk to his car when he found himself face to face with a short woman who was thin and had a sharp face with a look of distaste on it. He made a startled sound.

"Where's Doc Markham?" she asked.

Ryan took a deep breath and tried to get his heart rate to slow down. "Gainesville. Is there something I can...do?"

"It's a medical question. I would have been here before, but I had to cover the 4H equestrian event, and it's impossible to get away from a group of excited kids who think they might get their names in the newspaper. I barely escaped when I did. Are you the new doctor?"

God, the woman was abrasive. The last thing in the world Ryan wanted to do was admit he was, but he was also sure if he didn't, she'd make his life a misery. "Yes."

"Won't take that long." She pulled up her shirt and pulled down the waist of her pants a bit, and showed him a red spot on her skin. "I had a tick the other day, and does that look like that bull's eye thing that's bad news?"

Ryan was almost relieved. He knelt down to get a closer look. Sure enough, there was a definite ring around the tick bite. "When did this happen?"

"Four days ago."

"Yeah. You'll need…antibiotics. I can write…a script, but I'd like to get your file…"

"Well, shit. That's what I get for being out in the damn woods. The things I do for a story. I really don't have the time for this."

"You need to make the time," Ryan said curtly. He wouldn't let her not get the medical care she needed, but he also didn't have to be nice about it. He unlocked the front door, and they went in together. "What's your name?"

"Sheila Ward."

He found her file and made a notation in it about the tick bite, and after he wrote the prescription, he put the copy in the file.

"Take all of it. This early you'll probably catch it….not have any problems."

"Okay. Is this stuff going to be expensive? I don't have insurance."

Ryan took a deep breath. "No, it's amoxicillin. Generic and cheap."

"Good," she said and headed for the door.

They walked back out, and Ryan locked the door again. "Get that …. start taking it today. Don't wait."

"Yeah, yeah," she said as she walked away.

That woman probably poisoned the tick, Ryan thought as he headed for his car.

Chapter Eighteen

Ryan threw the tennis ball to the farthest corner of the back yard. Bonehead ran after it and caught it on the first bounce. Then he dashed back to Ryan carrying it in his mouth. The bright, neon ball was covered in leaf debris, dirt, and dog slobber. He grimaced as he took the ball from the dog, tossed it again, this time to another corner. This one Bonehead caught before it hit the ground.

Then he dropped to the ground to chew on the ball for a bit. He did that when he was tired and wanted to take a break. Ryan sat on the bottom steps that led to his apartment and waited for the dog to catch his breath and come back for more.

The Sheriff's car pulled up in the drive, and a moment later, the man himself wandered up to the gate. He took in the sight of Ryan and Bonehead.

"You wearing each other out?" he asked.

"I think we're both…weather is hot," replied Ryan. He grinned. "Pull up a piece of stair, Sheriff."

Jim laughed and opened the gate, and joined him at the steps, but instead of sitting, he leaned back against the garage wall. "I imagine it will take some getting used to. Though I hear that D.C. can be pretty hot and muggy in the summer."

"It can. That's not the problem. The smoke."

Jim nodded. "Yeah, it's getting to everyone. You having many patients with breathing problems?"

"A couple of asthma cases…… Most people are…staying indoors. Doc's got a few… he's worried about. Smokers. Work outdoors ….. can't escape it."

"Yeah, I've got a deputy who falls into that camp. I told him to keep his car closed up and use the air conditioning as much as possible."

Bonehead got up and carried his ball across the yard, then dropped it at Jim's feet. Jim picked it up, bounced it once in his hand, and then rifled it toward the chain link fence.

Bonehead followed the ball's trajectory, and when it rebounded hard off the fence and up into the air, he ran out, jumped, and came down with the ball in his mouth.

He trotted back to Jim and dropped the ball again.

Ryan whistled. "Never seen him do….that. Course, I can't throw like that."

Jim laughed. "I played baseball in high school. Center field. Always had a pretty good arm."

He threw the ball again, bouncing it off the fence in almost exactly the same place. Bonehead grabbed it out of the air and ran back to Jim. If a dog could be said to smile, he was doing it when he dropped the ball at Jim's feet.

"I played zero sports."

"You look like you work out."

Ryan felt a little jolt of self-consciousness. "Yeah. I…lift weights…a while ago. Is there a…place to do that here?"

"Pete's Gym. It's not fancy, but it's got weights and a couple of treadmills. I go there. Pete's a good guy."

Ryan took a breath. "I'll have to try it. I like to…keep strong."

"Tell Pete I sent you. He'll treat you right." He sent the ball rocketing toward the fence in the back. Bonehead read it exactly right and leaped, catching the ball. "Have you eaten, yet? I'm going to have to cook for Michael. No hardship to add another place at the table."

Ryan shook his head. "No, thanks. I ate. On call tonight."

Jim tossed him the sticky tennis ball. "Hope you have a quiet evening."

"Same to you, Sheriff."

Jim shook his head. "I need it."

Ryan watched him walk to the back door of his home and go inside. He couldn't help but like the man. He'd thought Jim might work out from his build. He had broad shoulders and well-defined arms, which usually indicated someone who lifted weights. More, though, he admired that for a big man, he had a quiet demeanor. Comfortable with showing affection for his son, and a good sense of humor. He'd made Ryan trust him since the first day they'd met.

He'd never expected to find himself friends with someone in law enforcement. Most of his interactions with law officers had been…formal.

The detective who'd taken the lead on his case in D.C. had been cordial and…gentle, but he had never been a friend. This really was a whole new world for him.

Bonehead dropped to the ground at his feet and panted. "You like him, too," he said to the dog. Then he laughed at himself and Bonehead. The dog grinned back.

Chapter Nineteen

Reynold Stendal lived in a nice house on a beautiful street in Valdosta, Georgia. Jim sat across from the two-story red brick structure and noted the car in the driveway. It had a baby carrier in the back seat and was a new model. The lawn was lush and green. Jim realized how odd a green yard looked to him. In Eden County, the drought had been so bad the only people with grass were ones who had irrigation systems, which pretty much left out ninety percent of the county.

A very pregnant woman came out of the house and walked down to the mailbox at the corner of the driveway. She gathered up the mail and went back into the house.

Jim looked at the papers Junior had gathered again. Reynold Stendal was 39. A Certified Public Accountant, he worked for a small company. He'd been with them since he'd graduated from the University of Georgia with his Master's degree. He had married five years ago to a woman who was eleven years younger than him. She taught school, algebra, at Valdosta High School. Currently, on maternity leave, she was expected to deliver any day.

They both had excellent credit. Last year Reynold had inherited a decent amount of money when his father died. His mother had died years before, and Reynold was an only child.

He was also well insured. And he was dying.

Jim took a deep breath and let it out slowly. The last thing he wanted to do was go and talk to this man. However, he had to do it. He knew that if he talked to Stendal, he wasn't likely to confess that he'd had Hatcher kidnapped and was planning on stealing the man's liver. But he wanted to see the man and talk to him, and get a sense of who he was.

The other thing was if Stendal wasn't there. If he was mysteriously "absent," it would be one more piece of the puzzle. At that point, Jim would have to get others involved. At the very least, the local Valdosta authorities.

He opened the car door and got out. He straightened his uniform. He'd decided he needed to be clear who he was when he talked with this man. If seeing Jim's uniform rattled him at all, it would just add strength to Jim's suspicions.

His knock on the front door was answered quickly by the pregnant woman. She looked surprised to see a law enforcement officer standing at her door.

"I'm looking to speak with Reynold Stendal. My name is Jim Sheppard."

She nodded and opened the door wider to let him in. "Reynold's upstairs. I'll go get him. You can have a seat in the living room," she said.

She had a soft Georgia accent, and had quickly gathered herself after her initial surprise. Jim moved toward the living room and saw her go up the stairs, calling to her husband as she went.

A few minutes later, a very thin man came into the living room. Jim stood up. Reynold Stendal looked far older than 39. His skin had a slight yellow cast, and he looked fragile. Jim had photos of him from several years ago, and he'd been a handsome man, if somewhat frail looking. Now he looked like what he was, a man who would not live much longer.

Jim held out his hand, "Mr. Stendal, I'm Jim Sheppard. I'm sorry to interrupt your day, but I need to speak with you."

Reynold Stendal shook his hand firmly. "Certainly, though I can't imagine why."

They sat down, Jim on the couch and Stendal in a nearby chair.

"I'm the Sheriff in Eden County, Florida. We've had a man go missing. A man whose blood type is AB Negative."

Stendal's eyes widened. "Oh." He rose from his chair. "Sheriff, if you'll excuse me just a moment. I'd like us to take this conversation into my study, where we can close the door. Do you mind?"

Jim was startled. "No. That's fine."

Stendal led him toward another room on the other side of the house. As they walked, Mrs. Stendal came down the hall.

"I was going to see if you'd like something to drink, Reynold," she said.

"No, we're fine, Wendy. It's about work, so we'll be in my office. The files I need are there."

She smiled. "Oh! All right. Let me know if you want something."

When they reached the office, Stendal closed the door and locked it. He motioned for Jim to take a seat in a chair near the desk. Instead of sitting behind the desk, he sat in a chair across from Jim.

"Did Dr. Clinton send you?" he asked.

"She gave me your name. She said you'd taken your name off the transplant list."

Stendal nodded. "And that coinciding with your man's disappearance led you here."

"Yes."

Stendal sat back and covered his face for a moment. When he began to speak again, his voice was very soft. He didn't want anyone to overhear what he said.

"I had nothing to do with your man's disappearance. I don't have anything to prove that, other than saying I haven't been anywhere but home for the past two weeks. I've been going through a bad time." Stendal stopped speaking.

The silence went on a long time, but Jim let it. He knew that Stendal needed to explain. He'd give him the time to do it.

"I've been sick for a long time. I have sclerosing cholangitis. For the past eight years, I've been in and out of hospitals. I've had an endless number of scans, tests, and twelve surgeries. After the last surgery, I realized that I was nearing the lifetime cap on my health insurance. If I have a transplant, I will hit that cap, and then I will go on needing medications, tests, scans and care for long after that. It will eat through every penny that I've saved, inherited, or could possibly earn."

Jim's mind reeled. Lifetime cap on health insurance. "But that's…"

"Impossible? No. It's really not. My policy had a $1 million cap. I'm within one hundred thousand of that right now. That wouldn't even cover the cost of my hospitalization for the transplant."

"God," Jim whispered.

"I made a decision. We have a child on the way. It's something we both really wanted. I won't be well, and I won't live long, but I'll live enough to know him. And when I do die, I won't have bankrupted his future."

"A son?" Jim asked.

Stendal smiled. "Yes. A son."

Jim reached for his wallet. He took out a photo of Michael. "I have a son, too. Michael."

Stendal smiled. "He's a good-looking boy." He handed back the photo to Jim.

They were both silent again.

Finally, Jim said, "I'm sorry."

Stendal shook his head. "It's the right decision. Wendy always knew there was a chance there would be no transplant, so when the end comes, she'll be fine."

"Thank you for explaining," Jim said.

They stood and shook hands. "I wouldn't want to cause you any delay. I hope you find the missing man."

"Me, too," said Jim.

Stendal started to go to the door, but then he turned back to Jim. "Don't tell Dr. Clinton. She's a wonderful doctor, but she'll try to talk me out of this plan."

"There are other ways...," Jim started.

Stendal shook his head. "To qualify for financial assistance, I'd have to have spent everything. I can't do that. This way, someone else gets a chance."

When Jim left the house and got into his car, he felt a crushing sorrow in his chest. He looked back at the beautiful brick home. You just never knew what kind of pain a house held. As Jim sat there a moment, he remembered his conversation with Bud. It seemed his prediction about Jim's soft side was coming true sooner than expected. It wouldn't kill him outright, but it would likely break him in ways he'd never imagined. He would never be able to forget the man who planned for his death so his son would have a good life.

Chapter Twenty

Jim stretched out on the couch and idly watched a baseball game. He didn't give a damn which team won, but it was easy on his mind, which he needed at the moment. He needed a break after the last few days. After his meeting with Reynold Stendal, Jim returned to Warren. He'd had no leads to follow up. He'd talked to Dr. Renaldi by phone and let him know that the tip from Savannah had turned into nothing. As promised, he hadn't elaborated on why.

The baseball game in the background allowed his thoughts about Hatcher, the body from the fire, and Buddy Bass to percolate. Maybe Bud Peterson was right. Maybe the fires were driving everyone bugshit crazy. God knows, the list of people who would want to hurt Buddy Bass was long. He'd worked hard to make himself the biggest pain in the ass he could possibly be.

Hatcher, however, was a complete mystery. He'd been the pastor at his little church for just over a year, and by all reports was popular with his congregation. Even the other ministers in town liked him. Other than his rare blood type, there didn't seem to be any reason to have a particular interest in Hatcher.

What possible connection could there be between the two men? The Bible verse proved the connection existed, but damned if Jim could find it.

It would be just like one of the half-assed idiots who hung around the Cedars to try to get rid of a body by putting it in the path of the wildfires, but he could not imagine one of them having a reason to take the preacher. Plus, he doubted any of them would think to leave a page of the Bible behind that would connect the two crimes.

He rubbed at his forehead and watched the current batter hit a pop fly that was caught by the first baseman. Both teams moved, one toward the field, the other toward their bench.

When the phone rang, Jim groaned out loud. He swung his feet off the couch and paused before he rose. If this was more bad news, he was going to seriously consider unplugging the damn phone, going to bed, and just letting everyone wait until the morning to find him.

As if that was an option.

When he picked up the phone, he heard Deputy Manny Sota's voice, "Sheriff, we've got an explosion and fire west of the Hammock Hunting Club."

"There are no fires west of the Hammock."

"There is now. Mike Rountree's meth lab blew up."

"That's where it was?"

"Yep."

Jim sighed deeply. This week just kept getting worse. "How bad?"

"Well, what was a bunch of scrub oak is now a forest fire. The Hammock's got a bunch of guys from Levy Timber out cutting firebreaks with bulldozers."

"I'll be there in twenty."

Jim hung up the phone. When he turned around, Michael stood in the hallway.

"You going out again?"

"Yeah," Jim walked over and put a hand on Michael's shoulder. His son was nearly his height and only sixteen. In another year, he'd be taller than Jim.

"Be careful," Michael said.

"Promise. You get to bed on time. You've still got finals."

Michael grinned. "I always go to bed on time."

Jim snorted. "Yeah, right."

He ruffled Michael's hair which earned him a squawk as he headed back into the kitchen to gather his keys.

* * *

The trailer was scrap metal and smoke when Jim arrived, but the woods all around it blazed with uncontrolled fire. Men from Levy Timber used shovels and chainsaws to try to contain what was burning. A bulldozed track from the road to the site had kept the fire from moving further north, and it would stop once it hit the beach to the west, but God only knew what was going on to the south and east.

Manny Soto was leaning against his patrol car, watching everything burn. Not that there was much he could do otherwise, but it still seemed weird to Jim.

He parked behind him, walked over to lean against the car next to him. He could feel the heat from the fire then. Manny was sweating. He'd opened his uniform shirt and tied a wet bandana around his neck.

"Hey, Sheriff," he said. He sipped at a large cola.

"Manny." Jim took a moment to look over the scene. He could see the frame of a truck behind what had been a decent-sized travel trailer. "You called for an arson team?"

"Yep. They said it'd be at least tomorrow before they could get here."

"You sure this was Rountree's place?"

Manny nodded. "You could smell the chemicals before the fire got out into the trees so bad. The trailer was burning when I got here, but the truck hadn't gone up, yet. I got around to one side so I could see the tag. It's Rountree's. Dumbass."

Jim had to agree. Only Rountree would be stupid enough to set up and cook meth in the middle of the woods during a drought. Of course, if he'd had two brain cells to rub together, he wouldn't be cooking the meth himself. Pretty much everyone knew that Rountree was his own best customer. He used more than he sold.

"The Hammock people dozing a firebreak south of this?"

"Yep. They said they would try to contain it down to County Road 361. They figure it'll burn to the Gulf on the west, but nothing we can do about it. It's only about three miles."

"What a mess," said Jim. "Hopefully, he didn't manage to kill anyone other than himself."

Manny shrugged. "Won't know until we get the arson team in. They said they didn't want FDLE mucking around in it until they finished. Bud Peterson sent word he wasn't making another trip out here today."

Jim laughed. "Yeah, I imagine he did. Damn, we don't really have the manpower to waste watching this scene."

The two men walked as close to the trailer as they could. The ground was hot, but they could get close enough to see that other than the base of the trailer and the concrete blocks it rested on, there wasn't much there.

"Call McNally's and have them bring out some concrete barriers. He's got a crane and a flatbed that can set them out across the firebreak. Stay here until it's done, then get back on your patrol."

Manny nodded. "That should work pretty well. At least keep the lookie-loos from driving in to see what's left."

"I'll head back into town and see if I can find his father."

"He's usually at the Cedars by this time of day, but since it's not open tonight, he might be over in Alachua County, or someplace that's got a bar. I know he's not at the Terrell's or Conseco's."

Jim sighed. "Lord, with any luck, his truck's broken down, and he's at home. I'll find him."

Jim headed back to his car. Nothing could be done here tonight. Once the way in was blocked off, at least the curious would be forced to walk in, and most of them wouldn't bother. Especially not with there being fire in the area.

* * *

When Jim found Elvin Rountree at home, he didn't get more than a moment to enjoy not having to search for the man. The door to the trailer slammed open, and Elvin stood there, a cigarette dangling from his lower lip. He was a thin man with a pot belly, and his Black Sabbath t-shirt didn't quite meet the belt of his pants.

"He ain't here," Elvin shouted, "so go on and just take yourself right on back out the way you came in."

Jim spoke quietly, "Elvin, Mike's lab out in the Hammock blew up tonight."

Elvin waved a hand at Jim, clearly not buying into what he was saying. "Bullshit. He ain't even got a lab out there."

"I saw it. His truck is there. Not that there's much left of it, either. He also set a good chunk of land on fire. It's the truth, Elvin."

"You find a body, then you come talk to me." Elvin stepped back inside his trailer and slammed the door.

Jim considered banging on it until Elvin opened up again, but knowing the man, he'd be armed this time, and the whole thing would escalate. Finally, he just shook his head and went back to his car. Once the arson team got in there, they'd find what was left of Mike Rountree, and then he'd come back and talk to Elvin. Until then, he didn't see any point to wasting his time. He'd just go home and get some sleep.

He got into his car and sat for a moment in the silence. He just felt sad. Two sons lost in two days. Sometimes his job just sucked.

Chapter Twenty-One

Ryan pulled up in front of Pete's gym around 7 pm. There were several other cars and trucks in the gravel parking lot. The building itself was clean, painted bright white. Big plate glass windows fronted it. He took a deep breath and grabbed his gym bag. He really hated going in to new places. "Well, asshole, you…moved," he said to himself softly.

He got out of his car and walked up to the door. When he opened it, he heard the clanging of weights accented by grunts and conversations. The smell was familiar. Metal, sweat, and Icy-Hot. The air was cool and flowing but not cold. He could see fans and hear the gentle rumble of central air conditioning.

A man a few inches shorter than Ryan walked up. His shaved head shone with a light sweat, but his smile was bright and unforced. He held out his hand. "Pete Jones. You're new here."

Ryan shook his hand. "Ryan Edwards."

Pete nodded. "New doc. Heard about you. You wanting to work out?"

Ryan nodded. "The Sheriff said this was….place to go."

Pete laughed loudly. "Yeah, unless you drive to another county, it's the only place to go. Come on in, and we'll get you set up."

Pete gave him a tour of the gym, explaining the setup and the rules. "Do you have a routine you want to work with?" Pete asked.

Ryan took out the small notebook he'd carried in his gym bag for the past year and a half. In it were records of the weights he was using, the settings of the machines, and what he'd done each time he'd been in the gym in Connecticut. His notations showed a steady increase in weight and repetitions as he'd gotten stronger with each passing week. He'd barely been out of the hospital two months when he'd begun the workouts. The minute he'd been cleared for exercise, he'd found a facility and hired a trainer, and started keeping his meticulous records.

"Well, I don't have these machines, but from this, I can help you design a workout plan that will give you the same results. That work for you?"

Ryan nodded. "Thanks. Yes."

They worked together for nearly an hour, with Pete showing him the exercises, correcting his form so that he would know how to do each one in a way that would maximize his effort and not cause injury.

Bench presses, and pull-ups were easy. The introduction to lunges left him exhausted. Curls and dips would work his arms in ways the machines had before. Pete knew his stuff, and Ryan felt grateful that Jim had prepared the way for him.

Ryan stood at the desk finishing up the paperwork for his membership when he heard a shout on the other side of the gym. Several men moved quickly to lift a bar off a man lying on a bench.

"Oh, no," said Pete softly, and he ran from the desk to where the men stood. Pete knelt next to the man on the bench, then turned his head and shouted to Ryan, "Doc! Quick!"

Ryan dropped everything and ran to him. It was obvious the minute he saw the man. The bar had dropped on his throat. His face was pale, and his arms flailed weakly. No sound came from his wide-open mouth.

Ryan pushed Pete aside. "Something sharp," he said. Pete got up and ran to the first aid cabinet at the desk, and three men pulled pocket knives out of gym bags.

Ryan took the one with the newest-looking blade. Pete came back with a couple of small, clean, white towels and a bottle of rubbing alcohol. Ryan said nothing, just poured the alcohol on the blade of the knife, wiped it with the towel. Then he used the towel to wipe the man's throat.

He felt for the thyroid cartilage, moved his finger down to locate the cricoid cartilage. Between the two, he made a small horizontal cut. He pushed his finger through. "I need ….hold this open, …..straw."

Pete shook his head. Then he held up a finger and rushed to his desk. He came back with a ballpoint pen with a bank's name on it.

"…..Bottom…..of that," Ryan said.

Pete unscrewed the pen's shell and handed it to Ryan, who set it into the hole. Another man offered him a roll of coach's tape. Ryan instructed him on tearing off some strips and used them to tape the pen to the skin around the hole.

Pete handed him the case of the ballpoint pen from the desk. Ryan inserted it into the hole and leaned over, and breathed into it.

He turned to Pete. "Ambulance."

"You got it, Doc," Pete said. He ran to his desk and dialed 911.

Everyone standing around began to cheer. The man lying on the bench reached out and grabbed Ryan's arm.

"You're okay," Ryan said. "Just breathe."

The man nodded slightly and smiled.

* * *

After the ambulance left, Ryan and Pete finally got back to the desk. Ryan took his wallet out of his gym bag to pay for his membership, but Pete waived him off.

"Doc, you have a free membership here as long as you want. You saved that guy's life, and probably my business. I don't know what I'd have done if he'd died."

Ryan shook his head, "The…ambulance…."

"Probably wouldn't have gotten here in time. You may have noticed that Eden County isn't exactly swimming in money. It took them fifteen minutes to get here after I called, and they came in with sirens. No, you saved him, and I owe you. So you're money's no good in here ever. You've got a lifetime membership, on me."

Ryan felt himself blushing. "Okay."

Pete slapped him on the shoulder. "And if you need someone to help you,

you let me know." He turned to the others in the gym. "You know you're not supposed to be lifting without a spotter! I catch any of you doing that again, you won't have to drop the bar on yourself. I'll drop it on you and then kick your ass out the door!" he said. There were some embarrassed nods and a little muttering. It wasn't likely that safety precaution would be forgotten in the near future.

* * *

Ryan had barely gotten into the driveway at the house when a car pulled up behind him. The woman with the tick bite got out of it. She stalked toward him so directly he had to stop himself from backing away from her.

A big man got out of the car behind her. He carried a camera and had a bag slung over one shoulder.

The woman motioned to the man without looking behind her. "Carl, get a shot of him here. I like this. This looks good." Her demand did not allow for any compromise.

Ryan stood perfectly still, feeling that he probably had a distinct "deer in the headlights" look on his face, but for the life of him, he couldn't change it.

The big man walked up to within a few feet of him and raised the camera, and snapped off a series of photos. When he lowered the camera, he stared into Ryan's eyes so intensely, he felt as though the man was trying to read his thoughts.

The woman pushed the photographer aside. "You remember me, Doc? Sheila Ward. I'm with the Eden Evening Star. I need to talk to you."

"Why?"

"You did surgery in Pete's Gym."

"What?"

"You saved a man," said the photographer. His voice was soft.

Ryan raised a hand defensively. "It wasn't...sur...surgery. I just opened... .airway."

"You cut into a guy with a pocket knife. That's surgery as far as the people around here are concerned. I need to talk to you. You living in the apartment there?"

Ryan nodded.

"Good. We'll do the interview there. Carl, get more photos. I'm going front page with this."

Ryan stood frozen. "No. No."

Sheila Ward marched past him. "Don't be a dumbshit. You're new here. You could use the good press. People don't trust anyone but that old fucker Markham. This will get them to like you, do you more good than being here for a couple of years."

She opened the gate and walked right up the stairs to his apartment. Carl stood quietly in front of Ryan, as though allowing him the courtesy of heading to his own apartment first. Ryan didn't give a damn who the woman was, or that she thought the good press would do him good at the practice, he really didn't like being bulldozed.

He looked at Carl. "Tell Ms. Ward…not startle…the dog." Then he walked to the front door of the Sheriff's house and went inside.

No one was home. Michael had admitted to Ryan that they never locked their doors. He said his dad figured it would just invite some dumb kid to break a window to get in, and they didn't have anything worth stealing. So he just left the place open.

Ryan locked the front door behind him, then went through to the kitchen and locked the back door. He stood to the side of the back door and watched Sheila Ward open the door to his apartment. He wasn't disappointed. Bonehead flew through the door and knocked her back against the rails at the top of the stairs. He then flew down the stairs and headed straight for the gate.

Ryan quickly unlocked the door, whistled, and Bonehead stopped, turned, and ran to the back door and inside. He closed the door, locked it again, and then sat down at the kitchen table. Bonehead sat on the floor next to him, tail thumping the leg of the table.

Ryan rubbed his head and ears. "Good dog," he said.

Bonehead smiled.

Sheila Ward made a lot of noise outside. She banged on the back door, then went around to the front and banged on the front door. Ryan and Bonehead just sat and waited for her to get tired and leave.

Finally, they heard cars pulling away from the front. Ryan went and looked out the window and saw that both Ward and the photographer were gone. He signed in relief. He unlocked the front door, and then he and Bonehead left through the back door.

He'd barely gotten into his apartment when his phone rang. He wasn't on call, so he thought about not answering, but he did.

"Ryan, what the hell did you do to set off Sheila Ward?" Doc Markham's voice was gruff. "She's at the front desk demanding to see me and says it's about you."

"Crap," Ryan said softly. "I'm sorry. I…" he struggled to find the word he wanted. "At the gym, a man, tracheotomy," he choked out.

"He die?"

"No. I saved him."

Doc sighed. "You just don't want to talk to her."

"Yes."

Ryan heard the thump of the Doc putting his feet up on his desk. "Will you talk to her if I'm there?"

Ryan ran his hands through his hair and took a deep breath. "Maybe. Should I?"

"It's either that or have her stalk you for the next few days."

Ryan groaned.

"All right. I'll get her settled down and call you back. Relax. Have a beer or something."

Doc Markham hung up, and Ryan dropped into a chair. Bonehead settled down on the rug he'd claimed as his own in the room. He raised his eyebrows and glanced up at Ryan. "I know. You did your best." Bonehead heaved a great sigh.

Chapter Twenty-Two

The arson investigator worked carefully through the debris of the burned trailer. Jim waited at the barriers. He had posted a deputy out on the road and walked in to talk to the man from the Fire Marshall's office in Ocala. The investigator had been on the scene for a couple of hours already.

Arson was rare enough in the county that Jim didn't really know any of the investigators from the regional office. He'd kept his own people off the site, and FDLE didn't want to send anyone in until after the arson guy had his look. No sense in mucking up each other's work.

Finally, the man made his way out of the ruins and walked over to Jim. He was a short, heavy-set man, but his bright blue eyes were sharp and intelligent. He held out his hand to Jim, "Dwayne Henry, Sheriff."

"Jim Sheppard, sir. Can you give me anything preliminary?"

Dwayne nodded. "Accidental explosion and fire from poorly ventilated space and volatile chemicals. In other words, your dumbshit left a lit cigarette in an ashtray while he was making meth."

"What about Rountree?"

"Not dead, as far as I know."

"He wasn't in there?"

"There's definitely no body. Maybe you're guy was outside for some reason when it went up."

"Shit," said Jim. "Thanks. Okay to turn it over to FDLE now?"

"Sure. I've gotten what I need for my report. You'll have it by late tomorrow. I've got some debris to test, but I don't think I'm going to find anything new."

The man walked past Jim, heading for his truck.

Jim stared at the ruins of the trailer. Well, Elvin would be happy because, apparently, his son wasn't dead.

Jim stopped at Russell's car. The older deputy had backed his car into the dirt track that led to the trailer. "I'm going to call the FDLE and have them send a team out. I'd like you to wait here and stay while they work."

"Yes, sir, Sheriff," Russell answered.

Jim looked out at the narrow road in front of them. There wouldn't be much traffic on it. It wouldn't be bow hunting season for another few weeks, which meant that the only people at the Hammock were those checking their feed lots and game cameras. That was both good and bad. Good, because it kept lookie-loos to a minimum, but bad because it meant there probably wouldn't any witnesses.

Damn Rountree. He'd made a hell of a mess, and they needed more fires like they needed extra assholes. They'd just been damn lucky that it hadn't spread more than it did. They'd lost a good three or four square miles of woods. It had probably driven a lot of game south, which was going to piss off a bunch of hunters in the Hammock.

"Fuck," Jim said aloud. Then he went and got into his car to head back to town.

He'd just reached the city limits when Junior called on the radio. "Sheriff, I called FDLE. They're sending a team out to the Hammock to look over that fire."

"Thanks, Junior. Let me know if something comes up. I'm going home to have a late lunch. Call the house if you need me."

Some leftover spaghetti called Jim's name as he drove up to his house. He could almost taste it. Then he saw the cars in his driveway. "What the hell?"

Jim pulled up in front of his house and got out of his car. He didn't want to block any of the other cars from leaving, because he was damn well going to be getting rid of them as soon as possible.

Bonehead stood on the inside of the gate to the back yard and barked and growled at Sheila Ward. She stood at the gate screaming for Ryan

Edwards to come control his dog. The photographer, Carl, stood behind Sheila silently, and Doc Markham sat on the hood of his car laughing.

"What is going on?" Jim asked.

"Sheila wants to interview Ryan, and the dog won't let her in the gate."

"Why?"

"Why Sheila or why the dog?"

"Either, both!"

At that, Sheila stomped down the drive to Jim and pointed a finger at him. "You! You get that dog and then get out of my way!"

Jim leaned against Doc's car. "If Dr. Edwards wanted to talk to you, he'd do it."

Sheila pointed at Doc. "You! You said he'd talk to me if we came here with you!"

Markham shrugged. "Maybe he doesn't know we're here?"

"Bullshit!" Sheila marched back to the gate and screamed up at the apartment. "Dr. Edwards, you promised!"

Doc turned to Jim, "Actually, he didn't, but that woman isn't going to listen to me."

Jim sighed. "What is going on?"

Doc laughed. "Ryan did an emergency tracheotomy at Pete's with a pocket knife and a ballpoint pen."

Jim whistled. "That's impressive."

Doc shrugged, "Not so much for the former whiz kid of Washington Hospital Center's ER. He's a great doctor, but the talking thing screwed up his career up there. We're damn lucky to get him."

Sheila continued screaming at the gate, and Bonehead continued barking.

Jim sighed. "I really ought to go up there."

Doc nodded. "Probably so."

Jim walked up to the gate and opened it. Bonehead backed away, tail wagging. Sheila tried to follow him through, and Bonehead lunged at her, backing her up on the other side of the gate.

Jim wanted to say, "Good dog," but he didn't want to hear Sheila start screaming again. Instead, he walked up the stairs to the apartment and opened the door.

Ryan was not in the living room. Jim looked through and could see him sitting in the rocking chair out on the screened-in porch off the bedroom.

"All right if I come in?"

Ryan motioned him in.

Jim took a seat in a nearby chair. The smell of smoke was heavy in the air, and the haze hung in the trees, blocking out the sun. Ryan's face was in shadow, but Jim could see the brightness in his eyes. "Bonehead's keeping Sheila Ward from coming up here, but I wouldn't put it past her to eventually shoot him. She's not one to let a story get away from her."

Ryan shook his head. "He really doesn't like her."

Jim snorted. "Smart dog. No one likes Sheila. But you'd be doing me a favor if you did the story. Any good news helps right now."

"Can't find your preacher?"

"Nope. And I've got a body, a missing bar owner, and a meth lab exploded and set the woods on fire south of town."

Ryan whistled.

"Any reason you don't want to talk to Sheila, other than the obvious, that she's a massive pain in the ass?"

"I don't like ... talking."

"Okay. I'll go run her off."

Jim started to get up.

"Is Doc Markham out there?" Ryan asked softly.

"Yep."

Ryan ran his hands through his hair and stood up. "Not fair to him."

"If it helps, I think he's amused by the stand-off."

Ryan smiled. "Good."

They walked down the steps together. Bonehead snapped at Sheila's fingers when she tried to unlatch the gate. She screamed in frustration. Then she saw Jim and Ryan.

"Well, it's about damn time."

Bonehead turned, saw Ryan, and came trotting over to him. Ryan reached down and rubbed the dog's ears. "It's okay," he said, "you did a good job."

The flash of a camera went off, startling both Jim and Ryan. Jim looked up at the photographer. The man's face was obscured by the camera as he focused intently on Ryan. The flash went off two more times, making Ryan turn his head away.

Doc Markham appeared next to the photographer and pushed the camera down. The flash went off toward the ground.

"Stop that," Doc said. He moved past Sheila and through the gate. "So, you want to do this up in your apartment or down here?"

"Down here," Ryan said.

Doc turned to Sheila, "Get in here, but stay away from the dog. I think he likes lizard meat."

Sheila huffed, but she came through the gate and stood a short distance away. "I need photos."

"You just got them."

The photographer stepped toward the gate, and Bonehead growled. He stopped and looked at the dog. "Sheila, I can't go in there."

"God save me from cowards," Sheila muttered.

Jim clapped Ryan on the shoulder. "I'm going to go eat lunch. Doc will handle it from here."

Ryan nodded but didn't look reassured. Jim happily escaped the annoying voice of Sheila and took himself inside.

Chapter Twenty-Three

Ryan hated to see Jim leave, but Doc was here, and he put up with no nonsense out of anyone. Someone would have to control this Sheila woman, and he knew he couldn't. Hell, Bonehead did a better job of controlling her than he did.

"All right, we'll just stand here, and you can ask your questions," said Doc.

"I'm going to record you," Sheila said, "that all right?"

Ryan shrugged.

"So what happened at Pete's?"

Ryan took a breath. "A man dropped a bar across his throat. His…. "

"Larynx," inserted Doc.

"Yes, it was crushed. He couldn't…get air. So I did a tracheotomy."

"He cut into him and created an airway," said Doc.

"I know what a tracheotomy is," said Sheila.

Bonehead growled at her tone. Ryan reached down and stroked the dog's head.

"Well, pardon me for trying to explain," said Doc.

"What did you use?" asked Sheila.

"Knife. Someone had a knife. And a pen…case thing."

"Pete said you saved the man's life."

Ryan nodded, "Maybe. The ambulance…"

"This is Eden County. I'd be more surprised if they showed up quickly," Sheila said. "So, why were you in the gym?"

Ryan looked surprised. "To work out."

Sheila looked at him, taking the time to view his body from head to toe.

"You don't look like a gym rat."

Ryan blushed.

Doc and Bonehead both growled.

"What brought you to Eden County?"

"I hired him," said Doc Markham.

"Yeah, but why would anyone who's a doctor move here? You were born here; you're just naturally stupid enough to like it," said Sheila.

"As were you," said Doc pointedly.

"I wanted a small town," said Ryan. "I wanted to…live somewhere quiet."

Sheila nearly snotted herself laughing. "Well, you sure as hell found that. At least until recently." She eyed Ryan suspiciously. "All of a sudden, we've got people disappearing."

"Oh Christ on a crutch, Sheila," said Doc, "don't start inventing some conspiracy crap about my partner."

Suddenly the photographer stepped up closer to the gate. "He saved a man, Sheila. He's not someone who hurts people."

They all three stared at him in surprise. He raised his camera and snapped a shot of Ryan.

"Oh, shut up, Carl," Sheila said sharply. She looked at Ryan. "I need more than this for a story."

Doc stepped in front of Ryan. "Go talk to the man he saved. That's your story. Leave Dr. Edwards alone, or I talk to Ed."

Sheila glared at Doc Markham.

"Don't try me, Sheila. I got no patience with you, and Ed's a fishing buddy. He'll listen to me. You mess with me or my partner, I'll have Ed give you the agricultural beat, and you'll spend the rest of your life covering Libby's Dairy Farm and the rates at the Farm Bureau."

For a moment, it seemed like Sheila was going to step forward, but she turned on her heel and walked back through the gate, shouting at the photographer as she went, "Come on, Carl. We've got things to do."

Carl shot one more photograph of Ryan, then turned and followed Sheila out to her car.

"I don't like her," Ryan said.

"Join the club. Whole damn town thinks she's a pain in the ass."

"Who's Ed?"

Doc Markham laughed, "Her publisher. He and I fish together, and he doesn't like Sheila either. But she's the only person in town who can spell that's willing to work for the money he pays."

"Oh," said Ryan.

Doc put a hand on his shoulder. "Go on back to your apartment. It's your day off, and you've had a hell of one so far."

Ryan nodded. "Thanks for being here."

Doc smiled broadly. "Wouldn't have missed it for the world. Nothing like a day where I can make Sheila Ward's life a little bit more miserable." He walked back to his car chuckling.

Bonehead looked up at Ryan expectantly. "What? You….earned something?"

The dog huffed.

"I guess you did," he said softly. They went upstairs to the apartment, the dog running up the stairs ahead of him. He knew the minute he opened the door, Bonehead was going to head straight for the kitchen and the treat box. The dog had no shame when it came to biscuits.

Ryan pulled three biscuits out of the box, looked down at Bonehead, who was smiling and wagging his tail in anticipation. He pulled out a fourth. "Thank you," he said as he handed them to the dog.

He left Bonehead chomping away on the biscuits on the kitchen floor and went to sit back down on the porch. The rocking chair's movement was soothing. Doing the tracheotomy at the gym had brought back to him all that he had lost that day in the parking garage.

Danielle had come to the ER to pick him up. It was a rare day that he was getting off a shift on time, and they planned to go to dinner and then go home for some private time. Danielle had arranged with a friend to have Bonehead walked and fed. That gave them two hours alone together that they rarely had.

The parking garage had been quiet. It was early, just four o'clock in the afternoon. Not a time that people generally would be in the garage or on their way out. Even the nursing staff would likely still be catching up in the transition between the day and the evening shift.

As they came out of the stairs, two men stepped in front of them. One of them had a baseball bat over his shoulder. The other carried a knife. He had stepped in front of Danielle, though he knew it would piss her off to no end. She hated to be treated as the weaker one.

"Excuse us, we're on our way to our car," Ryan said.

The man with the knife nodded, and the one with the baseball bat had swung at him before he even realized it was happening. He'd gotten his arm up between them, but the bat had broken his arm and hit him in the head.

Until he woke up three months later, he had no idea what happened next.

Danielle had pepper sprayed the man with the baseball bat, grabbed it from him, and gone after the man with the knife. A video camera captured it all. She got one good swing in, hitting the man's shoulder, and the knife had slashed her arm before she got another chance. She dropped the bat, but went after the man again, this time punching him with her keys. That brought her too close to him. He'd slashed her throat.

As she dropped and bled out, the man with the knife pushed the man who was still rubbing his streaming eyes, and they'd both run.

The police found them. A matter of days later, they had them both in custody, and once they saw the videotape they had agreed to a plea. One count of attempted murder and one of murder, sentences to be served concurrently.

Ryan insisted on seeing the video. He had to see it. He had to see her last moments. As he lay unconscious, she had tried to stop her bleeding. She couldn't do it. Likely no one could. She died only feet away from him.

He'd still be unconscious when they were found by someone going to their car about ten minutes later. It was too late for Danielle, but not for him. The man, a doctor, called for help from the ER, and the very people who had allowed him to leave a little bit early saved his life.

It was what they did. What he would have done. Nothing could be done for Danielle, but he was still alive and would remain that way.

Ryan started to cry silently. He could hear Bonehead happily chewing through the four biscuits that Ryan had given him. He'd leave slobber and crumbs on the floor. It was what he did.

Chapter Twenty-Four

Sunday dawned with a heavy overcast look. The smoke obscured the daylight enough to give the illusion of a cloudy day. Jim felt exhausted as he lowered himself into his office chair. The arson report hadn't come in yet. Mike Rountree hadn't turned up yet, either. He'd probably taken off to lay low outside the county. Jim figured he'd left his truck behind, thinking they'd be looking for him. Though that seemed unusually smart for Mike. Generally, he was dense as a post, and more than once, he'd walked into the local grocery store still wearing the goggles and respirator he used when he cooked meth.

The body from the fire out near the dairy had not been identified. They were still waiting for DNA. Dee had been right about Buddy's lack of dental records. But since there'd been no sign of Buddy, he was pretty sure it was going to turn out to be him.

As for Reverend Hatcher, Jim wondered if he should start looking into alien abduction. The man had disappeared into thin air.

He rubbed his face and felt his stomach burning. He grabbed the bottle of water he had brought in with him. His gut always suffered when he was stressed, and right now, he felt like he could spit fire from it. He needed caffeine, but he knew that cola or coffee would have him doubled up with pain in under a half-hour. So he made do. Water it was.

Junior walked into the doorway to his office. "Thought you might like to see this," he said, dropping the local newspaper onto Jim's desk.

On the front page was a photo of Ryan, Bonehead, and Jim. They all looked startled. The headline read: NEW DOCTOR SAVES LIFE WITH

PRIMITIVE SURGERY.

Jim lowered his head to his desk and tapped his forehead against the wood. "I hate that woman."

Junior laughed. "Mostly, she talked to the guy he saved. Well, didn't talk. He wrote notes on a whiteboard. He still can't talk."

"Poor Ryan," Jim said.

"Hey, he's a hero. He should like that."

Jim shook his head. "I don't think he likes attention. He is very private."

"Too bad," said Junior. Then he turned and made his way back to the front counter.

The phone rang, and Jim heard Junior answer, then his own phone buzzed. "Yeah, Junior?"

"Bud Peterson's on the line."

Jim punched the blinking line and heard the swirl of ice and liquid against plastic. "Bud."

"Jim, I actually have some information for you." There was a pause as he took a long drink of his tea. "We were finally able to get something out of the wallet on the body. Thank God the man had one of those thick leather things with the chain. Took a while to pry everything out of it, and a lot of it was damaged, but we found a driver's license and a credit card melted together in an inside flap. The body is definitely your Buddy Bass."

Jim's gut churned. He was going to have to go talk to Edna Bass now. Damn it.

"The coroner's going to release the body. Figured you'd want to let his mama know."

"Thanks, Bud."

Jim hung up the phone and laid his forehead back on his desk. He did not need this. He would have to go and talk to Edna, and he would have to find a way to ask her about who might want to break Buddy's neck. Edna was a nice woman. She hadn't deserved a son like Buddy, and she didn't deserve the grief she'd been suffering since he disappeared. This wouldn't lessen her pain a damn bit.

He picked up the phone and dialed Elsie Sanborne's number from memory. She'd called a couple of days ago and said that Hatcher's wife had gone to stay with her mother. She always let him know when she was available for "duty."

"Elsie, this is Jim. You up for helping me make a death call?" She agreed to meet him at Edna Bass' home.

The Duster was parked outside when Jim arrived. Elsie got out as Jim did, and together they went to the door. When Edna opened it and saw them both, she began to sob.

Elsie gathered Edna's bulk into her wiry arms and led her to her chair. Jim followed silently.

When Edna quieted, Jim spoke, "I'm sorry, Ms. Bass. We've found Buddy's body."

"Oh God, I knew it. I knew he was dead," she said softly.

"Ms. Sanborne here will be glad to stay with you and help in any way she can. I promise that I'll keep you up to date on what's happening with the case."

"When can I bury him?"

"The body is being released today. You'll be able to arrange his burial now."

Edna, her face red and wet with tears, nodded. "Thank you. You've always been good to me about Buddy over the years, Sheriff. I appreciate that. I know he was trouble to you, too."

"Never as much as he was to you, Ms. Bass," he said quietly.

Elsie motioned with her head for him to leave. Jim turned and went back out to his car. She had things in hand and would take it from there. Elsie was good like that.

* * *

The rest of Jim's day did not improve. He had the arson report from Dwayne Henry, which told him why the trailer exploded and burned and what items of interest were in the trailer and the truck outside.

Apparently, Rountree's wallet and a zippered plastic case of cash burned in the truck. Or mostly burned. There continued to be no evidence of a body.

Jim finally took a couple of Excedrin after reading the report five times and still not making sense of why Rountree wouldn't be in the trailer when it exploded.

Dwayne Henry noted in the report that Deputy Manny Soto stated the truck was not burning when he first arrived on the scene, but that it caught fire shortly after his arrival.

Jim called Junior into his office and had him read the report.

"Okay, I can see him getting out when the trailer exploded, but why didn't he get in his truck and get away?" Jim asked.

Junior considered this for a moment and then said, "Could he have been injured in the explosion and ended up wandering off somewhere?"

Jim looked at Junior and thought, not for the first time, that the man was too smart to be working for him. "I never thought of that. Damn."

"Want me to get whoever is not on duty together to go do a search?"

"Yeah. And can you call that ham radio group? The ones who helped us look for that Alzheimer's patient who wandered away from home last year? They do a great grid search."

Junior nodded and got up. "I'll get right on it."

An hour later, Jim had his deputies set out through the woods north of the trailer. The undergrowth was thick, but they had all come prepared, wearing heavy pants and high boots. Also, they were armed, so should they come across rattlesnakes or other problems, they would be able to deal with them.

The ham radio club he would have the search south of the trailer through the burned woods. If Mike Rountree had been confused and injured, he might have headed that way and could have been the cause of the fire spreading as quickly as it did if his clothing was burning.

The Hammock Hunt Club had already agreed to send men out on ATVs to check through the woods on the east side of the trailer. Once everyone had searched the immediate vicinity, then he would see if he could get some people out on the Gulf side to the west.

By seven-thirty, they were losing the light, and no one had found anything of Rountree. The deputies who had gotten off their shifts had switched places with those who needed to go on. The ham radio club had spent nearly six hours walking a grid pattern in the burned woods. They found no sign of a body, but there had been a lot of excitement for about twenty minutes when a mated pair of bobcats had made their way through the burned woods heading further south.

Everyone was filthy and sweat-soaked, and the heavy smoke in the air made the light of sunset darker than normal. Jim sent everyone home, and they all agreed they'd start again in the morning around eight.

Jim arrived home and saw both Michael's and Ryan's cars in the driveway. He wondered how Ryan had dealt with having his picture on the front page of the local paper. When he opened the door to the house, he could hear voices coming from the kitchen. Bonehead heard the door and came dashing out to greet him.

The big red dog's bushy tail batted things off the coffee table in the living room, which made Jim chuckle. "Hey boy, how are you?" Jim asked, reaching down to stroke the dog's ears. The dog chuffed at him and then turned to head back into the kitchen.

Michael came into the doorway. "Hey, Dad. You look like crap."

"Thank you. I feel like crap."

He walked into the kitchen, and Ryan sat at the table with a glass of iced tea. Michael went to the refrigerator and grabbed the pitcher of iced tea, but Ryan stopped him. "Get him water. Tea's a diuretic."

Michael looked confused. "This isn't diet. It's got sugar."

Ryan grinned, and Jim took a seat at the table.

"No, a diuretic…..it makes you pee," said Ryan.

"Some ice-cold water would be great, Michael," Jim said.

While Michael got him water, Jim turned to Ryan. "So, how's Warren's hero doing today?"

Ryan rolled his eyes. "Don't start," he said. Then he smiled. "….got…free lunch…Magnolia House."

Jim laughed, "Now that is worth it. What did you have?"

"Chicken and dumplings, fried okra...double chocolate cake."

Michael set his father's glass of water on the table and dropped into a chair. "Man, that makes me hungry just hearing about it."

"...Never had...okra. It's good....How...not have...their cholesterol."

"Only old people worry about cholesterol," Michael said.

"Yeah, and I'm old," said Jim. "Which is why I can only think about eating like that anymore."

Ryan shook his head. "You...hitting your prime."

Jim smiled, "I appreciate the thought, but today I'm feeling old."

"What's going on?" Michael asked.

"We're searching the woods around the Hammock to see if we can find Mike Rountree."

"There...that in the paper," Ryan said. "Meth lab...?"

"Yeah. His truck, or what's left of it, was still there, but no body in the trailer or the truck. So far, we've found nothing to indicate what happened to him."

"It's not like anyone's going to miss him," said Michael.

Jim spoke sharply, "No. That's not true. His father will miss him. Mike Rountree isn't my favorite person in the world, but he's Elvin's son, and he cares."

Michael nodded, "Sorry."

Jim reached out and put his hand on Michael's shoulder. "Not everyone is as lucky as I am. My son is a fine young man."

Michael grinned.

"So, what are you fixing your old man for supper?"

"Uh, pizza?"

Jim shook his head. "Yeah, you know how to order pizza. I'm well aware of that."

Ryan stood up. "I'll cook."

"You don't have to do that," said Jim.

Ryan laughed, "Yeah...I'm the big damn...guy today. I can do anything."

He and Michael busied themselves at the refrigerator, finding things to make a meal. Jim leaned back in his chair and drank his ice water slowly. It tasted damn good after the day he'd had.

Chapter Twenty-Five

Jim headed out a little after six the next morning. He had deputies coming and the ham radio guys again. Everyone met at the site of the burned trailer. Leaving their cars parked back on the road, they all walked in pretty much together.

Just as everyone started to head out to their respective search areas, another small group walked in. Elvin Rountree stopped just short of Jim and said, "You're searching for my boy."

"We are, Elvin."

"We want to help," he said, nodding toward the group of men behind him. They were all about Elvin's age, and none of them looked fit enough to be out in the woods. But they had bottles of water hooked to the belt loops of their pants, and they all wore boots, so he showed them an area on the map. One of the men pulled out a GPS unit and asked for the coordinates.

One of the ham radio guys gave him the information, and he programmed it into his device. He looked at Jim and said, "Been using it to hunt. Figured it would come in handy."

Jim agreed, and the men walked solemnly out into the woods to the northwest. Before they were out of sight, the deputies headed back north and the ham radio club to the south and west.

Jim went back to his car. His job was to monitor all the radios and let everyone know if anyone found something. He settled in for what he thought would be another long day. Less than thirty minutes later, Junior pulled up in his Lincoln Navigator. He got out and walked over to Jim's car, getting in on the passenger side.

"You're needed in town, Sheriff. I'll take over here. You catch me up on who's out, and I'll cover it."

Jim's surprise had to be written all over his face. Junior never went into the field. He'd been hired, taken over the desk at the office, and remained firmly in place for the past twelve years.

"What's going on?"

"We got a call from Riddick. They need you out at Montague Cemetery."

"Why? Someone defacing graves?"

Junior made it clear he didn't know anything else, or at least wasn't going to say anything else. Jim went over the maps with him and then called the leaders of each group by radio to let them know that Junior was taking over. He didn't want anyone panicking when they called in and didn't get him.

Junior got out of Jim's sedan and back into his SUV. Jim pulled out, and Junior pulled his vehicle into place.

The drive out to Montague took nearly forty-five minutes. It was on the other side of the county, east of Warren. One of the oldest cemeteries in the county, it had a special place in his heart. His great-grandparents, grandparents, and parents on both sides were buried there. It was quiet, covered by huge oaks and magnolias. It had a stately quality to it he'd always loved. He hoped like hell Matt Riddick hadn't found vandalism.

When he pulled through the cemetery gates, he could see Matt and his truck near the middle of the property, under a particularly beautiful magnolia tree. It was well away from Jim's family's graves, which relieved him greatly. Whatever was going on, he didn't want to think about it happening anywhere near where his family lay.

When he pulled up next to Matt's truck, he couldn't believe what he was seeing. A shrouded figure lay on the ledger stone over a grave under the tree. Jim got out of his truck and walked over to Matt.

"Is that...?"

"I think so." Matt looked pale beneath the dark tan of his face.

"Where...? How?"

Matt shook his head. "I drove in, heading for the Bass plot. Edna wants to bury Buddy next to his granddaddy. I saw this, and I come and stopped to see what it was. When I got close, I could smell it."

"Cinnamon and cloves," said Jim.

"I ain't touched it. I left the truck here so no one would see it that drove by and walked over to the minute market. I called your house, but Michael said you wasn't home, and I didn't want this to go out over the radio, so I called Junior. I knew he'd know where to find you. Michael said you was out in the woods looking for Mike Rountree."

"Yeah, over near the Hammock. Thanks for not letting this get out on the radio. God in heaven, what is going on in the world?"

Jim knelt next to the shrouded body, reaching out to touch it gently. It felt solid and stiff. He looked closely at the cloth covering and saw that it was stitched near the top of the head with large looping threads. He pulled out his pocket knife, took a deep breath, and carefully cut the threads. Then he peeled the cloth away from the face.

He felt his stomach lurch as soft brown hair and graying flesh were revealed, then past the eyes and down until the whole face showed.

"Merciful Lord Jesus Christ," whispered Matt.

Jim laid the cloth back over the face and stood up. "Matt, I need you to go back to that phone and call this number." Jim pulled out his notepad and wrote a number, then tore the sheet out to give to Matt. "It's Bud Peterson's personal number. I want you to tell him that I need him and a team, but nothing, absolutely nothing, is to go out by radio. I don't want anyone hearing about this. Not yet."

Matt nodded. "You know who it is?"

Jim nodded. "Yeah. Yeah, I do, Matt. Go on and make that call for me."

Matt took off running toward the road. Jim leaned back against the truck and tried to breathe deeply, get himself under control. Reverend Hatcher lay shrouded on the stone. Jim didn't know if there was any significance to the grave he was on, but he did recognize that whoever had done this had taken great care with the body. It reeked of ritual, and that scared the ever-loving shit out of him.

* * *

110

It took nearly two hours, but finally, Bud and a team arrived. They came in an unmarked car and a van that only had the markings of the lab. Jim appreciated the subtlety.

Matt had left his truck parked next to the body and gone back to the Bass plot to prep the new grave site. Jim wanted him close so he could answer any questions Bud and his people might have, but he also knew the man was uncomfortable being here, and he did have a job that needed to be completed.

Bud got out of his truck and walked over to Jim. He had his usual mug of tea. He looked at the body and then at Jim. "You been screwing with my crime scene? You know better than that."

"We weren't sure it was a body. For all I knew, it was a mannequin. I wasn't going to call you out for someone's prank."

Bud swigged his tea. "You know who it is?"

"Our missing preacher."

"Ah…hell," said Bud.

"Yeah," agreed Jim.

"Cinnamon and cloves. Probably bathed the body as well. We're not going to get shit off it." Bud knelt next to the grave and looked at the shroud. "This is an amateur's work. Sloppy stitching, and the bindings aren't right. Probably someone who looked it up in a book, but never had training."

"Great," Jim said, sighing.

Bud directed his team to get to work. Soon photos were being taken, a body bag was produced, and the shrouded figure placed in it. They scoured the ground around the grave, photographed the tablet stone, and looked for tire tracks other than Matt's and Jim's.

One young woman called to Bud from one of the paved trails through the grounds. Bud went over to where she stood, and Jim followed, wanting to know what she'd found. There were boot prints in the soft soil next to the road, and on the pavement and in the dirt were twigs of clove.

"He must have parked here and carried the body over," the woman said.

The pavement didn't have any evidence of tread patterns, but the boot prints were distinct. "Make a cast, pick up any debris you find in this area,

111

and then scour a direct line back to the grave where we found the body," Bud ordered.

"He didn't drive up next to the grave," said Jim.

"Yeah. He stayed on the pavement. You and Matt pulled up next to the grave, and you're on the grass."

Jim looked around. This road was the closest to the grave. Jim and Matt had both driven across the grass between graves to where the body lay.

"I think your guy didn't want to take a chance on desecrating any of these graves. He pulled up close as he could and carried the body in."

"Which must mean that grave means something. He picked it out."

Bud nodded. "Name on the grave's Casey. Mean anything to you?"

"Nope. Dammit. Wish it did."

Both men watched the team work, numbering, photographing, and picking up debris as they moved back toward the grave. The shrouded body of Hatcher was already in a body bag in the van. They would take it back for the medical examiner to autopsy. Bud and his team would study what little they'd found and hope that something gave them a clue.

The group made thorough work of everything, and Jim found himself alone in the graveyard. He stood looking at the tablet stone. One of Bud's people would check the background on the Casey name, but he needed to do some digging himself. The county library would still be open. It didn't close on Mondays until six. If God were merciful, the head librarian would be in. Annie White had a particular obsession with local history, and she would know where to point him on the Casey name.

Matt had finished his work at the Bass plot. The new grave was dug, the pile of dirt next to it covered with the astroturf-looking stuff. He'd have to contact Elsie to be sure he knew when the funeral was scheduled. It would also give him a chance to look over Bass' friends, or what passed for friends in his screwed-up world. Maybe one of them would have some idea of who had finally managed to kill him. Many had tried, and many had failed, and Lord, he needed to stop this whole thought process.

Jim rubbed his forehead. Yeah, he'd better head for the library.

Twenty minutes later, he stood watching Annie pull out rolls of microfiche from a large drawer in a back room. She was nearly as tall as he was, with short dark hair highlighted where she was going grey. She always smiled, and he thought of her as married to her library. Her passion for books and information knew no bounds.

"I had this stuff converted by a library over in Alachua County. Didn't have it in the budget here to get it done, so I paid for it, and they gave me a good rate. Bought the viewer from the state equipment sale. Got a great deal on it." She put a reel on the machine and rolled through it at a speed that made Jim dizzy. He had no idea how she had any idea what was flashing by. Finally, she stopped on an image of a news article from the early 1920s.

"Yep, there it is. Casey. He was hot shit during the Seminole wars. In 1849 he was involved in trying to negotiate with the Seminoles to leave Florida. In 1900, a local family claimed to be related to Casey. They bought a plot in the Montague cemetery and laid a tablet stone in it dedicated to his memory. The rest of the family was to be buried around the stone, but they fell on hard times, and it looks like they sold the plots."

"What was the name of the family?" Jim asked.

"Spiney."

"Never heard of them."

"Not much to them. They had a daughter. Looks like she married someone from Pensacola, became a Forenberry. Nothing after that."

Jim sat down next to Annie. "I was hoping for more."

"Why?"

"I think it might have a connection to a case I'm working on. Thanks, Annie. You're always the best. I don't know how you keep all that information in your head!"

She laughed, "I'm a compendium of trivia when it comes to Florida history. My family goes back eight generations here. Dirt poor every damn one of them, too. But we got history."

Chapter Twenty-Six

With the information from the library swimming in his brain, Jim drove back out to the Hammock, where the search for Mike Rountree progressed, even as it failed. He'd talked to Junior by radio, and no sign of the man had been found. He would have to call off the search soon. There had been no wind all day, and the smoke was lying heavily just above tree level. It made it hard to breathe, and in the heat, his searchers were going to start dropping if he didn't call them in.

He also had an autopsy to attend. Bud agreed that Jim really needed to be there. He hated autopsies. He'd managed over the years to attend very damn few of them. Eden County didn't have mysterious murders. It had drug dealers killing each other, husbands and wives killing each other, and on one particular occasion, a grandson beating his grandfather to death. Most of the time, the killer was still standing over the body, covered in blood, when he or she was caught.

Hatcher's death was different in any way from the ones Jim had experienced before. He needed to know more. He had to figure out why the man had been taken and why he'd ended up dead.

Pulling up next to Junior's SUV, Jim got out and opened the passenger door to the vehicle, and got in.

Junior handed Jim a bottle of water. "Didn't know if you'd be back."

"I'll go to Gainesville when they're doing the autopsy. They'll call.

Junior nodded. "Nobody's found anything. The smoke's getting worse."

Jim nodded. "Call everyone back in."

"What about Elvin?"

"I'll talk to him when he gets here. I don't think Mike's out there."

Junior sighed. "Me either. Maybe someone came and picked him up? That would explain his truck being here."

"But if he's somewhere else, why hasn't he called his dad? Mike's a lot of things, but he and Elvin actually love each other. He wouldn't worry his father like this."

Junior made the call over the radio to bring everyone in. There were no protests, not even from Elvin's group. It took nearly thirty minutes, but soon everyone was back at the trailhead. Everyone's eyes were red from smoke irritation, their noses ringed with black from breathing the polluted air.

Jim told everyone to go home, that he'd call them if he needed them again. Then he took Elvin aside.

"He ain't out there," Elvin said softly, "is he?"

"I don't think so."

Jim took a deep breath, then coughed deeply for several minutes. Elvin dragged out a cigarette and lit up. "There's a dealer down in Levy been wanting Mike to cook for him. Might be worth checking into."

"Got a name?"

"Billy. Billy Dustin. He's got a place outside of Williston, heading down toward Dunedin. Off 45, near Mountbrook."

Jim put his hand on Elvin's shoulder. "I'll check it out. Thank you, Elvin."

Elvin went back to his friends, and they walked out toward the road where their trucks were parked. For Elvin to share that kind of information, he had to be worried.

Once everyone was gone, Jim sent Junior back home. He walked back down the trail and stood in front of the burned-out trailer and truck. What the hell was going on in Eden County? First, it was the drought. Then the fires. Now he had two men dead and a third missing.

The smoke seemed to be dropping from up in the trees toward ground level. The scent of burned wood filled his head. He wondered if he would ever get rid of it.

BURNING EDEN

* * *

Once he was home, the smell of food cooking drew him to the kitchen. It was odd. He knew it couldn't be Michael cooking. His idea of a meal was a take-out menu. This smelled like real food.

When he stepped into the kitchen, Ryan was at the stove patiently instructing Michael on the use of a wok. Jim knew damn well he didn't own a wok, so it had to be Ryan's.

"That's it, gentle stirring, moving the vegetables around so they don't get limp or burned. This is why you cook the meat first. It gives you plenty of juices for the veggies, and really fills them with the flavor of the meat.

"Cool. Where'd you learn to do this?" Michael asked.

"I took a class when I was in college. Got tired of eating pizza and fast food."

"I never get tired of pizza and fast food," said Michael laughing.

"Yeah, because you're young and have a good metabolism," said Jim.

They both turned and smiled at him.

"Hey, Dad! Look at this! I'm cooking!"

Jim shook his head. "I'm thinking it's a hallucination."

"Okay, we're...done," said Ryan. "...Bowl."

With only a few stray pieces of vegetable dropping to the floor, they managed to get it into the corning ware dish that Jim knew was his. Bonehead quickly scarfed up the vegetables.

"Hope you don't mind," said Ryan. "I don't know how to...one....I asked Michael."

"Any time I don't have to cook, I'm good with it," said Jim.

Ryan pulled out a crock potlooking thing and dished rice out of it.

"I've never seen anyone make rice in a crock pot," said Jim.

"It's a rice cooker," Ryan said as he brought the bowl to the table.

Jim had never heard of such a thing. Why the hell would you need something special to make rice? But he had to admit, the rice that came out of it looked fluffier than anything he'd ever managed. Of course, minute rice was probably not the best thing to judge by.

116

Jim washed his hands at the sink and then joined Ryan and Michael at the table. He'd barely sat down when Michael exclaimed, "What is that?" He pointed to a spot on the back of Jim's arm, just above his elbow.

Jim tried to twist his arm to see it, and Ryan looked over. "Oh hell.....!" He got up and moved to get a closer look. "Tweezers. I need tweezers."

Michael ran to the bathroom and returned with tweezers.

"Get me something to put the tick in," Ryan said. He grabbed several paper towels and held Jim's arm with them. Carefully he grasped the body of the tick and pulled it. It seemed to Jim that it took forever, but finally, the tick was pulled from his arm.

Ryan dropped it into the jar that Michael held. He dropped the tweezers onto the table and screwed the cap on the jar and looked at it, and examined the bite on Jim's arm. "Good. Good. I got the head. Damn, these things are nasty."

Ryan wet some of the paper towels and cleaned the bite with soap and water. "I'm....write ......for antibiotics."

"Why?"

"Lyme's disease. I treated a tick...days ago...bull's eye on it. Sign of Lyme's....Where...?"

"We've been out near the Hammock doing a search.'

Ryan shook his head. "Must be deer.... The other...from woods in this area."

"Deer ticks cause this?"

"They're carriers."

"The Hammock is a hunting club. They've got feed lots all over down there. Lots of deer."

Ryan nodded. "...Would explain..."

Michael handed Ryan a band-aide. He covered the cleaned bite. "Get that...filled soon ...take all of it."

"I will. Now, do I get to eat?"

"Yes."

Michael held up the jar. "What do I do with this?"

Ryan took it from him. "Tested. If Lyme's here, Doc and I need to know."

"Someone will test that tick?"

"Yes. It's good…to have."

"Glad to know I've done my bit to further medicine in Eden County," said Jim.

Chapter Twenty-Seven

T he next afternoon Jim found himself back at Shands at the medical examiner's office. Because Hatcher's case was unusual, Bud had managed to get the M.E. to bump it up in the schedule. Jim hated autopsies, but this was too important to just leave to a report. He needed to see what had happened for himself. After that, he would make his notification call to Mrs. Hatcher. Right now, she was in Bradford County at her mother's home. He had deliberately waited until he could tell her more than just that her husband's body had been found. Twenty-four hours wouldn't make much of a difference, but the more he knew, perhaps the more information she would have in return.

The M.E., Dr. Eddington, carefully removed the shroud from the body. It would be examined for trace evidence and hopefully would yield some clues on its own. Photographs of the shroud and then the body were made.

The smell of cinnamon and cloves overwhelmed the normal chemical odors of the room. Careful swabs were taken of areas of the body.

"I'm sure we're going to find clove oil has been rubbed into the body," Eddington said. "That smell is way too strong for the few cloves we've found." Evidence of adhesive residue lay in small stripes on Hatcher's wrists, ankles, and around his chest. Hair had been pulled out when it had been removed, and the width of the marks left behind indicated it was probably duct tape.

When he finally opened Hatcher's mouth, he found it was packed with powdered cinnamon and cloves. He carefully cleaned it all out, putting samples away for further examination.

"This body is extremely clean other than the tape residue. I doubt we're going to find much trace on it other than the cleanser and the spices."

The autopsy progressed. The Y incision, the removal and weighing of organs. The stomach was nearly empty. The esophagus showed signs of stomach acid burns and had debris. When the lungs were examined, it became clear what had killed the young minister.

"Aspiration of vomitus," said Eddington flatly. "It's definitely food. There's corn kernels in it, and this looks like mashed potatoes. We'll test it to get a definitive answer."

He set samples of the tissue aside for further examination. There was slight bruising around the mouth, as though it had been held forcefully.

"Maybe someone covered his mouth to keep him from vomiting?" Jim asked.

"Possible," said the M.E. "Or someone was forcing food into the mouth. It's hard to tell because the mouth was washed out and packed with cinnamon and cloves. We'll see if there's anything stuck between the teeth."

Jim shook his head. "There was no sign of the Bible verse with the body?"

Eddington shrugged. "Nothing on the body except the shroud. I'll check it for anything we can see if there's any sign that something was there, but I doubt it."

"Peterson found the Bible verse highlighted in Hatcher's family Bible, and then a page torn out of the Bible with that verse was found at The Cedars where Bass was killed. Both times it was highlighted with O+ blood."

"We're trying to get DNA on the blood, but the report hasn't come in yet. But, yes, it was O+ on both. Other than that, we have nothing to connect the two deaths. Bass had his neck broken, and this man essentially drowned in food."

Jim looked at Hatcher's body, laid out on the table. "He dragged Bass' body into the path of a wildfire, and then he does this with Hatcher."

"Maybe Hatcher's death was an accident. He cleaned him, made him smell good, and then shrouded him and left him at a place where the dead are interred. Maybe he was trying to honor Hatcher?"

Jim thought for a moment. "Or apologize for it going wrong. He didn't mean for Hatcher to die. At least not like he did."

"Whoever is doing this, he has a plan. He's not killing just to kill. These deaths mean something to him," said Eddington.

"Bass was a sinner. No one would argue with that. But Hatcher was a preacher."

"The soul that sinneth, it shall die," said Eddington.

"I hate fucking riddles!" Jim stepped back from the table and clapped his hand over his mouth.

Eddington shook his head. "Don't be embarrassed. This is why I like the science. I don't have to figure out the riddles. I just supply evidence."

Jim left the autopsy feeling more confused and frustrated than ever. Donald Hatcher had been taken, held for days, and died from inhaling food he tried to vomit. It was a skewed puzzle, and Jim didn't have any idea where to start.

He remembered the verse that had been highlighted with blood in the Bible. This was one sick bastard. That was the only thing he knew for sure.

* * *

The visit with Mrs. Hatcher went about as well as Jim expected. She'd sobbed in her mother's arms. The man she had loved and called her husband would never return. It wasn't the kind of thing a young woman ever expected. In this case, it seemed more capricious than it had a right to be.

Jim left the house feeling depressed and useless. The man had been missing for a week when he'd turned up in that cemetery. He should have been able to do something. Now they had his body, and he still didn't have a clue as to who had taken the man.

The drive back to Eden County was missing time when Jim pulled into his driveway. He had no idea how he'd gotten home. That shook him as much as anything. He'd never lost time like that.

As he headed into the house, he heard Ryan call to him. He turned and saw him walking across the yard with Bonehead on a six-foot lead. The dog slowed as he got nearer Jim, as though he could sense that something was wrong.

Ryan touched Jim's shoulder. "What's wrong?"

Jim shook his head. "Nothing. I'm fine."

"No, you're not. You're pale and sweating." Ryan reached up and touched his forehead. "Crap, you're going into shock." He took Jim's arm and hurried him into the house.

Ryan unclipped Bonehead's leash and let the dog wander as he quickly got Jim to lie down, raising his feet slightly. "Blankets. Where can I find blankets?"

Jim motioned toward the hall. Ryan disappeared, and Jim realized he was shivering. He felt numb and cold.

Ryan returned with a couple of blankets. He wrapped them around Jim and tucked them under him at the edges. "You stay here."

Jim heard the back door open and close. Bonehead sat at the end of the couch by his feet, staring at him. The dog's expression was serious. Jim wondered if somehow he knew that Jim was...well, not right. They said animals could sense things. Smell chemical changes in the body.

Before he could fully formulate those thoughts, Ryan was back. He had his doctor's bag with him. He took one of Jim's arms out from under the blanket, wrapped a blood pressure cuff around his arm, and took a reading.

"Your blood pressure's too low. I'm going to give you some fluids. Try to raise your pressure." He efficiently began an IV. Jim didn't even feel the needle going in. He could see it, but he couldn't feel it. In fact, other than cold, he felt like everything was very distant.

Ryan had a small green canister he pulled out of the bag. He slipped some tubing on it and put a mask over Jim's nose and mouth. The metallic smell of compressed oxygen filled the mask.

"Jim, can you talk to me?" Ryan asked.

Jim tried to think of something to say. "Your dog is staring at me."

Ryan laughed. "He does that. He's not much for talking...champion at staring."

"What's wrong with me?" Jim asked.

"You're shocky. Your blood pressure is low, and your temperature's......

wonky."

"Wonky. Is that a medical term?"

"You bet," Ryan said. "What were you doing…?"

"Death call. I had to tell a woman her husband is dead."

Ryan sighed. "…Sucks."

"I've made those calls before. But this one…this one was different. Never lost someone like this."

"Want to talk…?"

"Shouldn't. Open case." Jim's thoughts wandered for a bit. He felt warmer. His head didn't feel quite as foggy.

"It's all right."

Jim felt his eyes getting suspiciously moist. He swallowed hard. "I hate my job sometimes."

Ryan laid a warm hand on his shoulder. "Understand. Sometimes…I… mine."

Thumping noises interrupted them, and the door swung open to reveal Michael. His expression went immediately to one of alarm upon seeing Jim lying on the couch with Ryan sitting on the floor next to him.

"Dad?"

"Hey, it's okay. I just got a little…wonky."

Ryan snickered, and Jim smiled.

"What happened?"

Ryan moved away to give Michael room to kneel next to the couch.

"I had to make a death call. This one was really hard."

Ryan interrupted, "He was…shocky. I'm giving him fluids and…..oxygen. He'll be fine."

Jim did feel better. The world had come back into focus, and he was warm again.

"Who died?" Michael asked.

Jim shook his head. "I can't talk about it right now. Open case."

Michael nodded. "Okay. But you're all right? You feel better?"

Jim nodded. "Yeah, Ryan fixed me right up."

"Good. Okay if I get something to eat?"

"Go ahead," Jim said. "I wouldn't want you to collapse from hunger. Poor Ryan would have to go to work again."

Michael laughed, and, taking his backpack, headed into the kitchen.

"Take this whole bag… You have the time…..?" Ryan asked.

"Yeah. Honestly, I feel like I just want to take a long nap."

"Go right on. I'll check…in a bit."

Jim closed his eyes and allowed himself to sink into that state of drowsiness where everything felt a little soft. He was warm, and he could hear Michael and Ryan talking in the kitchen. He heard a shuffling noise and opened his eyes. Bonehead had stretched out on the floor next to the couch. He cut his eyes up, looking at Jim from under his raised eyebrows. "We'll both take a nap," Jim said quietly. Then he let himself drift off.

Chapter Twenty-Eight

Michael had made a sandwich for himself in the kitchen. (Though Ryan wondered if something that elaborate could be called just a sandwich.) A thick layer of chicken breasts lay on a slice of bread, and on top of that were tomatoes, some kind of garden salad mix, pickles, cucumber, banana peppers, onions, a thick layer of mustard, and another slice of bread. Michael picked it up and somehow managed to get his mouth around it to take a huge bite. Ryan had to admit he was impressed.

"Want some?" mumbled Michael as he chewed.

"No, thanks. I don't eat…bigger than my head," said Ryan.

Michael laughed. He finished chewing and began to stuff the things that had escaped the bread back into it. "Thanks for looking after Dad."

"Glad to do it. I like your father."

Michael grinned. "Most people do. He's a good guy." His face turned serious for a moment. "He is going to be okay, right?"

"I promise. I think…something really bothered him. His blood pressure is…back up, and he's sleeping…he'll be fine."

Michael nodded. "Yeah, he hates death calls, but I've never seen him like this." He paused and then looked thoughtful. "I bet his preacher is dead."

"What?"

"He said he had to tell a woman her husband was dead. He's had this case, a missing preacher. I bet they found his body." Then Michael realized what he'd said. "Oh, shit! Don't tell anybody, okay?"

Ryan nodded. "I won't. If it's an active….thing…I know it needs to be kept quiet. You're ...good at putting things together. Do you...law enforcement?"

Michael looked thoughtful. "Yeah. Dad doesn't want me to do it."

"Why not?"

Michael set his sandwich down. "If I talk to you about this, you promise to keep it just between us?"

Ryan was curious now. "Doctor/patient privilege."

Michael took a drink of milk, swallowed, and took a deep breath. "Grandpa was the Sheriff here forever, and before that, his father was Sheriff. He figured Dad would be the Sheriff after him, so he hired him as a deputy. Grandpa used to say that I would be the next Sheriff, because Sheppards have always been sheriffs. But Dad has always said that I get to be whatever I want to be. I think maybe this isn't what he would have chosen, you know?"

Ryan did know. His father was an architect, and his mother was a surgeon. It had been assumed by the family that he would choose one of those professions. Fortunately, he'd really liked medicine, though his mother was still pretty horrified he'd chosen emergency medicine over private practice.

"He's good with people, and I know that the deputies like him. No one has even run against him in an election. It's not anything he's ever said; it's just the way he would look when Grandpa would start talking about it. It was like he just closed himself off and let Grandpa talk."

"He doesn't...unhappy," Ryan said.

Michael shrugged. "Who knows? He doesn't talk to me about this stuff."

"Is there anyone he does talk to?" Ryan asked.

Michael shook his head. "Not that I know of. Dad pretty much keeps everything about himself to himself. I mean, it's easy to know how he feels about someone else 'cause he shows it. He's good that way. But he doesn't talk about himself at all."

Ryan understood that. Sometimes it was the only way to deal with who you were and what you couldn't talk about. Not to anyone. Not even the dog.

"My dad was going for a Masters in History," Michael said. "Mom wasn't interested in college at all, so she didn't go, but Dad loved it. I buy him books about history for like Christmas and stuff. He loves reading about that stuff."

"Doesn't seem like…a sheriff."

Michael laughed. "I know! I've been thinking about Criminal Justice. I know mostly pre-law takes it, but Dad will have a fit if I don't get a bachelor's, and it looks the most interesting to me."

"So you want to be a Sheriff?"

"I want to be a Deputy. We'll see about Sheriff once I've done that. Wouldn't it be weird if I ended up hating it? I mean, I think Dad kinda does, and he studied history. But if I get a degree in Criminal Science and then hate it, what would I do?"

"Become a lawyer?"

Michael looked horrified. "Do you want him to have a heart attack?"

"There's all kinds of law. My mother…..cardiac surgeon. Her face when…..I wanted to work in the ER. She…..shit herself."

Michael shook his head. "Parents are weird."

Ryan nodded. Parents seemed to want what had made themselves happy. Maybe because it was so hard to imagine anything else working. Or maybe, to them, success was defined by the work they did, and they couldn't imagine their child doing anything else.

"Danielle's father represented…Ivory Coast…International Monetary Fund, and she…..a contracts lawyer. They loved…… what she did. Marrying me was…weirdest thing she ever did."

Michael was quiet. "What happened with her?"

"She was killed. Same attack…..gave me bum brain."

"I'm sorry."

"Me, too," said Ryan said. "Bonehead was hers. She wanted a dog….came home with him. Lo and behold, I…a dog owner."

"You never had a dog before?"

Ryan laughed softly. "My father…architect. Fastidious people. I'm surprised they had a kid."

Bonehead must have heard his name because he wandered into the kitchen and leaned against Michael's chair. "What do you want, dog? Huh?"

Bonehead plopped his head on Michael's knee. "Yeah, you don't seem much like a dog guy."

"I'm trying," he said. "But before I…got hurt, I never had time. He….thinks me….got way too much of her attention."

Ryan checked his watch and got up from the table. "I'm going to check…..IV. You pet the dog. He likes you better…traitorous animal!"

The bag was nearly empty when Ryan checked it. He removed the needle from Jim's arm and cleaned and put a Band-Aid on the site. Jim stayed sound asleep. He made sure he was covered, and then he went back to the kitchen.

"I'd better take…for a walk and feed him. Your dad is sleeping. Just let him. He's…exhausted. It's…crazy here."

Michael agreed. "I'll get my homework done. Then I'll order a pizza."

"God! Will you ever learn to fix food?"

Michael smiled. "Not if I can help it."

Ryan headed out the back door. Bonehead followed. Outside, he found a tennis ball and carried it up to the apartment. The moment the leash came out, he dropped it and sat. The one thing Bonehead loved more than tennis balls was a walk.

They headed down the steps outside toward town. Ryan never went toward the graveyard anymore. Besides, Bonehead loved a burger from McDonald's as an appetizer for his dinner.

Chapter Twenty-Nine

The next day there was a lead to follow in the disappearance of Mike Rountree, and Buddy Bass' funeral to attend. Jim really needed to be at the funeral, but he didn't want to let Billy Dustin get by with another day of no questions. He sat at his desk and looked at his log sheet to see who he might be able to spare to head down to Levy County.

Dee would be his best bet. He had her on traffic out on 27, but he could pull Bobby Dale off the beach patrol and send him out to cover traffic.

If there were answers to be gotten, Dee would get them. He'd seen her go toe to toe with everything and everyone Eden County had.

Bobby Dale, on the other hand, had half a brain on a good day. He worked hard, and he meant well, but he tended to be a step or two behind. He was great on the routines. He did fine with traffic. He was also honest and hardworking.

Dee might be the smarter deputy, but Jim knew he could do a whole lot worse than a force of Bobby Dales.

Jim actually hated to waste Dee on traffic, but everyone took their turn with it. He had 800 square miles to cover, and he had less than 100 deputies to do it. It didn't make any kind of sense, and there was no way to do it well, so he had shifts where he had three deputies and shifts where he had six, and none of it was enough. The biggest problem he had with deputies in Eden County was finding people he could hire. The small population and the lack of education in Eden kept the pool of possible hires small. Finding someone who would willingly move to Eden to be a deputy was near on to impossible.

The good thing was that large areas of the county were nothing but woods and swamp. The bad thing was that there were idiots who could manage to make trouble even there. Of the deputies he had, Manny Soto and Dee Jackson were his best, and Bobby Dale was his worst. All things considered, he had a lot to be grateful for.

So he'd send Dee to Levy County, and he'd attend the funeral. He needed to be at the funeral. Edna Bass would be hurt if he wasn't there, and he needed to get a look at who showed up. Dee couldn't replace him there.

He picked up his phone and made a call to the Sheriff's office in Levy County. If he was going to send Dee down there to talk to one of their meth dealers, he wanted to be sure he didn't step on any toes.

* * *

Jim couldn't help but find his attention drifting off toward the Casey ledger stone just a short distance away.

The minister did his best to give a decent send off to Buddy. There were more mourners than Jim had expected, but most of them were older. He figured more than a few of them were men and women who used to go to the Cedars when Edna was young and running it by herself. He found himself looking at the men and wondering if any of them was the father of Buddy. No one had ever known who fathered Buddy. Edna had never said, and no man had ever come forward to claim him.

There were a few big men. Edna had been a plump, feisty young woman, but she was tiny. Her father hadn't been a big man. So clearly, Buddy's father had to have been tall and broad. Jim realized he couldn't quite picture Buddy's face. None of the men here brought the picture into focus, so it was likely the man wasn't here.

Linda Roman's patrol car was parked a short distance from the Bass plot, and she was taking photos of everyone there. Jim mentally started ticking names off. There was no one present who had actively tried to bust open Buddy's head, but there were a few of the bar regulars whom Jim knew had never been on particularly good terms with him. He would check into them later.

At the very back of the crowd, Jim noticed someone who really looked out of place. It was the photographer who'd been with Sheila. He had his camera, and it occurred to Jim it'd be just like Sheila to want a photo of the funeral so she could do a piece on it. She enjoyed writing high-profile stories, and a murdered man and two missing men had made her damn month.

Thinking about Sheila aggravated him. She worried a damn story to death until she got it to roll over and give up to her. She never met a fact she couldn't twist or a situation she couldn't make worse just by being there.

When the graveside service had ended, Jim went to Edna and paid his respects. She wept openly, but as always, thanked Jim for his kindness. He wished he could give her more.

Quietly he made his way over to Sheila's photographer. "Are you here officially?" Jim asked softly.

The man looked startled. "No, sir."

"I'm sorry I don't remember your name."

"Carl Basinger, sir." He held his hand out, and Jim shook it.

"You're not from here."

"No, sir. Just moved here a few months ago when I took the job at the paper." Basinger had thin blond hair and watery blue eyes. He was tall and broad-shouldered. Easily Jim's height.

"I thought maybe Sheila had sent you to take photos at the funeral."

Carl looked upset. "No, sir. I'm just paying my respects."

"Did you know Buddy?"

Carl nodded. "I'd met him. He and Sheila had a run-in a little bit ago. He caught her snooping around his bar, and he threatened her."

"Sounds like both of them," said Jim.

Carl smiled. "Yes, sir."

"You were with her?"

"Yes, sir. She thought he was selling drugs out of the bar, and she wanted me to get photos of him out back with some other men. I did, but he caught us. The two of them got into it. I had to step between them to get her away."

Jim sighed. "That woman is going to be the death of someone." Then he thought about the photos. "Do you have those photos?"

Carl nodded.

"Would you mind giving me copies? Might help me figure out who else had it in for Buddy. And could you not tell Sheila?"

"Certainly, sir. Be glad to. I can drop them by your office tonight."

"Thanks. That would be great."

Jim made his way to his deputy. Linda handed over the digital camera. Jim had paid for it out of his own pocket. The cost for one had finally dropped below a thousand dollars. Before that, his team had used disposable cameras and had them developed at the local drugstore. It was slow, costly, and never confidential. After finding out that copies of a domestic murder had been shared by the lab in Gainesville, he'd been determined to go digital. It also made him feel they were a little less behind the curve having it.

He'd also used it to take photos of Michael playing baseball. It was his, after all.

* * *

When he returned to the office, Jim found Dee at a desk filling out a report. Junior just held his hands up as though he was surrendering. When it came to Dee, Junior kept himself safely in neutral territory.

"Dee," Jim said.

She looked up, and he saw the lingering annoyance displayed on her face. "Sheriff." She went back to writing her report.

"Did you talk to Billy Dustin?"

"He's in the interrogation room. You can talk to him yourself."

Uh-oh, thought Jim. "Is he under arrest?"

"Yes, sir," Dee said without looking up.

"What charge?"

"Assaulting an officer and animal cruelty."

"Witnesses?"

"Levy County Deputy Timothy Mackey."

"Okay."

Dee finished writing and handed Jim the report. "I'll type it up in the computer after you've had a chance to talk to Dustin," she said.

Jim scanned the report. Dee always wrote her reports out by hand first. She said it gave her time to think and be more accurate. He had better sense than to argue with her about it, and since he barely knew how to turn on the computers, he wasn't really the person to argue the point anyway. "All right. Now tell me what happened," he said.

Dee took a calming breath. "I checked in with the Levy County Sheriff's office, and they sent me out to Dustin's place with a deputy. Tim Mackey and I drove together in his car to a trailer in Mountbrook. Dustin was outside sitting in a lawn chair, had the dog tied to it. The rope was barely long enough for her to put her head on the ground."

Jim winced. He hated that kind of cruelty. Dee despised it.

"We walked up, and Deputy Mackey introduced me and said I needed to ask him some questions. Dustin responded that he didn't talk to black bitches, he owned them. Then he jerked on the rope, and the dog stood up. He told the dog to smile pretty at me. She bared her fangs. He thought he was clever teaching her to do that. I told him I wasn't tied on a short rope and helpless, but I was black. He stood and walked up to me and pushed me using both hands against my chest. He was quite surprised that I didn't move."

Dee was smart and capable, and when she took a bladed stance in front of you, you had a snowball's chance in hell of moving her.

"I explained to him that if he touched me like that again, I would consider it an aggressive action and arrest him for assault on a law enforcement officer, which is a felony. He laughed and tried to punch me in the face."

"How bad did you hurt him?"

"He's not bleeding, and it's not like he needs to be breeding."

"The dog?"

"Deputy Mackey said he would take her to a vet and had her in the car with Dustin."

"So you haven't had a chance to question him about Mike Rountree?"

"No, sir, we didn't do any talking once I arrested him. Well, he did some talking, but I didn't respond. It was mostly rhetorical on his part."

Jim grinned. He was sure it was. "After I talk to him, you can take him over to the jail."

"Yes, sir."

Jim decided not to say anything else. He walked to the interrogation room and found Billy Dustin sitting in a chair, looking slightly pale and definitely angry.

"Mr. Dustin, I'm Sheriff Sheppard."

"Fuck you and your bitch," Dustin responded. With his buzz-cut hair and tall, wiry body, Dustin probably intimidated a lot of people. He had bruises on either side of his head where Dee had boxed his ears, but he could sit up straight, so probably his testicles had not been crushed, just warped temporarily. This was good. Dee had obviously not made any real effort to hurt him, just stunned him so she could get him cuffed.

"I'm not here to talk about your arrest. I wanted to ask you if you'd been in touch with Mike Rountree recently. If you want a lawyer, let me know, and I'll leave. Either way, you're going to jail."

Dustin shrugged. "Fuck Rountree, too."

"So you have seen him?"

"We had a beer together at the Cedars about a month ago. Haven't talked to him since, and don't want to."

"I heard you were maybe looking for Mike to do some work for you."

"Yeah, well, that didn't happen, Sheriff. Dumbshit couldn't leave his Daddy. When he grows a pair, I won't be interested."

Jim nodded. That sounded like the truth. "All right." Jim turned to leave.

"You're really going to let that bitch charge me?"

Jim glanced back at Dustin. "Even I don't argue with Dee Jackson," he said.

* * *

In the early evening, Basinger dropped by copies of his photos from the night at the Cedars. The prints were black and white, and in some, the light had been very low, but he could make out faces. He began to cross-reference them with the photos he had from the funeral.

He'd been more than a little surprised to see Billy Dustin and Mike Rountree sitting at a table in the bar. It was like all of his problems had decided to make an appearance in the same evening.

Several of the men and women from the funeral were in the photos. He noted that Basinger had put the date on the photos, and it had been a night slightly over a month ago. That gave more credence to Billy Dustin's story. Jim had a feeling that Dustin had nothing to do with Rountree's disappearance. What he'd said about Mike was true. He wouldn't have left his Daddy. Whatever Mike and Elvin might be, they had loved each other.

The photos in the back of the bar were clearer. Buddy stood with two men, and it wasn't a friendly conversation. There were lots of threatening gestures in the photos. Finally, both men had left in a Ford F-450. That was an expensive damn truck, and most people in Eden couldn't afford one. Fortunately, the tag on the back of the truck was visible. Jim made a note of it. He'd run it and see what he came up with.

The last two photos showed Sheila Ward getting right in Buddy Bass' face. One thing about Sheila, she had guts. She and Buddy were jabbing fingers and shouting. It must have escalated at that point for Basinger to step in, as there were no photos after that.

This gave him a couple of starting points. He would talk to Sheila, though God knows, it was the last thing he thought he'd ever say. He would run the tags on the truck and see if he could find the two men Buddy was arguing with before Sheila. If God was merciful, maybe these two men would be the connection he need to everything that had happened.

Somewhere in all this mess, there had to be a lead toward Buddy's and Hatcher's killer. Jim would find it.

Chapter Thirty

Ryan was sitting on the opposite side of Doc's desk, finishing up his notes in the files for the day, when he remembered he'd never written up the prescription for Jim. It needed to be documented. Not documenting care and prescriptions was a good way for a doctor to end up with his ass in a sling. His years in the ER made him very disciplined about his records.

He went to the records room and retrieved Jim's file. When he got back to Doc's office, the man himself was in his chair.

"What are you doing with Jim's file?" Doc asked.

"I wrote...script...antibiotic."

"He sick?"

Ryan shook his head. "Tick bite. Second time I've seen one here."

"Who else?"

"Sheila Ward."

Doc snorted. "I'm surprised her blood didn't kill the tick."

Ryan grinned. "Maybe it did."

They continued their work until Claire stuck her head into the office doorway. "Hey, Doc, I'm heading home. Everything's all locked up."

Doc waved her off. "Have a good evening."

When the door closed, Ryan remembered that he wanted to talk to Doc about Filly. "Do you mind...what we're paying Filly?"

Doc shrugged, "We're paying her $22 an hour."

"She's worth more."

Doc laughed. "Yes, she is. But it's all we can afford."

"She's doing more…"

Doc smiled. "You think you put a burden on her?"

Ryan nodded.

"She says you're easier than I am," Doc said. He set down his pen. "She could make more if she went over to Gainesville and worked at Shands, or even in a private practice over there. She's good. But she likes working here. I'm cranky and forgetful, and you can't talk worth shit. I think between us, you are easier. Now let's finish up these files, and I'll take you home for dinner. I caught two fine red drum the other day, and I will happily share."

"I need to get home and let Bonehead out."

"Pick him up and bring him with you. I'll cook him a burger."

Ryan smiled. "All right."

They continued working a minute, and then Doc said, "Filly loves those fancy flowers, Bird of Prey or something."

"Bird of Paradise?" Ryan asked.

"They orange and spiky?"

"Yes."

"Thanks."

They worked in silence for a while longer when Ryan broke the silence again. "What if I gave up…..some salary?"

Doc looked shocked. "You serious?"

"Yes. I can afford it. I'm paying …..for the apartment. Bonehead is happy there. There was life insuranc…and some other things."

"How much can you give up?"

"$200 a week."

Doc sat back in his chair. "What if I give $150 of that to Filly and $50 of it to Claire."

"Sure. It probably wouldn't be fair to give Filly a ….more and not give Claire something. She works hard, too."

Doc held out his hand, and Ryan shook it. "I'm going to have to have the accountant write something up for you to sign. Just so he won't be all over my ass."

"I understand."

"Damn. Filly's likely to want to kiss someone. I'm going to make sure it's you."

Ryan laughed. He felt lighter than he had in a long time. Danielle's life insurance had been a half million. He hadn't touched it because he hadn't needed to. He'd grown up in a wealthy family and never wanted for anything. It occurred to him that this was really his first time in giving something away.

When he worked in the ER, he'd felt he'd earned his role. He was good, and had been highly sought after his residency Northwestern in Chicago. The job in DC belonged to him. The money he earned meant recognition of that.

As the only child of wealthy parents, it had never occurred to him to even think about what the nurses and other support people made.

"God, I used to be such a ….prick."

"What?"

"I never…I had money, and didn't—"

"You never thought about what people who worked with you made?"

"Not people who were not doctors." Ryan blushed.

"Yeah, you were a prick," Doc said. Then he smiled. "Sometimes we change. Seems like you've changed. You're a good man, Ryan. I probably wouldn't have hired the man you were before. I wanted the man you are now."

Ryan smiled and felt a warmth in his chest. He was different. He might not be able to talk as well, but he was a better person. It surprised him, because he'd never thought about what he'd been like before his injury.

Chapter Thirty-One

The tag on the truck came back as registered to Nick Bowman. Bowman had a sheet which included arrests for burglary, dealing in stolen goods, and misdemeanor assault. Jim hadn't recognized him because all his arrests were in Gulf County, up in the panhandle. Jim hated when criminals moved in from another county. They needed more idiots like they needed additional buttholes.

The man with him looked to be a known associate named Kenny Wilson, who also had a record. Most of his charges included such highlights as attempted rape, DUI, and thirteen counts of domestic battery. How the hell the guy wasn't in prison, Jim didn't know, but he wasn't. And he was in Eden County. Dammit.

Currently, neither had active warrants, which was a shame, because it would make it easier to talk to them both. They lived out off Baden-Powell, way north of Libby's Dairy.

Jim didn't believe in coincidence, and that the wildfire south of the dairy was between the Cedars and their recent home made it all the more likely they would know something about Buddy's death.

Having better sense than to go out and try to talk to the two men alone, Jim looked over the current schedule to see who was on duty he could hijack. The one that made the most sense was Bobby Dale. He would do. Bobby at least wouldn't do anything until Jim told him to, unless someone started shooting. Oddly enough, Bobby Dale was a good shot. The man loved to hunt, and he filled his wife's freezer with enough venison and duck to keep them in meat throughout the year.

They drove in separate cars, and Jim pulled up in front of Bobby Dale so they had a second venue of escape should it be needed. It was late morning, and he could hear a television on in the house. Jim knocked on the door, and Bobby Dale stood by his car as backup.

Kenny Wilson opened the door. He had on jeans and nothing else. He scratched his big, hairy belly as he leaned against the door frame.

"Yeah?"

Jim noted that at least Wilson was a big target if he needed to use his new taser. "I'm Jim Sheppard, the Sheriff of Eden County. I'd like to ask you and Mr. Bowman a few questions about Buddy Bass."

Wilson didn't even turn around. He just shouted, "Nick. There's some county cop here to talk to you."

Nick Bowman stumbled into the room behind Wilson, followed close behind by a young woman wrapped in a sheet. Jim recognized her. Fifteen-year-old Dawn Hollis. Son-of-a-bitch, he thought.

Dawn saw Jim and quickly disappeared back into the room.

"What the fuck you want?" Bowman growled.

Jim wanted to punch both these assholes and grab Dawn Hollis and take her home, but he had to do this right. He keyed on his radio, knowing that Junior would listen in and make the appropriate calls. "I would like to speak with you both about Buddy Bass, but first, I'm going to ask that you tell the young woman to get her clothes on and come out here."

Bowman shrugged. "Done with her anyway." He turned and yelled into the room. A moment later, Dawn came out, mostly dressed. She crossed the room to Jim.

"Hey, Sheriff."

"Ms. Hollis, would you please go outside and stay with Deputy Dale?"

She nodded and walked out past him. Jim kept his eyes on Bowman and Wilson. "You the only one who had sex with her?" he asked Bowman.

Wilson laughed. "That one was up for anything. She took us both on before we even got her home."

Fuck, Jim thought. This was going to get really complicated really fast. "Both of you were recently seen to be arguing with Buddy Bass."

140

Bowman laughed. "Shit. You think we had something to do with killing him?"

"Did you?"

Wilson stepped away from the door and retrieved a cup of coffee he had on a nearby table. "Not likely. That dickhead wasn't worth our time."

"Look, Sheriff, we just moved down here. We got no interest in getting ourselves into any trouble. We went to the Cedars, and Bass hassled us for wanting to fuck one of his waitresses in the bathroom. He seemed to be under the impression we should be paying for it, you know? Only Kenny and me, we never pay for sex. We don't have to."

Jim heard the crunch of tires pulling up. Two car doors opened. "Can you tell me where you were the night Buddy disappeared?"

"Yeah," said Kenny. "We spent most of last week over in Gainesville. Found some nice college 'tang. It was sweet."

"Anyone who'll attest to that?"

Bowman nodded. "Yeah. We took a room over there. They'll remember us."

Jim had no doubt they would. He heard footsteps coming up behind him. Bowman and Wilson had noticed the arrival of the two other deputies.

"I'll need the name of that motel."

"Knights Inn," said Bowman. "I even got a receipt somewhere around here."

Jim nodded. "Good." He turned around and saw Will Hester and Tommy Barton. "Good. I think that takes care of that part of the conversation. Now, Mr. Bowman and Mr. Wilson, if you'll both step out here, please."

"What the fuck for?" asked Wilson.

"Indulge me."

The two looked confused. Jim wondered if maybe they didn't know what indulge meant. But they both finally moved out onto the front porch of the frame house. They saw the two deputies standing there.

"What the hell is this?" Bowman asked.

Jim nodded to the two deputies who stepped up onto the porch and moved toward each of the men. "You are both under arrest for statutory rape."

"Rape?" Bowman's voice went up an octave. "That girl wanted us. You could see we didn't make her be here. Hell, we let her leave when you asked."

"Yes, sir, I saw that," Jim responded. "But the young woman in question is fifteen years old."

Wilson turned to where Dawn Hollis stood with Bobby Dale. "You little cunt!" he screamed.

The men allowed themselves to be cuffed without saying anything more. Jim told the deputies to read them their rights and get them to the jail.

He walked out to the car where Bobby Dale and Dawn stood.

"I'm going to have Bobby Dale take you to Doc's. I'm going to call your mother and have her meet you there."

"What for?"

"I'd like Doc to look you over and make sure they didn't hurt you."

Dawn rolled her eyes. "I'm fine. Didn't do nothing I didn't want to do."

"Fine."

She got into the back seat of Bobby's patrol car, and he closed the door. "I'll get her there," Bobby said.

Jim nodded. As soon as everyone was gone, he went to the door of the house, closed it, and sealed it with crime scene tape. He'd get FDLE to come and go over the house.

As he drove back to the station, he felt the headache building behind his eyes. He hated that guys like that existed and that girls like Dawn found them. She was full of teenage rebellion and a bad case of the "no way outs." Her mother had been the same way when they were in high school together. Legacies in a small town could be good and bad. At least his had been good.

The call with Sue Hollis was brief. She agreed to go to Doc's to pick up Dawn, but she told Jim flat out she wasn't paying for the visit. She had Dawn on the pill, she'd said, so there was nothing to worry about.

Jim's headache bloomed into blinding after the call. Sue didn't have any more sense now than she'd had when they were kids. There was damn worse shit than getting pregnant.

He'd just settled into his desk when Junior passed along a phone call to him. When he heard the M.E.'s voice, he paid close attention to what the man said.

"I found exactly what was in Hatcher's lungs. Roast chicken, brown gravy, mashed potatoes, and kernel corn. Simple meal, but he'd inhaled the bulk of it, just a few traces in the stomach."

Jim felt his stomach lurch. He hadn't eaten anything since breakfast, but it wanted to make another appearance. He swallowed hard. "Thanks for letting me know."

"Anything else?" Jim asked.

"Not right now. I'll let you know when we get the DNA on the O+ blood."

Jim hung up the phone and pulled his trash can out from under his desk. He leaned over it and took deep breaths. He could feel the sharpness under his tongue, and his stomach convulsed. Nothing came up, but he spit into the trash bag. He swallowed again, trying to keep from vomiting.

What the fuck was going on? Hatcher had died from inhaling a pretty average meal. It could have been made by anyone in the county. Goddamn. This was not something he was fit to deal with. He didn't have the expertise, the support, or the manpower for this kind of shit.

Jim heard Junior from his door, "Sheriff, are you all right?"

Jim shook his head and spat again. He didn't dare speak yet.

Junior left the door and returned a minute later. He handed Jim a ginger ale. "Take a sip of that. It should help."

Jim didn't have the heart to tell Junior that he was afraid to open his mouth at the moment. He brought the can up to his mouth, and he could smell the ginger. He took a deep breath, took a tiny sip. He swallowed hard several times, and finally, the bile seemed to back out of his throat.

He took another sip of the ginger ale. "Thanks, Junior." The Vernors was strong. Junior swore by it for indigestion, so he kept a six-pack of the cans in the office refrigerator.

A few minutes later, he was able to sit up and take a few more sips from the can. Junior sat down in the chair on the other side of his desk.

"What did the M.E. say?" Junior asked.

"Hatcher suffocated on food. Roast chicken, mash potatoes with brown gravy and kernel corn," Jim said.

"That's crazy."

Jim nodded. "Tell me about it."

"Poor Reverend Hatcher."

Jim didn't bother to respond to that.

Junior stood up. "Rountree's still missing. There's a woman over in Alachua County that's got a cadaver dog. I read about her. I'll find out if she'll come over here and help us look."

"Junior, I don't even know where we'd start. We've been through the woods all around there."

"There's got to be something we can do."

Jim sat back in his chair. "God, I wish I knew what it was."

Junior sat back down. "Give me something to do, Sheriff."

Jim smiled. "I need to talk to Sheila Ward."

Junior grimaced. "Oh, hell no, Sheriff."

Jim nodded.

"I'll go call the paper and see where she is."

"Thanks."

Junior got up and headed back to his desk. Jim kicked his trash can back under his desk and drank the rest of the ginger ale. He was going to need to settle his stomach, especially since he had to talk to Sheila Ward.

Chapter Thirty-Two

Friday afternoon passed quickly, and Ryan felt good leaving the office. At his apartment, Bonehead greeted him at the door with boundless energy. Ryan grabbed a beer and followed the dog down the stairs to the back yard. He began tossing tennis balls into the grass and letting Bonehead retrieve them. He couldn't bounce them off the fence like Jim, but he could get them going fast enough that Bonehead would ricochet off the fence himself as he grabbed the ball and ran back to drop it at Ryan's feet.

By the time he finished his beer, he had a mild buzz, and the dog was exhausted. They made their way back up the steps, and both collapsed in the living room. Bonehead claimed the couch, and Jim took the easy chair.

This was Doc's weekend of call, which meant he didn't have to be anywhere or responsible to anyone else until Monday morning. His plan at the moment was to spend most of the weekend sleeping. Though there would be a break or two for food and tossing tennis balls to Bonehead.

But first, he decided, he needed food. He had actually prepared in advance for this weekend. He'd stocked up on beer, put in some snacks, and bought himself a nice steak with all the good sides. It wasn't the healthiest meal, but it was something he'd promised himself for his first weekend off. He would have an exorbitant meal, and then he would sleep like the dead. He popped a potato into the microwave and then dragged out his George Foreman grill.

For just a moment, he thought about the argument the gift of this grill had caused. He paused and touched it lightly. Yeah, he'd learned that cooking appliances were not a good birthday gift for some people. Danielle had made that very damn clear. He brushed aside the memory and plugged it in. He liked his steaks grilled.

As he opened a package of fresh broccoli for steaming, Bonehead raised his head. Then he flew off the couch toward the door and seemed to attack it, snarling and growling and barking.

Ryan set down the package of broccoli and went to the door. He flipped on the outside light and looked through a side window, but he couldn't see anyone. The angle from the window didn't allow him to see all of the landing at the door. He could see that the gate below hung open. He knew he'd closed it before he came upstairs to let Bonehead out.

He went to the door to open it, and Bonehead blocked him, continuing to snarl at the door.

"Dog, let me check," he said, but Bonehead continued to put his body between Ryan and the door.

Then Ryan heard footsteps running down the steps. He pushed past Bonehead and pulled the door open. The dog shot past him and ran down the steps. Ryan followed him, but when they reached the gate, all Ryan saw was the blur of a figure disappearing around the house across the street.

Bonehead started to follow him, but Ryan called, and much to his surprise, Bonehead turned around and came back to him. He scratched the side of the dog's head and murmured to him.

Jim pulled up in the driveway. As he got out of his car, he called hello to Ryan. "Everything all right?"

Ryan shook his head. "Someone on the porch...Bonehead went nuts...he ran away."

"Which way?"

Ryan pointed across the street. "Around that house."

"Damn," Jim said. "Let me call it in."

Ryan stopped him. "Jim, no, it's okay. He won't try it...now he knows I have a dog."

He could tell that Jim didn't like the idea, but he let Ryan have his way. "Keep your door locked. I wouldn't normally advise that, but I there's some crazy things happening in town. I'd rather you be safe."

"You…take your own advice?" Ryan asked. He knew from experience that Jim didn't lock his doors.

Jim grinned. "If I do, will you?"

Ryan laughed. "Yeah…you've got Michael and no dog."

Jim's face grew serious. "Yeah."

"You want a beer?" Ryan asked. "I was making…supper. I wouldn't mind the company for a while."

Jim agreed, and they went back up the steps. Ryan grabbed two beers and gave one to Jim, and looked at his dinner. "Enough here…for two, and…Michael's not home," he said.

"If you're offering, I wouldn't turn it down."

Ryan popped a second potato in the microwave and continued with his dinner preparation. Jim took a seat at the butcher block table, and Bonehead had already gone back to sleep on the couch.

"How was your day?" Ryan asked.

"Lovely. I attended the arraignment of two men who had sex with a fifteen-year-old girl. Spent another fruitless day trying to get Sheila Ward to talk to me—"

"Why would you…that woman?" Ryan asked.

"Ah, it's an open case," said Jim.

"Can't talk about it?"

"Not really."

Jim worked on his beer, and Ryan started heating the water to steam the broccoli. Ryan could feel Jim watching him work. He glanced up. "What?"

"If I tell you something in confidence…," Jim started.

"Yeah, I can keep it confidential." Ryan leaned against the counter as he waited for the water to boil.

"I've had some pretty ugly twists come up lately. I know you used to work in an emergency room in a big city, so probably this will seem pretty tame to you."

"Try me."

Jim fiddled with his beer bottle. "You know we found Buddy Bass' body out in a fire zone. That's not where it ends, though. We found the body of

Reverend Hatcher, and he died from inhaling a meal he was throwing up."

"Whoa."

"Yeah."

Ryan dumped the broccoli into the steamer and closed it. "I can't...that weirdness. I did have a guy bite off his own index finger...spit it at me."

"Why?"

"He was high as hell on PCP."

"What did you do?"

"Five of us...into restraints, packed finger in ice and sent him......surgery to have the finger re-attached. They had...a local...anesthesiologist wouldn't put him under. Figured he'd die if they did."

"I got hit in the face with a bag of dog shit once," Jim said. Then he snickered. That was the only word for it.

Ryan had to ask. "Okay, spill."

"Two men got into it over a dog taking dumps. Seems that the owner of the dog wasn't picking it up, and the owner of the yard was tired of stepping in it. So, he went to the dog guy's house and was banging on his door, demanding he come out. We get a 911 call, and I head over there. The yard guy does not take kindly to my suggestion that he leave before I have to arrest him, so he swings this plastic bag he has in his hand at me, and it comes open, and I get a face full of dog shit he'd collected from his yard for the past week."

"Yuck."

"Yuck doesn't begin to cover it."

"Did you arrest him?"

"Yeah. I charged him with assault of a law officer. He pled down to misdemeanor battery, because my dad thought it was stupid for a felony charge. But I was pissed about it."

They both laughed. The light on the grill went out, and Ryan put the steak on. "How do you like steak? And please....not well done."

"Rare."

"Hot damn. I may marry you!" Ryan said. Then he blushed. "Sorry."

Jim laughed. "Hell, it's the best offer I've had in years."

CHAPTER THIRTY-TWO

Ryan laughed and finished cooking their meal.

When they finished eating, Jim leaned back in his chair. "That was excellent. Thank you. I'll do the dishes."

Ryan shook his head. "You don't have to.......dishwasher right there."

Jim snorted. "Man, you wouldn't believe the fight we had about that damn dishwasher."

"You and Michael?"

"Me, Dad, and Mom. She wanted it. He didn't. I made the mistake of having it installed when this place was being refinished. Mom didn't tell me Dad didn't want it. I thought he was going to whip both of us."

"Did she...do the dishes?"

"No. He did. But he never did them to suit her. Plus, she liked them dried and put away, which he thought was a waste of time, since they were just going to take them out again at the next meal. The two of them stood up here yelling at each other, with me stuck in the middle, not saying a damn thing."

"But it stayed."

"Oh, hell, yeah. Once Mom decided she wanted something, she always got it. Dad should've given up, but when it came to arguing, he was not one to back down. If there'd been something up here to throw, shit would have been flying. It was one of their biggest fights."

"They fight a lot?"

Jim laughed. "No, they just aggravated each other a lot. Seriously, they were good. Dad would have laid down and died for her, and she would've let him."

Ryan laughed. "My parents...never argued. I don't think they were...with each other. They are both workaholics."

Jim pointed to the photo on the wall behind Ryan. "Looks like you were married once."

Ryan didn't even look. He took a long sip of his beer. "Danielle. We were married for two years."

"Didn't work out?"

"She died. When I got this," Ryan said as he pointed to his scar.

"I'm sorry. She was beautiful."

"She was. Smart and beautiful."

"The dog was hers."

"Yes. I…think he thinks…I was…she never came home again."

"He's accepted you now?"

"I'd call it…detente."

Bonehead chose that moment to walk to the door and turn and look at Ryan. "Not my fault you don't have opposable thumbs. Bring that up with God." He got up from the table and opened the door, and Bonehead headed out. They listened to his nails clicking down the wooden stairs.

"You don't talk to him like he's a dog."

"He still resents…English with me. Danielle only spoke to him in French."

"Where was she from?"

"Ivory Coast. But she'd went…college here. Her father…he likes me less than the dog does. …….white boyfriend."

"Yeah, it'd never go over well here in Warren."

Ryan snickered. "No one knows…Danielle. Doc knows…killed, but he doesn't know she was black."

"He wouldn't give a shit."

"Yeah, but…some would. And I don't like to talk…..People always want to know how it happened, and that's…not their business."

"You're right. People are nosy. Took me years of refusing to talk about it before people quit asking me what the hell was Annie doing on the road with the baby that night."

A comfortable silence settled on them. Then Ryan raised his beer. "To Annie and Danielle."

"To Annie and Danielle."

Chapter Thirty-Three

Saturday, just before noon, Dee Jackson brought Sheila Ward into the office. Neither of them looked happy, but Sheila wasn't in cuffs or bleeding, and Dee didn't have a pen stuck in her heart, so Jim figured they'd come to an agreement.

"So, now the police state of Eden County wants to compromise the first amendment," Sheila said, standing toe to toe with Jim.

"I just want to talk to you about your trip to the Cedars on Friday, May 8th."

Sheila huffed. "Fine. Whatever. Where do you want to talk?"

"My office?"

"Leave the door open," Sheila said as she stomped off.

Dee looked at Jim. "You know if I shot her, everyone in town would call it justifiable."

Jim smiled and followed Sheila. He took a seat at his desk and pulled out the folder holding the photographs. "I talked to Carl Basinger. He gave me copies of the photos he took that night. He said you believed that Buddy sold drugs out of the Cedars."

"Fucking Carl! These are confidential to my story!"

"I'm not showing them to people, Sheila. So, you thought Buddy was selling drugs."

"He was. I just couldn't prove it."

"Did you watch him any other night than that one?"

Sheila leaned back in her chair. "I watched him for weeks. The one night I didn't watch him, he fucking gets himself killed. I should have had that

151

story."

"You were there every night?"

"No," she admitted. "But more often than not."

"Did you always take someone with you?"

"No. The one time I did take that idiot, Carl, his fucking camera catches the light, and Buddy goes postal. He charged across that parking lot like his ass was on fire. I tracked down the two assholes he talked to, but they were both worthless. Unless you wanted to write about their tag team action on every woman they came across."

"Mike Rountree was in the bar that night. Was Buddy dealing for him?"

Sheila laughed. "Hell, even Mike was smarter than that. Half his shit was being dealt in the parking lot of the VFW."

Jim must have let his surprise show.

"Yeah, the VFW. He had a couple of old geezers selling for him right out of the parking lot. I think they're friends with his old man."

"And you never thought to report this?"

"Not yet. I was building a story. When I broke it, I'd give you what I had."

Jim felt the flush on the back of his neck. He wanted to strangle Sheila. If she'd talked to him, he could have busted Mike a month ago. "So, exactly how much meth do you think got sold while you investigated your story?"

Sheila, oblivious as always, said, "Hell if I know. But there's a regular pipeline between the VFW and the high school. Dawn Hollis has been selling at the school for months."

Dee, who'd been standing outside the door stepped in. "Sheriff, would you like me to go pick up Dawn Hollis?"

Jim pushed his rage down and nodded.

Dee looked at Sheila Ward. "I'd suggest you turn over your notes right now, because if you don't, there's a shitload of obstruction charges the Sheriff could file."

Sheila seemed to swell up. "I don't have to reveal my sources. I've got rights!"

Dee shook her head. "Well, I tried," she said. Then she turned and left.

Sheila looked at Jim. "That's bullshit."

Jim smiled and picked up his phone. He dialed the newspaper office. "This is Sheriff Sheppard. Is Carl Basinger available? Thank you, I'll hold."

"What are you doing?"

When Carl answered Jim asked him, "Mr. Basinger, I'm with Sheila Ward. She's made several statements regarding drug dealing she says is going on at the VFW, and by a high school student by the name of Dawn Hollis. Do you have photo evidence of any of this?"

"Shut up, Carl! Don't tell him anything!" Sheila shrieked.

Basinger's voice was quiet. "Yes, sir. Would you like me to bring it to your office?"

"Yes, I would. Thank you."

"Carl! You jackass!"

Jim hung up the phone.

Sheila stood up. "Fuck you. I don't have to stay here and talk to you. I was cooperating."

"All right, Ms. Ward."

She looked surprised. "You're not going to arrest me?"

Jim shrugged. "You're free to leave."

Sheila sat back down. She sulked for a moment, then she said, "I want the exclusive on whatever busts you make."

Jim just smiled.

* * *

Sue Hollis sat next to her daughter. Jim asked her if she wanted a lawyer for Dawn, but she'd told him, "Fuck it," and he'd decided to let it go. He knew Junior was taping the interview, so he felt safe going ahead and asking his questions.

Jim handed Dawn photos of her selling meth to several high school students. The bags of chunky crystals were visible.

Dawn shrugged and handed the photos back. "So."

"If I bring in the others in this photo, what do you suppose they're going to tell me?"

153

"Nothing."

Sue slapped Dawn. "You think those kids are going to lie for you? Don't be a fool."

Jim made a motion toward the window, and a moment later, the door opened, and Dee Jackson stood there.

"Deputy, would you please remove Sue Hollis and put her under arrest for child abuse?"

Sue looked at him like he'd lost his mind. "Why? 'Cause I slapped her? I was trying to help."

Dee stepped in and took Sue by the arm, and led her out.

Dawn grinned and stretched out in her chair. "All right. Now that's justice. I like that."

"Good, then you'll like that I'm charging you with distribution of a controlled substance."

"Bring it on. All they're going to do is send me to juvie."

Jim knew damn well that Dawn had never been arrested before, so she had no idea what she was in for once she was put into the system. He also knew there was little he could do for her. She was a kid, but she'd gotten herself deep into the adult world of trouble.

"You get the meth from Mike Rountree?"

Dawn sat back and pretended to zip her mouth shut. "Or did you buy it from Arch Biggers at the VFW?"

Jim handed her the photo of Arch handing her a handful of baggies with the chunky crystals in them.

She continued to stare at him. "Fine. I'll talk to Arch. He's older and a lot less stupid. He'll flip on you in a heartbeat to get charges reduced."

Dawn grinned, and Jim's heart sank. Yep, he was too late to do anything to save this one. "Interview ended at 2:38 pm," Jim said. He stood up and walked out of the room.

Junior had left the camera running, as was policy when a suspect was in the interrogation room alone. He looked at Jim. "What do you want me to do, Sheriff?"

"Get Linda Roman in here. I don't want Dawn taken to the jail by a male deputy."

Junior nodded and headed back to his desk.

Jim went back to his office. Depression settled on him like a thick morning fog. He hated that Mike Rountree's meth had ended up ruining so many lives. Arch Biggers had been in Vietnam. Mostly he was a harmless drunk. The other guy in the photos from the VFW parking lot was Tim Potter. He was a WWII vet living on social security. Jim figured he'd started dealing for Mike simply because he needed the money.

He'd had no idea this was happening in his own town, and it made him feel both stupid and useless. Now it was in the high school as well. He'd recognized one of the football players in the photos of kids buying the meth.

The fact that he'd had deputies actively looking for Mike Rountree's meth lab for two months didn't mean anything. Manny Soto and Waylon Forest had spent hours talking with known users, trying to get a lead on it, and they'd never gotten close to the whole VFW thing.

This made him angry. The department coped with limited supplies. They made do with being short of the people they needed. They stretched every hour of the day to its limit, trying to keep crime down, get to the kids in trouble, cover the roads, the emergencies, and yet, here he sat with this mess.

With Rountree gone, at least for the moment, the drugs would dry up for a while. But there would be some young entrepreneur who would find a supply out of Alachua County or Levy County, and it would all start up again.

Junior appeared in his door. "Linda's coming in to take Dawn to the jail. Do you want Arch and Ray picked up? Manny says he can get them both."

It was enough to make a grown man weep. "Yeah, go ahead."

Junior paused. "Why don't you go home, Sheriff. They've called off all the games this weekend, so Michael's probably hanging around the house."

Jim shook his head. "No, I've got to get ahead of this thing, Junior. I need to talk to the VFW Commander and then with the high school principal."

Junior sighed. "Want me to get you their phone numbers?"

"Yeah." Junior headed back to his desk, and Jim thought once again how lucky he was to have Junior, Dee, Manny, and all the others. Even Bobby Dale, bless his pointed little head. They were good people, and they gave more than their share to the county.

Jim rubbed his face, took a deep breath, and let go of his self-pity. He had a damn job to do, and he'd get it done.

Chapter Thirty-Four

After a weekend of arrests, arraignments, search warrants, seizures, and endless damn reports after endless damn interviews and interrogations, Jim found Monday morning a relief. They would be running a skeleton crew all day, because otherwise, he'd have to get justification for overtime. Which would then make the County Commissioners ask questions about how come all these arrests had to happen at the same time.

There were still photographs to go through that Carl Basinger had turned over. Sheila had truly done a masterful job of investigating. He just wished to hell she'd let him in on some of it. Manny Soto and Ivan Culpepper had volunteered to take the photos and continue reviewing them, even if Jim couldn't pay them. It was clear Manny took it personally that Sheila had gotten information he had not been able to get with months of work.

Jim just wasn't up for the headache of trying to justify overtime, so he prayed that Monday gave all of them a break and was quiet. The minute his phone rang, he knew that his prayers were for naught.

To his great surprise, the call was from Dr. Eddington, the M.E.

"I've got a body that I think you need to see," Eddington said. "Its neck is broken, left-handed perpetrator, head practically twisted off the neck. Also, there was a page from a Bible stuck in the pocket of his shirt with a verse highlighted in O+ blood."

Jim felt his stomach lurch. "I'll come that way as soon as I notify my office."

"I'll be here," he said.

Junior answered the phone. "Do you ever go home?" Jim asked.

Junior laughed. "I go home lots. You just never notice," he said.

"I've got to drive over to Gainesville to see the medical examiner. Call there if you need me and can't raise me on the radio."

"Yes, sir."

The drive into Gainesville was quiet. The ground on either side of the highway, where there had been grass or trees, was blackened and barren. The peat in the swamps still burned actively, so the smoke hung heavy on the road. Jim took his time. Whoever's body was at the M.E.'s wouldn't be going anywhere, and he had no desire to get in a hurry and join it.

Jim parked in the visitor's lot and made his way into Shands to the Medical Examiner's office. Dr. Eddington made a quick appearance and led Jim back to the morgue. He pulled out a drawer and drew back the draping.

It was Mike Rountree. There was some decomposition, but not enough to destroy the face.

"Shit," said Jim.

"You know him?"

"Mike Rountree. He's been missing. When and where was he found?"

Eddington checked his notes. "He was found yesterday on the Gilchrist County side of the Suwannee River."

"He went missing two days before that. Cause of death?"

Eddington nodded. "Same as Bass. Did Bass and this guy have a connection?"

"Buddy Bass owned a bar, and Mike Rountree cooked and sold meth. They both grew up in Eden County. Buddy may have been doing some dealing of Mike's product, but I don't know that for a fact."

The M.E. covered Mike's face again and closed the drawer. "I'd like to get information on the next of kin."

Jim nodded. "I'll do the notification of death. I know his father."

Jim left a short time later with a copy of the report and a stomach full of dread. Elvin Rountree and his son had caused him endless headaches over the years, but they loved each other. Elvin's wife had died when Mike was a child, so it had just been the two of them for most of Mike's life.

Jim went to Elvin's trailer as soon as he hit town. When he knocked on the door, Elvin answered. He took one look at Jim's face, and his head dropped to his chest. "He's dead, ain't he?"

"I'm sorry, Elvin."

"Where is he?"

"At Shands. I gave them your contact information. Here's the number to call to follow up with them." Jim handed him a note with instructions and a phone number.

"You know who done it?"

Jim shook his head. "Not yet. But I'll find out."

Elvin shrugged. "Just one less drug dealer, I guess."

Jim reached out and put his hand on Elvin's shoulder. "No, Elvin. I will do everything I can to find who did this."

Elvin grinned, his eyes shining with tears. "No offense, Sheriff, but you never could find Mike's lab. Not sure you're going to be any better at this."

"I'm going to put Dee on this with me," Jim said.

Elvin nodded. "She is a darn sight smarter than you." He swiped at his face and then stuck his cigarette back into his mouth. "You let me know." He went back inside his trailer and closed the door.

Jim fervently hoped that Elvin would grieve at home instead of going out to tie one on with his buddies. He didn't want to have to arrest him. Not today.

* * *

The front desk stood unattended. Jim had sent Junior home. He could answer the phones as he went over the file on Mike Rountree. Dee, unlike Junior, had the good sense to take the day off when he'd told her to on Sunday. He'd go over the file with her tomorrow.

Shortly after lunchtime, Manny and Ivan came rushing into the office and stood in the bullpen clutching photos. They both had huge bright smiles on their faces, which faded the minute they saw Jim's face.

"What's going on?" Manny asked.

"Mike Rountree's dead. Turned out his body's been at the medical examiner's office in Gainesville for the last 24 hours."

"Then this may be even more important than we thought," Manny said. He set the photos on a desk. "We've been going through the photos that Sheila had that photographer take. Look at this."

Manny laid out a series of photos of Mike Rountree's meth lab/travel trailer in the woods. The photos showed the trailer, with Mike getting supplies out of his truck and taking them inside.

Jim instantly made the connection. "These are before it blew up. They knew where the lab was."

"They sure did. And they were probably the only ones that did, since even Elvin didn't know it was out there."

Jim flipped the photos over and looked at the neat penciled date on the back. The photo had been taken on May 30th. "And it all leads back to Sheila and the photographer, Carl."

Ivan whistled quietly. "Suppose one of them's crazy?" he asked.

"Maybe both," said Manny.

"We don't know if it's them or not," said Jim. "But it may be connected to them. Maybe someone they know, or someone in their lives."

Manny asked, "Sheila got a boyfriend?"

Ivan snorted.

Jim shrugged. "No idea. I don't think anyone wants to get close enough to her to find out if she has a private life."

Manny left the photos on the table. "Want us to go pick them up and bring them back here for questioning? One way or the other, we'll find out what's going on."

Jim put his hand on Manny's shoulder. "Yeah, pick up Sheila and the photographer. But be careful. If it is one of them...."

"We'll be careful," Manny said.

* * *

Sheila was predictably irate at being brought in - again - for questioning. She bristled as she sat in Jim's office. The photographer, Carl Basinger, looked abashed. Jim didn't know if his embarrassment was caused by Sheila's behavior or by finding himself once again the subject of the Sheriff's attention.

"This is bullshit," Sheila stated. She crossed her arms over her chest and leaned back in her chair, getting as much distance between herself and Jim as she could.

"All I'm asking is who else might have known about Mike Rountree's lab. He's dead. I've got two men dead now, and in one case, you and Carl managed to be close by not long before the man ended up dead. Certainly, you can see why we'd want to talk to you about this," said Jim.

"What I can see is you grasping at straws because you've got two bodies and no leads and no damn experience investigating murder." Sheila's mouth curled in a self-satisfied sneer.

"Sheila!" Carl said softly.

Jim looked at Carl. "Carl, is there anything you can tell us? Was there someone else at the paper who could have seen the photographs?"

Carl seemed to think hard about that for a moment. "I don't know. I mean, I guess it's possible. Other people do use the darkroom. I wasn't hiding what I was doing, but I didn't see anyone looking at the photographs."

Jim looked back at Sheila. She sighed. "No, I've got nothing for you. Not even Ronnie knew about Rountree's lab. I knew if I told him, he'd have a fit."

Ronnie Weeks's reaction would be predictable. His sister had gotten into meth and been in and out of treatment a half dozen times. It wouldn't be likely he'd allow Sheila to keep the location of Rountree's lab under wraps, even for a big story. He might be editor of the paper, but his feelings about meth were very personal.

"Did you see Mike talking with anyone in particular, other than the people dealing for him?"

Sheila and Carl both looked at each other, then Sheila said, "There was some dealer down in Levy County we saw him talk to a couple of times."

"Billy Dustin?" Jim asked.

Sheila nodded.

"How recently?"

"Two weeks?" Carl said.

Sheila shrugged. "I don't remember. I just know he's the only guy Mike talked with who wasn't family or one of his dealers. Mike didn't meet the regular customers himself. Mostly because I don't think he could remember to collect the money from them. He was always high as hell," said Sheila.

"Thanks. It gives us something to start with," said Jim.

Sheila got up from her chair and left. Carl paused after he stood up. He said, "I'm sorry, Sheriff. Sheila's got a good heart, even if it doesn't show."

Carl hurried to follow Sheila out.

"Guess we need to talk to Billy Dustin again," said Manny. He and Ivan were both leaning against the far wall of Jim's office so they could be in on the conversation with Sheila and Carl.

Jim rubbed his face. "I'll go over to the jail and talk to him. Are you done with the photos that Carl gave us?"

Ivan shook his head. "That man must take pictures every few seconds. We've still got a stack yay-high to get through," said Ivan, holding his hands about a foot apart.

"Why don't you finish that up while I talk to Dustin. See if you can find anything that might be a link between Buddy Bass and Rountree."

They headed back to Manny's, and Jim picked up the phone to call Junior. He hated to do it, but someone needed to cover the office while he went to the County jail.

* * *

Billy Dustin's temperament had not been improved by his time in the County jail. Jim had been surprised that he hadn't bonded out. He didn't ask him about it, though, because he figured it definitely wouldn't make Dustin more amenable to talking to him.

"What the fuck do you want?" Dustin asked.

"I've got a witness who says you were in Eden County talking to Mike Rountree within the last two weeks," Jim said.

Dustin looked genuinely shocked. "What the fuck? I told you I hadn't seen the guy in a month. I haven't been in Eden County since I met him at the Cedars, and he told me he couldn't leave his daddy to come work for me. Who told you they saw me?"

"Right now, that doesn't matter. What does matter is that I need to know where you were Friday, June 5th."

Dustin looked confused. "June 5th?" He thought for a minute then he started laughing. "Oh man, this is too good."

"Mind letting me in on the joke?"

"I was under arrest at the Williston Police Department. I busted a guy's face up at the Hardee's for shorting me on his payment."

"When?"

"They arrested me around two o'clock. I was at the station for a couple of hours and then had my ass dragged down to the courthouse to be arraigned. Finally got bonded out around nine that night. I was pissed off and bitched out my bondsman, which is why my ass is still in jail now. Bastard won't take my bond, and the dumbass lawyer says he can't find anyone that will take it."

Hell's bells, thought Jim. "You didn't have anyone come up here to bring Mike down to talk to you?"

Dustin laughed. "I told you, I gave up on that guy. Cooks can be found. I didn't need to go courting Rountree."

Jim stopped at the main office on his way out of the jail and checked Dustin's record. Sure enough, he had been arrested the afternoon of June 5th in Levy County and charged with simple battery, a misdemeanor. Damn. Unless he could find someone that Dustin might have sent to get Rountree, this was going nowhere fast.

He'd make some calls to the Williston Police Department and the Levy County Sheriff's office and see if they could point him to someone. It was going to be another long day.

* * *

163

Jim ended up driving to Williston and talking with both the police and the Levy County Sheriff's Department. The same Deputy Mackey who'd gone with Dee to interview Billy Dustin took him around to a few of Dustin's known "crew." One of them had a brain, and she had no interest in doing Dustin any favors. Manuela Ortiz made it clear she hoped Eden County kept Billy Dustin for a while.

"Could he have arranged for someone to kill Mike Rountree?" Jim asked her.

She sneered. "He can barely bother to get up in the morning. He has the motivation of a rock and about as much sense. You're doing me a favor keeping him in jail."

Mackey grinned at Jim. "Told you."

"The way he tells it, he can't get bonded out," said Jim.

Manuela smiled broadly. "Yeah, too bad about that."

Her eyes were dark and cold, and Jim had to suppress the urge to shudder. He thought maybe they were doing Dustin the bigger favor keeping him in jail. Now that Manuela had gotten her foot in the door with his crew, he doubted very much she'd ever let him have it back.

"If I could get him for a murder charge, it'd keep him in jail a lot longer," said Jim.

She shrugged. "Yeah, but I got nothing. I can tell you that bolsa de basura doesn't have it in him. If it's not female and helpless, he lacks the cojones."

As Deputy Mackey drove Jim back to the station to pick up his car, he asked about Dee Jackson.

Mackey said, "I like her. She had Dustin on the ground and in cuffs, with his ears ringing and his balls in his throat faster than lickety-split. She seeing anyone?"

Jim looked over at the ginger-haired, white deputy and tried not to choke. "You'd have to ask her."

"Think I will. She's fine."

Jim couldn't respond. He didn't think there was anything he could say to that. He briefly thought about warning Dee, but that might be dangerous. While she cut Jim a lot of slack about some things, her personal life was carefully guarded.

He would just let this ride.

Chapter Thirty-Five

Pete's Gym had started to feel comfortable to Ryan. He had to admit that part of it was the welcome he got from Pete every time he walked in, but it wasn't just that. The other men and the women in the gym were all friendly.

Unlike his gym in Connecticut, where everyone kept a cool distance except people who actually knew each other, here geniality was the rule. Guys offered to spot him. Both men and women would help him correct his form.

His comfort with the free weights increased with each visit, and he no longer felt at sea with the various exercises Pete had given him to do.

"Hey, Doc Ryan!" a guy named Bill called out when he came in.

Yeah, he liked this. They couldn't call him Doc, because everyone in town called Doc Markham by that name, so he'd been dubbed "Doc Ryan" by his fellow gym rats.

"How are you, Bill?" Ryan called back.

"Working on the guns!" Bill said, laughing. He struck a pose showing off his huge biceps.

Pete snorted at the front desk. "Huge arms and no calves. I tell these guys to work it all, but do they listen? No, sir."

Ryan grinned and went to one of the cubbies to drop off his bag. He made a mental note to be sure he worked his legs. With the Florida heat, he'd want to wear shorts at some point, and he didn't want to hear Pete's snort applied to his own physique.

He went through his exercise routine at a decent pace and then spent thirty minutes on the treadmill. He enjoyed doing something aerobic. He liked for his workouts to tire him enough to feel he was making progress. Plus, it helped him sleep at night. He'd gotten to the stage he had enough endurance to not only walk Bonehead, but spend a good thirty minutes a day throwing the tennis ball for him. Bonehead appreciated that.

He'd gathered up his things and left the gym for his car when he saw the photographer standing by it. That startled him. He stopped walking and the man saw him.

"Dr. Edwards," he said. "Carl Basinger, the photographer with the newspaper."

"I remember."

Carl smiled. "I saw you were working out here, and I thought I'd stop and see if maybe I could buy you a cup of coffee or something. I want to apologize for the whole thing with Sheila."

Carl took a couple of steps toward Ryan. Ryan found himself backing up a couple of steps. "I'd rather not."

Carl started to get closer, and the door to the gym opened, and Pete stepped out. "Hey, Doc Ryan, can I borrow you a sec?"

Ryan turned slightly and said, "Sure." He looked back at Carl and then just turned and headed back into the gym.

When Ryan stepped inside, Pete motioned him over to one of the women who worked out regularly at the gym. She'd been introduced as Phoebe, and she trained for bodybuilding competitions.

Pete smiled, "Look, I hope you don't mind, but Phoebe's having some trouble with her right wrist. Maybe you could take a look at it?"

"Be glad to," said Ryan. He glanced over his shoulder. Carl Basinger stood at the door watching. He dropped his bag to the floor and took Phoebe's arm in his hands, and began to examine her wrist carefully. Might as well take his time, he thought.

Chapter Thirty-Six

Tuesday morning Dee Jackson sat across from Jim at his desk, reading over the file and looking through the photographs that Manny and Ivan had found. She and Jim couldn't find any new angles. He could tell it frustrated her as much as it did him.

"I'd love to lay this on Billy Dustin, but I don't see any way that this is his doing. He's a dumbass. I doubt he had enough of a reading capacity to know the Bible well enough to find Ezekiel, and I have to agree with Ortiz's statement that he doesn't have the balls."

"Yeah, I can see him shooting someone, or hitting them over the head with something, but not this shit. He wouldn't take the preacher." Dee sat back in her chair. "I know Sheila thought Buddy was dealing, and maybe that could lead back to Dustin. But none of this makes sense with the Bible verse and Hatcher."

They both stared at the file and the photos and were silent. Then Jim said, "It's another damn dead end, isn't it?"

Dee closed the folder on Billy Dustin and tossed it across the desk. "It is."

Dee got up from her chair. "All right, let's see what else we have."

She walked out into the bullpen and began to spread out photos and files on the desk. She laid them out in a timeline. First, they had the photos from the bar. The photos of Buddy Bass' body took the space between the photos of the bar and the photos of the meth lab. The meth lab explosion and disappearance of Mike Rountree followed Sheila and Carl, finding Rountree's trailer. She pushed another desk against the first and continued making a straight line with the files and photos. Mike Rountree's autopsy report. Finally, she laid down the file on Billy Dustin.

"I'll leave Billy in there since he's a piece of it, though we have eliminated him as our murderer. I think he was dropped into our laps to keep us distracted."

Jim thought about that. "Then we need to put in the file on Bowman and Wilson. I arrested them after we saw the first photos of the bar. They were probably just another distraction."

"Then we have the Hatcher case," said Dee.

Jim dropped the Hatcher file after Buddy's and Rountree's files.

"Did you have anything on it at first?"

"Nothing that led to anything." Jim walked into his office and took out the file he'd made on Reynold Stendal. "I followed up another dead-end early on. Hatcher's got a rare blood type."

Dee nodded. "Look for someone who might need it?"

"Transplant lists. Thought I might have something, but it was nothing in the end."

He placed the two files into their rudimentary timeline. They both studied the information carefully. When Jim looked it like this, he felt a little better about what he'd managed to do. Considering he'd never had a case like this, much less three cases tied up into one, his department had covered a lot of ground and eliminated a lot of leads. It didn't bring back any of the lost men, but at least he could see he really hadn't been doing nothing.

"Sheriff, this is one crazy ass case. You've got a Pentecostal preacher, who, by all accounts, was a decent guy, and two of the biggest criminal problems in the county. There is no connection between these three guys."

"Other than that, two of them are dead, and the Bible verse that first appeared at Donald Hatcher's home."

"Bass and Rountree were both being stalked by Sheila Ward and her photographer. And it was the photos from the bar that night that tipped you to Bowman and Wilson."

"But the Dustin lead came from Elvin Rountree."

"What about your transplant thing?"

"Doc put me in touch with a guy at Shands who made a connection to another doctor up in Savannah."

"So Bass, Rountree, Bowman, Wilson, and let us not forget Dawn Hollis and the two old guys from the VFW were all part of Sheila Ward's investigation."

Jim picked up Hatcher's photo. "If we could tie Hatcher to Sheila...."

Dee smiled. "Why don't we go ask? Ronnie Weeks might know."

"Worth asking anyway," said Jim.

As they left the office, a man got out of a pick-up truck parked at the curb. He smiled at them, and Jim wondered why the guy looked familiar.

"Sergeant Jackson, Sheriff. I hope you don't mind me dropping by the office. Hoped I might catch the Sergeant here."

It was Deputy Mackey from Levy County. Dee went still as stone next to Jim. Jim took a deep breath. This could go spectacularly bad in about ten seconds.

"I brought you something, Sergeant."

Mackey went around to the passenger side of the truck and opened the door. "C'mon, sweetheart. She's right here."

A black dog, the size of a small bear, appeared at the end of a leash that Mackey held.

Dee's face broke into a huge smile. "Is that her?"

"Sure is," Mackey replied. "I got her out of the pound. Couldn't let a beauty like this have nowhere to call home."

The dog pulled toward Dee. Dee dropped to her knees, and Mackey let the leash go. The dog ran straight into Dee's arms. "Hello, baby. You're looking good. Yes, we got you away from that nasty man. You sweet thing."

The dog licked Dee's face and pushed its huge head under her chin. She petted the dog and talked to it softly.

"I don't know if you have a place for her, and if you don't, I'll be happy to take care of her. But I thought, you know, since you saved her that you ought to have first dibs."

Dee looked at Mackey and beamed him a smile Jim hadn't seen since the day she'd gotten to ticket the Colonel for parking in a handicapped space. The Colonel had literally turned purple, and Dee had smiled at him like he'd just given her a million dollars.

Jim let out his breath. Okay, so she wasn't going to kill Mackey. Yet.

"I'd love to take her. I've got plenty of space. Thank you."

"Tim," said Mackey. "Tim."

"Thank you, Tim. The Sheriff and I are heading out right now, so I can't...."

Mackey shook his head. "Hey, no worries. I can hang out. I'm off today. Don't go in until tomorrow. You let me know when you'll be back. We'll go take a walk and get something to eat."

Dee rubbed her face against the dog's fur. "She got a name?"

"They were calling her Blackie at the pound. No imagination, those guys. I been calling her Jackie. She reminds me of you, sort of. She's beautiful, and she's tough."

Jim swore that Dee was blushing. He had never seen her blush, and she was dark enough that he couldn't swear to it, but her color seemed to heighten.

"Yeah, I like it. Jackie suits her. She's got that Pam Grier cool about her. Yeah, you're Jackie Brown, aren't you, baby?"

The dog licked Dee's face, and she laughed.

Jim bit the inside of his mouth to keep from grinning. If Dee saw him grin, this would go to shit immediately. Mackey, bless his soul, had found the way into the woman's heart, and by God, he was not going to do anything that screwed that up.

He looked at the red-headed, freckled deputy and marveled at the universe's ability to make something unexpected happen at the oddest times.

"Great. Jackie and I'll just hang out until you get back."

Dee nodded. "It could be a while. Let me tell Junior that if you need to come in to let you sit in the office. Jackie'll be good. Won't you, girl?"

Dee disappeared into the office.

Mackey smiled at Jim. "She's something. I never met anyone like her."

Jim let his grin out just a little. "I can say the same about you."

The man shook himself and petted Jackie. "I been thinking and thinking, and I had gone in to the pound to see how Jackie was doing. I thought maybe the Sergeant would like to have her."

"Yeah, seems so," Jim said.

Dee came out of the office. "You're good to go. If you need a place to sit that's not in the heat and smoke, just go on in. Junior's expecting you."

"Cool," said Mackey. "I'll take Jackie for a little walk, and then we'll come back here."

He nodded at them both and then led the dog away.

Jim and Dee got into her car. She buckled her seat belt and spoke without looking at Jim. "Don't say a word."

"I wasn't going to!"

"He's sweet."

"So's the dog."

"Yes, she is."

Dee pulled out of her parking space, and they headed out to the Eden Evening Star offices.

* * *

Ronnie Weeks looked up and rolled his eyes wearily when he saw Jim and Dee standing in the door of his office. "What has Sheila done now?"

"Nothing that I know of," said Jim. "Can you tell me if there was a connection between the Reverend Donald Hatcher and Sheila Ward before his disappearance?"

Weeks sat back in his chair. "You mean had she done a story on him? Yeah. About three months ago. She was doing a series on local sources for help for alcohol and drug addiction. She interviewed Hatcher about the AA and Al-Anon meetings at his church. People used to have to drive to another county before he took over at Holy Fire of God. For a Pentecostal, he was a very liberal guy. He even was talking with the County Commission to see if he could set up a shelter for battered women and abused kids. He'd gotten a church member to donate an old house outside of town for him to use."

Jim felt his gut twist again at the loss of Hatcher. Of all the preachers in the county to lose, it had to be the one who was actually trying to do something concrete to help.

"Were any photos taken?" Dee asked.

Ronnie nodded. He got up from his desk and went to a large set of drawers against one wall. He pulled out a drawer and took out a flat copy of the local page, which featured the story on Hatcher. He laid it on a nearby table.

Dee and Jim stepped up to examine it. The photo was of a smiling Hatcher and his wife, and taken in front of his home.

"Can we get a copy of this, Ronnie?"

Ronnie shrugged. "Sure, hold on, and I'll go pull a copy for you."

Ronnie left the office, and Jim turned to Dee. "Sheila wrote a story about Hatcher, and he disappears. Whoever took him could have seen the article."

When Ronnie returned with a copy of the article, Jim asked, "Is Basinger around today?"

Ronnie shook his head, "No, he and Sheila have been out beating the bushes about something. You know how she is. She always has some super-secret story she's working on. Carl's become her pet photographer. Sometimes I'm not sure he knows he really works for me."

"He's been helpful. Given us information that Sheila wouldn't have given up on a bet. If you hear from him, would you ask him to give me a call? I'd like to see if he can tell us anything about the article."

"Sure, Jim. Happy to do that. Might not be today. You know how Sheila is once she's got her nose to the ground. Sometimes I don't hear from her for days."

"Thanks, Ronnie. Anytime would be good. You can give him my home number," said Jim.

As Dee and Jim walked back out to his car, Dee asked, "So our killer may have targeted Hatcher because of Sheila's article?"

"It's a possibility. If we're lucky, Basinger may know something. Maybe Sheila was contacted by someone to get information."

"Want me to put out the word to look for him?" asked Dee.

"No. If we do that Sheila will find out and turn it into some kind of conspiracy. You take the car," Jim said. "I'll walk back to the office."

She saluted him, accepted his keys, and got into his sedan. Jim watched her drive away, knowing that she would go back and spend time with her new dog and maybe new friend. He would take his time and give them a chance to get out of the office before he got back.

Chapter Thirty-Seven

"How are you feeling today, Mr. Robertson?" Ryan asked the thin, ancient man who sat in the chair next to the small desk in the examining room.

"I'm older than dirt. How do you think I fucking feel? Everything hurts. Nothing works right. I piss fifteen times a night, can't see shit, can't hear shit without these damn aids, and all my friends are dead."

Filly touched Mr. Robertson on the shoulder. "How are those grandkids of yours? Isn't Shantal graduating this year?"

The man's wrinkled face broke into a huge smile, "Summa cum laude. She's the top of her class. Got eight different medical schools courting her. She's making up her mind which one she wants. She's not sure she could deal with the snow up to Harvard, so she's thinking she'll go to Stanford. Figures California won't be so cold."

Ryan realized his mouth had dropped open. He closed it.

"Dr. Edwards, his blood pressure is 118 over 80, and his A1C is 6." Filly smiled at Mr. Robertson. "You been listening to Shantal."

"She's smart. She tells me to do something, I do it. I got to live long enough to see her get that M.D., you know. I'm saving up for a plane ticket."

Ryan looked at Robertson's chart. The man was 87. But he wasn't diabetic, he showed no signs of heart disease and he got regular checkups and all testing recommended, and had for years. It was more than a little stunning. Ryan had started to get used to patients who didn't do anything he told them to do.

"Mr. Robertson's Shantal will be the second doctor in the family. Her

175

older brother is finishing up at Northwestern."

Mr. Robertson laughed, "He ain't as bright as his sister, but he's no dummy. But that Shantal, she going to be something. She's talking about Gerontology. Said she's got used to talking to old people like me, and she kinda likes it."

"Sounds like you're feeling," Ryan said.

"Proud, right, Mr. Robertson?" Filly completed Ryan's sentence.

"Yeah. I worked the watermelon fields, but I made sure every one of my kids went to school. I got two teachers, an EMT, and three nurses. Now I'm going to have two doctors! Giving 'em all my good genes, too. They're going to be like my side of the family and live to be older than dirt."

Ryan laughed. "I think I'd like to have your genes."

Robertson looked at him and snorted. "White boy, you couldn't handle my genes."

Filly snorted and Ryan smiled. "Probably not, sir. Probably not….I…envy."

Robertson nodded. "I suppose you're going to want to refill that prescription for the pressure pills."

"Yes, sir, I am. We've got…graduations you need to…get to."

"Yeah, that's right," Robertson said. "Already got enough saved for Chicago. But I think it'll cost me more to go to California. But I got some years for that."

Ryan wrote out the prescription and handed it to the man. "I'll see you…in six months unless you have a problem."

"Hell, only problem I got is being old. Ain't nothing you can do about that." Robertson got up, and Filly showed him to the door as Ryan finished up his notes in the chart. She came back a few minutes later.

"He had six children?"

"And he's got ten grandchildren. Shantal and her brother are the oldest. No telling what will happen with the rest, but I'd put money on them turning into something. That family's got grit."

"His wife?"

"Oh, she's alive. You'll see her next month. The good genes come from both of them. She worked in the watermelon fields, too. They're legends around here."

They walked out of the examination room together, and Ryan put the chart on the counter for Claire to file. Mr. Robertson was the last patient of the day, and it was time to close the office. The cleaning crew would be in shortly to scrub the floors and bathrooms and make sure all the public areas shone before they opened the next morning.

Before Claire could lock the front door, it opened, and Jim Sheppard walked in.

"Evening, Claire, Filly. I was hoping I could catch a ride home with you, Ryan."

"Sure. Your car...?"

"No, I loaned it to my Sergeant. She's taking care of something. I thought I'd go home and have supper before I have to connect up with her again. Michael can run me back to the office."

Filly pushed Ryan toward his tiny office. "Get your stuff. Don't keep the Sheriff waiting."

Ryan slowed his steps as he rounded the corner. Filly didn't make a habit of getting rid of him unless she had something to say she didn't want him to hear. He'd figured that out one day when he'd made a quick U-turn to get something he'd forgotten and overheard her talking to Doc.

"I heard about Dee Jackson and that dog."

"You want to know about the white boy that brought her the dog, you better talk to her. I am not involved in Dee Jackson's personal life."

"You better not be, because you know how this town will react if she gets herself into a mixed relationship."

Jim's derisive snort was loud enough that even Ryan heard it. "Dee can make up her own mind. If she decides to take up with a white boy, it's no one's business but hers."

"That's bullshit, and you know it, Jim Sheppard. Outside of Eden County, things may have changed, but they have not changed here."

"Are you saying that if Dee Jackson had a white boyfriend that it would be anyone's business? Because if you are, let me remind you that she works for me. She's an officer of the law in this county, and I will damn well not put up with any bullshit from either side of that damn argument. Are we clear on that?"

There was a short silence.

"Just because you think it's okay doesn't mean anyone else would."

"Would that anyone else include you?"

"We can't afford to lose a black deputy in this county. You know that."

"And we won't, unless she graduates and decides she's had enough of the stupidity that goes on around here. I'm staying out of Dee's personal life. I like my balls right where they are."

Suddenly Filly burst out laughing. "Good. That's what I wanted to hear. You just make sure that everyone else knows that. You hear me, Jim Sheppard? I do not want that woman dealing with some of these backwoods ignoramuses because I will be the one walking around with your balls in my pocket if that happens. Are we clear on that?"

"Yeah, we're clear. And how the hell did you hear about this? The man just brought the dog to her today!"

"I do not reveal my sources."

"Junior. Your nephew called you?"

There was a short silence, then Filly said quietly, "No. His daddy called me."

"Good Lord, you tell Senior to keep out of this, and I'll tell Junior if he does any more talking about it, I'm going to let Dee take care of him."

"All right."

Ryan retrieved his keys and headed back into the waiting room. Filly and Jim still stood, facing off with each other. Claire appeared to be hiding behind the ficus tree in the corner.

"Ready, Jim?"

"Yep."

When Ryan had the car headed toward the house, he broke the silence. "Why would Filly care who Dee Jackson...saw?"

"Mixing races isn't just an issue with whites. Dee comes from a mixed family. Her mother was Hispanic black, and her father was from Warren. I don't think anyone in town ever got over his marriage, though she was the one that actually raised the kids. The fact that she didn't speak English well was enough to annoy people on both sides."

"I would have never…Filly…like that."

Jim shrugged. "She likes Dee. Doesn't want to see her get more alienated in the community. But I'm going to kick Junior's ass for talking to his father about it. Senior and Filly are brother and sister. Hopefully, it won't go past them."

"So she's interested in this white man?"

"He's interested in her. Brought her a dog she saved when she was down in Levy County. He's a deputy there. He's got a hell of a crush, and I think this was the start of his attempt to court her."

Ryan shook his head.

"You and Danielle have any problems with either set of parents?"

Ryan laughed. "Her father nearly had a stroke…when she brought me home. They're African. They were not…a white boy from Connecticut as a son-in-law."

"Your parents?"

"My parents are Connecticut liberals. They didn't even flinch."

Jim leaned his head back against the headrest. "That must have been nice."

"It was. Once her father…realized I was a doctor, he didn't…hate me too much. Her mother liked me. When they buried her…I was in a coma. They bought the plot next to her for me. In case I didn't make it."

"Car accident?"

Ryan shook his head. The only person he'd talked to at all about what had happened was Doc, and then only the minimum. "We were attacked… Baseball bat and a knife."

"Bat hit you."

"Yeah. I was knocked out…the knife got her."

"I'm sorry."

"Thanks."

They were quiet the rest of the way home. When they reached the house, Ryan parked, and Jim offered to feed him in exchange for the ride. Ryan refused politely. Right now, all he wanted was to get some time to himself. He'd take Bonehead for a walk.

He watched Jim head into the house. Michael's car was in the drive, so there would be homey chatter and a quick dinner before Jim headed out to work again. Warmth and love filled the Sheppard house.

Thinking about it made Ryan's chest ache.

Chapter Thirty-Eight

Dinner had been a quick sandwich. Michael dropped him off at the office on his way to a study group for a calculus exam. Dee and Tim Mackey sat in the bullpen with Jackie when he walked in the door. Junior picked up his phone and pretended to be on the phone with the Colonel. Jim pointed a finger at him. "You, later." Junior nodded and continued his non-existent conversation.

Jim motioned for Dee to come into his office, and Tim followed with Jackie right behind him. As he sat at his desk, he looked at the three. "This is a case, Deputy Mackey."

Mackey nodded. "I know."

Jim looked at Dee. "I read him in while we were talking."

"You read him in?"

Dee smiled. "Yes, sir."

Jim shook his head and rubbed his face. "Sergeant...."

"He already knew about looking for Rountree's killer. Only made sense to let him know there was more to it. We might need cooperation down in Levy County before this is over. He'll be our liaison."

She and Tim took a seat, and Jackie dropped to lie on the floor beside them.

"Did you deputize her, too?"

Dee grinned. "She'll be working with me."

"Anyone seen Sheila?"

"No one has seen her. I even called her mother. She could be out of the county. She does that sometimes. Makes a contact and goes outside the

181

county to dig up background or information on whatever she's working on."

"Anyone check her house?"

"I sent Deputy Wills. He found no sign of her there."

Wills carried lock picks, so Jim was sure exigent circumstances had demanded an entry and search. Dee knew everyone's skills as well as he did, and she wouldn't hesitate to use whatever she thought was necessary. She had been an MP in Iraq. She knew life and death situations better than anyone, including him, when it came to law enforcement.

"No telling what kind of story she's into now."

Deputy Mackey said, "Seems like she may be helping point your killer?"

"She could be, but not deliberately. As much as we all dislike the woman, I can't see her being involved in anything like this," said Dee.

Jim leaned back in his chair and rubbed his face. "She's single-minded enough to not think anything about this connects to her. I'll ask Ronnie to let us know if he hears from her."

"I'll see if anyone's seen her in Levy County. She's not won any fans down there either," said Tim. "I've got a couple of friends over in Alachua County who can keep an eye out as well."

Dee stood up, and Jackie jumped to her feet. The dog had already tuned into her. "If you don't need me any further, Sheriff. Deputy Mackey and I were going to take Jackie back to my place."

Jim's eyebrows nearly met his hairline, but he quickly got his expression under control when he saw Dee's mouth turn into a grim line. "Of course, Sergeant! Past time for you to be gone. Have a nice evening. Good to see you again, Deputy Mackey."

Dee nodded and turned on her heel. Mackey grinned at Jim. "You take care, now, Sheriff."

* * *

Jim dragged himself home and found Michael had ordered a pizza.

"I heard you'd be worn out. Thought I'd make supper tonight," Michael said.

Jim's breathing loosened a little to see Michael smiling and relaxed, sitting at the kitchen table. "Ordering pizza is not making supper."

Michael grinned. "It is when I'm in charge."

Jim saw Ryan and Bonehead clattering up the stairs to his apartment. Ryan was red-faced and sweating. Bonehead bounced up the steps. That meant they'd been for a long walk. The dog always came back looking energized while Ryan looked beat.

Michael snickered. "Looks like they had their usual adventure out tonight."

Jim witnessed the walk once and had to go inside to keep from laughing where Ryan would hear it. Bonehead would pull on the leash, dragging Ryan behind him. The smoky air didn't seem to bother the dog at all, but Ryan would be wheezing within yards.

"I think Bonehead needs more exercise," said Jim.

Michael laughed. "Hey, I threw the ball to him for over an hour this afternoon. I think exercise just gets him worked up."

Jim wondered if Ryan might be willing to spend the night at the house. Having the dog around would make him feel that both were safer. He shook the idea out of his head. He would make Michael lock up the house tonight. He knew that Ryan had the big city habit of always locking his doors.

Jim took a deep breath. He liked having Ryan in his father's old apartment. Michael, still living at home, gave him someone to come home to each night. But in just a few short years, Michael would be off to college. Probably in a few weeks, Ryan would find himself a permanent residence, and Jim would not have this comfort.

His home refuge could not last forever. He had to hope it would outlast the fires and whatever craziness was going on in Eden County.

A knock at the front door startled him. Michael ran to answer it before he could make himself move, but it was the pizza delivery. His stomach felt sour, and his eyes throbbed. Today had been too long, and it wasn't over, yet.

"All right!" Michael said. He set the pizza box on the table and grabbed two plates and a roll of paper towels.

"Oh, we're going classy tonight," said Jim.

Michael laughed. "Nothing but the best. It's got pretty much everything on it. Paper plates wouldn't hold it."

Jim flipped the box open and pulled out a couple of slices that he slid onto the plate Michael held. Then he put one on his own plate. He could feel the indigestion starting already. The pizza looked like someone had up-ended the kitchen on it.

"You in for the night?" Michael mumbled through a mouthful of pizza.

At least, that's what Jim thought he'd said. "No, I've got to get back to the station."

Michael swallowed and squinted at his father. "What's going on?"

"Nothing you need to know about. But keep the doors locked tonight, okay?"

"Sure," Michael said. "What are you worried about?"

"Just feeling protective. Nothing to worry about."

"Yeah, right. That might have worked if you didn't look like you were going to throw up on your pizza. This is about the murders."

"You are too smart for your own good."

"It's in my blood."

"My boot's about to be in your ass. Your coach called me about your play."

Michael shook his head. "Un-huh. It's about the murders. I don't think the coach thinks my center fielding is that bad, Dad."

Jim snorted a laugh. "Maybe it's your batting average."

"C'mon. Talk to me. You know I won't tell anyone."

Jim thought about it for a moment, then he said, "We're trying to locate someone that might be able to help us with the murders. They probably don't even realize they know something."

"That sucks. You think the murderer's got them?"

Jim sighed. "No, nothing like that. Just aggravating to not be able to get some information."

Michael swallowed the last of his second slice and reached for another. "You'll find them. I know you, and I know your department. They're probably all out looking right now, half of them in their personal vehicles to keep a low profile."

"Yeah," Jim said. "I think I've even got a guy down in Levy County looking."

"The guy who brought the dog up for Dee?

"How did you hear about that?

"Dad, a white guy from Levy County, drove into town and waited around the station for Dee. I think the only person who doesn't know about him and the dog is maybe that blind guy that plays the accordion in front of the grocery. And I'm sure his dog did see it and tried to communicate it to him through telepathy."

Jim shook his head. "Who told you?"

"Junior's cousin."

"Dee is going to kick Junior's ass."

"Target's big. It's not like she can miss. Do you want me to get you some ginger ale and crackers?"

"Do I look that bad?"

"Yes, and I'm going to eat that slice of pizza before it goes to waste."

Jim pushed his plate over to Michael. "Thanks."

Michael got the ginger ale and saltines, and Jim managed to eat a few and drink about half a glass before he pushed it away. "I should get back to the station."

Michael reached out and put his hand on his father's arm. "I promised to keep the doors locked and not answer unless it's Ryan. That okay?"

"Yes, that would help. I can't be worrying about you."

"School's over for me. I'm exempt from my finals, so I'll stick close to home. Other than being at Ryan's, or being in the backyard with Bonehead, I promise to not go anywhere. You know Bonehead won't let anyone get near me or Ryan."

"That's true, and I'd appreciate it."

"In exchange, you promise me that you'll be careful. Don't take any risks you don't have to, please?"

"I promise."

Jim and Michael both stood up and hugged each other close. Michael had grown up with law enforcement being the family business. He understood the risks probably as well as Jim did.

"If you need me, call Junior. If I can, I'll call you back."

"Sounds good. But I won't need anything, so don't worry."

And hopefully, no one else would die in the meantime, Jim prayed silently.

Chapter Thirty-Nine

Ryan parked behind the office and sat in the car a moment, finishing his coffee. He never took the travel mug inside. If he did, he knew he'd forget to take it home, and it would disappear into the detritus of the office kitchen and he would never see it again. He liked this travel mug. It was the perfect size to hold exactly one cup of coffee with a nice layer of cream, and he wasn't going to lose it. He'd spent weeks looking for just the perfect one when he'd started in the ER at George Washington. Unlike most of his co-workers, he didn't drink coffee all day. He had one perfect cup on his way into work, regardless of what shift it was, and that was it.

He'd always been a runner, and too much caffeine could throw off his heartbeat. He'd learned that all the way back in high school when he ran cross country. One bad race after too much coffee convinced him he needed more than moderation. He needed to be downright stingy with the stuff.

Most travel mugs held two cups and sometimes more. Too much for him, and the extra space just gave the coffee air to cool it. He'd found a one-cup travel mug with just enough space to add cream, and he'd carried it with him ever since.

Danielle teased him about it. She thought one cup was insufficient for survival. She started with a pot of coffee each morning and kept it up all day. She could drink coffee right before bed and sleep like she'd drunk water.

Her father told her he believed it explained how dark her skin was. She'd begun sneaking sips from his cup as a child. She and her father both took their coffee black and sugar-free.

187

Ryan swallowed the last of the coffee and shut down the memories. It was time to start his day. One of the good things about being in private practice was the regular hours. He liked getting to the office at 7 am. The doors didn't open until 8, which gave him enough time to read over his charts for the day and get himself set. That was a luxury no doctor had in the emergency room. He considered himself lucky if he didn't walk through the door into an immediate disaster.

Just as he stepped out of the car, a large van pulled up next to him. He didn't recognize it, and he couldn't see the driver. The side door of the van slid open. He saw the photographer from the newspaper.

Before Ryan could say anything, the man grabbed his right arm and pulled him into the van. Ryan's legs slammed against the frame of the van, and he cried out in pain and surprise. He tried to pull away, but with his feet on the gravel of the parking area, he couldn't get any purchase as he struggled to pull away.

He yelled, and a hand clamped firmly over his mouth.

He took advantage of having one hand free and grabbed the door of the van, and pulled hard. All those months of lifting weights, every minute of focusing on building a layer of muscle came into play, and Ryan pulled himself out of the man's hold on his other arm.

But the hand on his mouth jerked his head back, and the second hand came up and grabbed him around the neck.

Ryan fought. He bit the hand over his mouth and gouged at the man's face with his fingers. The hand over his mouth disappeared, and Ryan grabbed for the door of the van again, pulling as hard as he could to get away.

Then he felt himself being pushed forward. For a second, he thought he'd gotten away, then he felt the force behind it. His face slammed into the edge of the door, and blinding pain split across his face. He felt the gush of hot blood, and the world greyed out.

Hands grabbed his arms and pulled, and though he kicked and tried to stop his movement, he was pulled into the van. He heard the door slam shut, and he tried to sit up. His hair was pulled painfully, and he felt the pain of his head being beaten against the metal floor of the van. Then nothing.

Chapter Forty

Jim came out of the bathroom after shaving when his phone began ringing. Muttering to himself, he answered it, expecting to hear Junior's voice. Instead, it was a very panicked Filly.

"Jim, someone took Ryan," Filly shouted. "You've got to get people over here now."

"Took Ryan?"

"Claire just got here, and she said Ryan's car door is wide open, his keys are on the ground, and there's blood out there."

"Call 911 now."

"Claire's already done that. We need you."

"I'll be right there."

Jim hung up, then called Junior. "Call Bud Peterson. Get him and his team here as soon as they can get here. It looks like someone's grabbed Ryan Edwards in back of Doc's office. We'll need a full team. Call Dee at home and get her over there right away."

Michael came out of the kitchen and walked to where Jim could see him.

"I'm headed over there now. If you need me, use the radio."

Jim hung up and looked at his son.

"Someone grabbed Ryan?" Michael asked, his eyes wide.

"Looks like it. You stay home. Keep the doors locked. In fact, go up to Ryan's place and get Bonehead. Bring him down here and lock him in with you. Got it?"

"Yes, sir."

Michael took off for the back door, and Jim went to his bedroom to grab his duty belt and gun. He didn't bother to put on his gear. He ran out to his car and flipped on his siren, and drove straight to Doc's. Everyone pulled off the side of the road as he drove through town, and he didn't give a shit that there would be questions about it later.

When Jim stopped behind Doc's office, he could see Ryan's car, the driver's door open. He got out and circled the area as he put on his duty belt. He could see that the gravel next to Ryan's car was all kicked up. There were tire tracks next to that. What looked like blood puddled on the ground next to the tire tracks.

Claire Garvin's car had pulled up behind Ryan's and stopped short of pulling into the open space. Jim was grateful for Claire's intelligence. Someone else might have pulled on in and then wondered. She'd obviously seen something was wrong and stopped short of the scene. It made him want to go in and give her a hug.

Jim heard a siren in the distance, and just moments later, Dee Jackson pulled up in her patrol car. Her hair wasn't in its usual neat bun, just pulled back and loose in a tight band. She only had on half her uniform. Her shirt looked wrinkled, but it was official. Her jeans and sneakers most definitely weren't, and he'd never been gladder to see her in his life.

"Sheriff," she said briskly.

"Claire Garvin. She's inside. That's her car. Talk to her first, then get everyone's statements. See if we can figure out when this happened."

"Yes, sir." She turned quickly and ran toward the front door of the office.

Jim went to his car and pulled several traffic cones out of the trunk. He set them at the entrance of the parking lot to keep anyone else from pulling in. He wanted this area as clear as possible for the crime scene techs.

He walked the perimeter of the lot, scanning for anything that was out of place. Then he looked at the surrounding businesses. Nothing on the street behind Doc's office was open yet. The bank's ATM machine faced the lot. "Oh hell, yeah," Jim said to himself. He called Junior on the radio.

"Find Joe Sanders or Patricia Jenkins and get them to the bank as quickly as you can."

"Yes, sir. What do you want me to tell them?"

"I want the footage from the bank machine. It faces Doc's parking lot."

"All right!" Junior crowed. "You got it, Sheriff."

Jim paced back and forth on the side of the street. It couldn't have been too long. The office didn't open until 8. It was 7:20. Ryan couldn't have been here that long ago. Jim found himself saying another prayer, despite the failure of his earlier ones. This one was more urgent to him personally. This one, God had a better answer. Jim couldn't take one more death. Not one more.

Chapter Forty-One

Ryan came back to consciousness in a dimly lit room. His face throbbed, and his head pounded, the pain from one in counterpoint to the other. He could taste blood in his mouth. He could only breathe with his mouth open, which probably meant he'd broken his nose. His right eye was swollen almost completely shut, but he could see pretty well out of his left eye.

He could hear the hum of an air conditioner, and he felt a little cool. He realized he was naked, sitting up in a chair, with his arms, legs, and chest duct taped to the frame. A towel lay across his lap, providing him with some modesty, but the frame of the seat was open beneath him.

He tried to clear his head enough to get a better sense of where he was. A potty chair. An adult potty chair. That was what he was strapped to, which meant that the guy who'd grabbed him, that photographer guy, didn't plan on letting him out of the room. His heart rate zoomed, and he took several deep breaths. Crap. Crap. He needed to not panic. He needed to calm down. He wasn't doing himself any good. Calm, calm, breathe, breathe. He forced himself to take slow deep breaths. His mouth felt dry. He stopped, swallowed a couple of times, and then took a couple more slow, deep breaths.

Okay, think, think. He had to think. He focused, searching the room visually for anything that might help, or at least give him information he might need. The room was bare. Vinyl floor. Plaster walls. The windows were covered with plywood, except over the window unit air conditioner. Everything seemed yellowed with age, so that probably meant this was an older house, but he knew so damn little about this area that he had no idea what older might mean.

There was one door, wooden. The light in the room came from a ceiling light. It was dusty, and the bulb was not bright, making the room dim and yellow. Accordion doors in one wall probably meant a closet. So likely, this was a bedroom.

A bedroom meant a house, but where? Neighbors? He thought no. No, neighbors would be a problem. They'd notice things like boarded-up windows, and since he had no gag, there couldn't be anyone close enough to hear him if he yelled. That meant he had to get out of here, wherever here was.

Ryan's feet were on the floor, and the aluminum frame of the chair was light. He leaned forward slightly and tilted the chair up. He was standing, albeit in a crouched position, and still taped to the chair. His hands were free. The tape wrapped around his wrist and forearms, and his legs were taped at the shins to the chair legs.

One thing for sure, he was not going die taped to a fucking potty chair. He'd survived brain damage and the death of Danielle. He'd spent the last year building muscle and strength. He would not die like some incontinent old man.

He moved to the door and twisted the knob. It turned. He almost wanted to cry with relief. He pulled the door slightly open, and he could see the hallway beyond. It was daylight. He could see light in the hallway coming from a room at the other end.

Okay, okay. He had to take his time. He needed to listen. He needed to be sure that he didn't meet up with the photographer while he was still taped to the damn chair.

After a moment, Ryan heard someone moving around in another area of the house. Footsteps. He carefully closed the door, then made his way back to the middle of the room and sat down in the chair. He would have to be patient. He had no idea how long he'd been here. The sun that fell into the hall was bright, but whether that meant morning, mid-day, whatever, he couldn't know without understanding in which direction the house was oriented.

It could still be early morning, and his captor could have put him in here a short time ago. He might not be expecting Ryan to be awake, yet. But if he checked, it would be best to appear disoriented, if not still unconscious.

He wished the pounding in his head would lessen even just fractionally. He didn't feel dizzy, which meant he might be lucky. He might not have a concussion.

Ryan nearly laughed when he looked down and realized he had fingers crossed on both hands. An unconscious action to attempt to ensure good luck. Man, wouldn't Danielle laugh at him. She'd been a great believer in luck. She had little superstitions, wearing the right color for a meeting. Eating the right food on New Year's Day. He'd always said luck didn't exist. He stopped himself. Couldn't let his mind wander. He had to focus. Focus on now. Not the past, now.

He heard footsteps and the crackling of the old vinyl floor outside the door.

Ryan dropped his head, closed his eyes, and began to breathe slowly, feigning sleep. His heart hammered in his chest as the doorknob clicked and the door opened.

Chapter Forty-Two

Dee stood with Jim as they reviewed the recording from the ATM machine. They were able to isolate the time period from the statements Dee had gotten from the staff at Doc's office. Filly had come in at 6:45. She had been the lone car parked in the lot at that time. Doc was in Gainesville visiting patients in the hospital.

Claire Garvin had arrived at 6:55. She had to be in the office by 7 am, and the doors to the practice opened at 8. When she'd started to pull into the lot next to Ryan's car, she'd seen the open car door and the keys on the ground. She'd parked her car behind his and slightly across the space between his car and Filly's to keep out of the disturbed gravel of the lot.

She'd gone straight into the office and called 911.

That gave them a ten-minute window when Ryan could have been taken. It made it very simple to search the recording. They fast-forwarded to 6:45 and watched carefully.

At 6:48, Ryan had pulled into the lot. He'd sat in his car until 6:50, drinking coffee. Then he'd opened the door, and as he got out of the car, a white van pulled into the lot, coming from the west. Seconds later, the side door of the van slid open and thick arms reached out of the van and grabbed Ryan by the left arm, pulling him into the van.

The struggle had been short, but fierce. Ryan had fought, grabbing the side of the van to pull away. He had nearly been out of the van when they saw Ryan go limp. Then he'd disappeared into the van, his legs pulled in. The door had closed, and seconds later, the van backed out and disappeared the way it had come.

It was 6:52 when the van disappeared from sight.

"Lord," Dee said. "That was scary fast."

Jim felt anxiety, like something crawling under his skin. Ryan was a tall guy with decent strength. Whoever did this had to be strong as well. Had to be a big man. "I can't see the tag on the van."

Dee nodded. "Too far away, and the resolution is for shit."

"Van's white. That helps. Big arms. Which could fit more than half the men in Eden County."

Dee put a hand on Jim's arm. "We can't be sure this is connected to what's going on. This could be about something that happened at the practice. Doc's had problems before."

"It'd be a crazy coincidence. Two men in Eden grabbing people right now?"

"Crazier things have happened here. It's Eden, Jim. Crazy is the norm."

Jim took a breath. "But it could be."

Dee got up from her seat. "I'll start with registrations on white vans for the county. It didn't have any business logos, so we'll be able to narrow it down some from that."

Jim stood. "Take this with you. Give it to Bud Peterson's people and see if they can get anything more."

"Will do, sir." Dee took the disk out of the machine and left.

Jim stepped out of the security room and found Patricia Jenkins waiting for him. She wore her usual suit and white blouse. He'd never seen her not put together. But there were tense lines around her eyes.

"Is it any help?" she asked.

"It is. Thanks for letting us get to it right away."

"He seems like a nice man," she said. "He treated Ricky for his asthma last week. Was really good with him."

That was right, Jim remembered. Her son. Ricky was in elementary school. "The smoke hurting him a lot?"

Patricia grimaced. "Yes. But he'll be all right. Just need to keep him indoors. He hates it. All his friends are outdoors playing."

Jim grinned. "Yeah, Michael's chaffing about it, too. The end of the baseball season got canceled."

Patricia nodded. "Let me know if there's anything we can do."

"I will. Thanks again."

He left the bank and walked across the street to Doc's office. Doc had gotten in. There were patients, but anyone that could be rescheduled had been called. Doc was only seeing the sick today.

The tension in the air of the office was nearly as thick as the smoke that hung in the trees outside. Claire's eyes were red, and her nose ran. She dabbed at it with a wadded tissue.

"Can I speak with Doc?" Jim asked.

She nodded and got up to get him. When she spoke after returning, her voice quavered. "You can wait in his office. He'll be right in."

Jim reached out and took Claire's hand. "You made a huge difference, Claire. We have evidence. We've got a window of time, and all of it is because you thought quickly. Thank you."

Tears rolled down her face. "He's nice to me," she said softly. "Please find him."

Jim squeezed her hand gently. "We will. We will find him."

He released her hand and went on to Doc's office. When Doc came in it was clear he wasn't in much better shape than Claire.

"What do you know?" he asked.

"We know it was a white van. We know exactly when and how it happened. Do you know anyone who might want to do this?" Jim asked.

"No. People have liked him. Haven't had a single complaint. Hell, that damn newspaper article had people coming in just to meet him. Only person I know who didn't like him was Sheila, but she hates everyone."

Jim sat down in the chair in front of Doc's desk. "She was at the house not that long ago. She could know his schedule."

Doc shook his head. "Ryan treated her for a tick bite a few weeks back. Had to give her a prescription for antibiotics. He said she was pissed that he insisted."

"Tick bite? Like the one I had?"

Doc sat back in his chair. "Yeah. Yeah, said she got it while she was out on a story. You got yours out by Rountree's trailer, right?"

"I did. Shit. When did he treat her?"

Doc picked up the phone and called Claire. "Get me Sheila Ward's medical file. I need to see it now."

Claire appeared with the file and handed it to Doc. He looked at her, "Thank you, Claire."

"Does this have to do with Ryan?"

"Claire," said Doc.

"If she had anything to do with this…" she started.

"Claire, let Jim do his job, and don't go saying anything to anyone. Got it?"

Claire nodded and left the room.

"I swear that girl's got a crush on the man…," Doc muttered as he looked through the file.

"Yeah, here it is. June 2nd."

"Mike Rountree's trailer burned on June 4th."

"And your tick bite?"

"June 4th."

"You think Sheila has something to do with this?"

"I don't know. Sheila doesn't seem like she would, but she's got a connection to everybody involved in the shit going on in Eden."

Doc nodded.

They stared at each other for a moment in silence. Then Jim stood up. "We'll find him, Doc."

"You'd better," Doc said. His voice wavered just as Claire's had. He coughed and cleared his throat. His voice came out firmer. "I can't retire without that man, you know."

Jim put a hand on Doc's shoulder. "I know, Doc. I know."

Chapter Forty-Three

Ryan forced himself to keep his eyes closed and his breathing slow as he listened to someone come into the room. There was complete silence for a few minutes, hands gently arranged the towel back over his lap. Ryan flinched at the touch and desperately tried to cover it by shifting his body and moaning softly, hoping the person would believe he had simply shifted in his unconscious state.

Apparently, he sold it, because footsteps retreated and then the door closed again. He waited, counting the seconds until at least five minutes had passed before he cracked open his good eye. The room was empty again.

He took a deep breath of relief, and the trembling of his body as the adrenaline rush left him made him feel weak. Okay, okay. He couldn't be sure if it was the photographer who'd come in or not, since he couldn't afford to look. The steps sounded heavy, like a man, so he would operate under the assumption that the photographer operated alone.

That meant there might be a good opportunity for escape in the future. One man could not spend 24 hours a day with him. He had a job. It was a Wednesday. He would have to go to work.

Ryan could be patient. He'd learned patience during the long months of rehab after his injury. He would do this. He would survive this, too. He bit his lip when he realized he wanted to laugh. Yeah, he'd survived before, so what were the odds that he'd find himself in this position? One in a million? One in two million? Surviving one murder attempt seemed like more than enough in one lifetime.

It wasn't like he was famous, or a criminal. He was a freaking doctor. He'd spent his life patching people back together, not taking them apart. Plus, Bonehead would be really pissed off if he disappeared.

Though the dog did like Michael. Maybe Jim would let him take Bonehead in. That way, he wouldn't be orphaned. Well, he would be an orphan, but he wouldn't stay one.

If Ryan had had a hand free, he would have smacked his forehead. What the hell? Worrying about the damn dog while he sat taped, naked, to a potty chair by someone who probably was some kind of psychopath. He needed to have his head examined.

And if he died here, it would be. In depth. Some other doctor would cut into his skull, remove his brain and examine it in detail. They'd find the damage done by the first attempt on his life. What else would they find?

Ryan took a deep breath and shook his head slowly. Shaking it too hard would really hurt. He needed to keep his mind on the now. Live in the present. Think about how to keep living in the present. Not going off on tangents about what would happen to his brain if he died.

Ryan bit the inside of his cheek and silenced himself again. He had to listen, pay attention, and look for his opportunity. He stopped biting the inside of his cheek. Okay. He could do this. He could, and he would.

Chapter Forty-Four

They'd pushed together several tables in the bullpen to make a big surface for what information they had. Bud Peterson sat in a chair at a nearby desk, talking on the phone to his laboratory. Dee had images from the recording by the ATM laid out. They had a timeline drawn.

They had moved and stacked the files and timeline from the Hatcher case to another desk so they could work on Ryan's disappearance.

Not for the first time, Jim looked at the layout on the tables and wished he could afford one of those fancy whiteboard things they always showed cops using on TV.

Of course, you couldn't lean down on whiteboard like you could a table, so maybe it was just as well, Jim thought as he leaned on his hands against the table. He examined the photos from the ATM recording. He couldn't see the driver, just a figure in the driver's seat. The tag was illegible in all the shots. It looked like there were a couple of decals on the bumper, but he couldn't read any of them.

Bud hung up the phone and wheeled the chair over to the other side of the tables. "Okay. The blood on the ground is Edwards.' It does match what's in Edwards's records with Dr. Markham. I'm going to be heading back to the lab. You can call me if you come up with anything new. Until then, I'm going to go work with what we've got. I don't think we can do anything with the ATM recording, but I'll have my guys look at it." Bud got up from his chair and headed for the restroom. It wasn't his first trip since he'd arrived, and it confirmed what he'd said about having to piss every fifteen minutes. He was right on schedule.

The fax machine began to chime, and Dee went to it and gathered up the sheets being printed out. "These are our van registrations," she called out.

"We need to be watching for anyone who could be connected to any of the murders. With the Bible verse thing, maybe it's someone in Hatcher's church. The list of members is here, so we'll need to crosscheck them against that.."

Jim motioned to her, and she handed half of them to Jim. They sat together with the list of Holy Fire of God members between them so they could both check the names.

"Jim, Tommy Barton's on this list of church members," Dee said.

"Shit." Jim rubbed his forehead. How had he not noticed that? Probably because the last time he'd looked at the list had been the day after Hatcher had disappeared.

"He'd know Bass and Rountree. I know he brought both of them in more than once," said Dee.

"Junior, radio Barton. I think he's working south along 98 today. Tell him we need him here at the office asap."

"Yes, sir," Junior said.

* * *

Tommy Barton walked into the office thirty minutes later, looking very nervous, which made Jim nervous. He motioned for Tommy to follow him into the interrogation room. He had already set up for Junior to tape their conversation. Jim felt he had to treat the man as a suspect. He certainly would know Hatcher, and he would know both Bass and Rountree.

Everyone in the department knew that Hatcher had disappeared during the night. Only a few details had been held back. One—that Hatcher had been naked when taken, two—where Hatcher had been found, and three—that a Bible verse connected him to two other murders.

Bud Peterson and Dee Jackson stood in the viewing room on the other side of the one-way glass. Jim had set up taping because he couldn't always have witnesses. His staff was stretched too thin to have someone in the office and manning the phones. So he relied on the taping of the interviews to prove that no coercion or leading had taken place.

This time he wanted witnesses in addition to the tape. He needed help getting a read on Tommy's answers. He'd never had to question one of his own Deputies before. He remembered that his father had on a few occasions. In the thirty-five years, his father had been sheriff, there had been incidences of theft, dereliction of duty, and twice with false evidence. He remembered how angry his father had been at each man involved.

"What's going on, Sheriff?" Tommy asked.

"You knew Donald Hatcher. You're a member of his church."

Tommy looked surprised. "Yes, sir. Me and Judy have been members for almost two years."

"I'm wondering why you didn't mention it when he went missing."

Tommy swallowed and stared down at his hands.

"I'm waiting, Deputy Barton."

Tommy spoke in a whisper. "I like...liked Reverend Hatcher. He helped us with Eddie."

"Your son."

"Yes, sir. When I heard he was missing, I didn't know what to think, and honestly, I never thought it mattered that I knew him. I just hoped he could be found and that he would be all right."

"I checked, and you were working that night. You were on the midnight to seven shift."

"Yes, sir."

"What can you tell me about this?" Jim slid a piece of paper across the table.

Tommy read it. "Is this a Bible verse?"

"What do you think?"

"Probably Old Testament. They're always talking about smiting this and that. Though Revelations does have some talking about what happens to sinners. I don't know it. Me and Judy aren't much for Bible reading. She's got one, her mother gave it to her."

"What does it mean to you?"

Tommy Barton moved his lips when he read. Jim gave him time. "I guess it means that God takes care of believers, but the ones that don't believe, they die."

"Have you seen it before?"

Tommy looked surprised. "I don't think so, sir. I mean, there's lots of things like this in the Bible, but I don't know this verse. I know the 23rd Psalm, and John 3:16. I mean, I guess most everyone ever went to Sunday School knows them. But this one isn't one I know."

Jim took the paper back. "What do you know about Reverend Hatcher's disappearance?"

Tommy clasped his hands together. "The call went out that morning. I was at home, but I had my radio on. I remember it said that Reverend Hatcher had been taken from his home sometime during the night. I know he was dead when he was found, and…well, he's going to be buried with his people up in New Hampshire. Least that's what they were saying at the church."

"Anything else anyone at the church was saying?"

"Said his wife wasn't coming back here. She's going to stay with her Mama up in Glen St. Mary. There's some of us that are going to pack up their things from the house and take them up to here. I can't go with them 'cause I'm scheduled to work traffic that day. Judy and some other women were going to take Velma Crossing's truck up. She's got a rocking chair won't fit in anyone's car with her other stuff."

Jim didn't know what he should do. He heard someone tap at the one-way glass.

Tommy didn't move.

Jim got up and left the interrogation room. Bud and Dee were in the hall.

Bud swirled the iced tea in his mug. "I don't think he's your man, Jim. But I also don't think you can have him out there working with no one keeping track of him."

Dee nodded. "I agree. I know we're short, but you have to send him home."

"All right, I can do that. I don't think he's involved, but there have been too damn many surprises lately. Who can we put on his house? I don't want him having his patrol car and I don't want him going anywhere without us knowing about it."

"Nestor Donda."

Nestor made sense. He was older and cool-headed. Jim went back into the interrogation room. Tommy looked terrified.

"I'm going to have someone take you home, and I want you to leave your weapon here in your locker."

"You're firing me?" Tommy's voice shook.

"No, Tommy, it's leave with pay. I can't have you working right now. Not until we figure out what's going on here and see how all of it connects up. You're not fired, but until we get this cleared up, I can't have you out working as a deputy."

Tommy seemed relieved. "Thank you, sir. I'll stay home. Judy's got a list of things she's always wanting me to do at the house. I can keep busy and stay out of the way. I promise."

Jim nodded. "I'd appreciate that, Tommy."

Jim left the room and saw that Dee had hustled Junior from behind the desk. "Junior's going to take him home. I called Nestor. He's heading that way now. He'll keep an eye on the house and Tommy."

"Thanks."

Bud headed for the restroom. Dee motioned for Junior to go into the interrogation room. Jim headed for the table and their lists.

"When we find some vans to search, what are we going to search for?" Manny asked.

Bud returned from the bathroom at that point. "Luminol," he suggested. "Even if the van's been washed, there's probably enough trace to light up with Luminol. I can get enough out of my truck to set up your people with the Luminol so they can use it when they do their searches."

The door to the building opened, and four deputies walked in. They walked over and stood in front of Jim. Buck Neville spoke. "What can we do?"

"I can't pay you," Jim said. "It's not in the budget."

Buck looked annoyed. "What can we do?"

Dee smiled at Jim. "They're volunteering."

Jim handed them part of his list and motioned for Dee to hand over part of hers as well. They opened the interrogation room and grabbed space where they could, and began to go over the lists carefully.

Jim couldn't help but feel proud. These were his people. They worked because they cared. A man couldn't ask for more than that. Jim gave himself a moment to be proud of the people who worked for him. Then he turned back to the table and the information they had.

The last kidnap victim in Eden had ended up dead and ritually prepared for burial. That could not happen to Ryan. Jim found himself hoping it was just a pissed-off patient. That would make it a little less scary. But the realist in him didn't believe that.

Deputies called names out to each other, getting together lists they would each check by areas of the county. Eighty-six vans didn't sound like many, but for them, the project could take hours.

Jim felt a surge of emotion rise again in his chest as he watched them work. These were his people. They came in, not for overtime pay, but because they were damn well going to find Ryan Edwards. They'd work this list until they'd checked each van, where it was, and who had access to it. It made him think of his father, who used to say that no one became a deputy in Eden for the money. They did it because Eden County was their home. They all gave everything to their jobs. Eden was no kind of paradise, but each of them was devoted to making it the best and safest place it could be.

Dee came in and touched his shoulder. He looked at her and she simply shook her head. Then she said, "We got this, sir."

He nodded and dropped his head so she wouldn't see that his eyes blurred with tears that he would not let fall. They didn't have time for that. No time for comforting. It was time to work.

Chapter Forty-Five

Ryan heard the sound of a door closing. It sounded heavy. Maybe it was the front door? He felt hopeful.

Once again, he leaned forward, got his feet on the ground under him, and stood up in the awkward bent position. He shuffled to the door and opened it a crack. He waited, counting the seconds.

After two minutes, he heard the sound of a motor and the whine of a reverse gear. He took a deep breath and began counting again. He allowed three minutes. There was no sound.

He opened the door further and made his way into the hall. He had to move carefully. He didn't want to ding the walls with the chair or knock anything over that he wouldn't be able to pick up. If he couldn't get free and get out of the house, he still needed his captor to think he was helpless.

He got to the front door, and his heart sank. A double-keyed deadbolt. There would be no opening that and making his way out. He had to move more carefully through the living room. There were tables with books and magazines and knick-knacks on them.

It was a slow process getting through to the kitchen and to the back door. There he found another double-keyed deadbolt. He cursed silently.

The kitchen was narrow, so he had to turn very slowly to be sure the chair didn't strike or catch on something. He didn't see a phone. There had to be a phone somewhere in the house.

His back ached from crouching to walk with the chair. He set it down and sat down for a minute. The towel had shifted down across his knees again. He had no way to straighten it and didn't really care right now.

He breathed hard. Between his anxiety and the difficulty of moving with the chair, he was tiring quickly. He could continue searching for a phone, or he could try to find a way to get separated from the chair. He decided getting separated from the chair was his first priority.

He got his fingers on a drawer pull and moved backwards a bit. No knives. Dish towels. Crap. He continued the process until he finally found a drawer with silverware. The problem was, the knives were in the very back of the drawer. Nothing could be easy.

He pulled the drawer out as far as it would go, leaning his body and the side of the chair against the kitchen counter, and tried to get his hands high enough to reach into the drawer. He stretched up on his toes, and could just get the tips of his fingers onto the end of the knives, but he couldn't pick one up.

The chair leg's rubber tips rubbed across the countertop. He looked over his shoulder and could see slight traces. He had to keep trying. He tried to tip a knife up, to flip it out of the drawer, but nothing. They moved, but he could not get one to move enough where he could grasp it.

He set the chair back on the floor and rested for several minutes. This was a waste of his time. He needed to look for the phone. He leaned against the drawer and shut it. Then he began to move back toward the hallway. Maybe the phone was in another bedroom.

It took a long time to make his way into the other rooms. First he found the bathroom, which made him kind of giggle hysterically. It wasn't like he needed it, what with the potty chair he was carrying around.

Opening and then closing doors was an exhausting process. One door opened into a closet. Finally, the last door opened into a bedroom. He used his shoulder to flip on the overhead light. There was no phone in this room either.

He set the chair down in the doorway and let himself mourn. He had hoped for a phone. If nothing else, he could get the receiver off and dial 911. But no luck. No joy.

There had to be something he could do. He could not, would not, sit in this place and let someone else control his fate. He hadn't fought his way through rehab and grief to end up a victim of some other sociopath. He would get himself out of here. He would not die here. That space in the graveyard next to Danielle would have to wait until he was damned ready to die.

He made himself take the time to think. Maybe he could pick up one of the knives some other way. He took a couple of deep breaths, raised himself up into a crouch again, and closed the bedroom door as he left.

Two steps down the hall, he heard a car pulling up outside. As quickly as he could manage, he headed back to the room where he was supposed to be imprisoned. He had shut the door and made it back to the spot his chair should be when he heard the front door slam shut.

That had been way too fucking close.

Chapter Forty-Six

Two hours later, Dee and the deputies presented Jim with their list of possible van registrations. They had it narrowed down to sixty vans. It hardly seemed possible that there could be sixty white vans in the county. The thing was, the dairy farm had twenty, and none of them had a sign on them. They were white utility vans used on the farm for transport. Tanker trucks took the milk to a processing plant.

Twenty of them could possibly allow someone from the dairy to borrow one, and it not be missed right away. And since Buddy's body had been disposed of in the fire next to the dairy, well, that just increased the odds.

Bobby Dale raised his hand.

"Yes, Bobby?"

"My brother manages the garage at the dairy. Why don't I take one other guy and get that stuff Bud's going to give us and check the dairy vans?"

Jim smiled. "That would be great, Bobby. But we do need to get permission."

Bobby laughed. "Any reason my brother can't give me permission?"

"No, I see no reason he couldn't. Take Driscoll with you."

Bobby Dale looked really happy.

Dee looked through the list. "We'll split up the list. We've got forty left. We should be able to eliminate vans pretty fast," she said.

"Make it happen, Dee," Jim said.

He stepped into his office and sat down at his desk. It was noon. They'd narrowed their suspect pool down to a relatively small group in a short amount of time. A run to the Dollar Store had netted them six cheap plastic spray bottles, which Bud had the deputies wrap in black trash bags to protect the fluid from light.

He'd taken the bottles and the Luminol into the men's room, turned off the lights, and filled each wrapped bottle with enough to check the interior of the vans. He'd carefully instructed each of them on how they had to block as much light as possible from the area they were spraying and then look for the blue chemiluminescence of the Luminol. It wouldn't last long, and he warned them not to spray it more than once. Either they got something, or they didn't.

Bobby Dale had written notes.

Six deputies left the station carrying their black-covered bottles in a black plastic bag along with more black plastic bags to tape to windows to black out the inside of the vans. Jim hoped like hell that they found something.

Chapter Forty-Seven

The locks clicked, and the door thumped against the wall as it opened. Ryan listened for footsteps and heard the scuffing of shoes through the front room. A moment later, he could hear noise coming from the kitchen. He hadn't heard the front door close or the locks, and he wished fervently he'd been able to get free of the chair. Naked or not, he'd make a run for that door. But there would be no running, yet.

He kept quiet. If the photographer came in, he would not feign unconsciousness again. He would face the man. He needed to get some sense of what was going on.

The smell came to him before he even heard footsteps. Was the guy cooking? No, probably warming up food. The smell of chicken permeated the air, and his mouth started to water. It must have been hours since he'd eaten breakfast. His stomach rumbled.

The door opened, and there he stood, holding a tray. Ryan couldn't see what was on it other than a glass of milk, but he could smell the food. His stomach rumbled again.

"Oh good, you're hungry," he said, smiling.

What was the name? Ryan knew he'd heard the name. Carl! "Guess it's been a while since breakfast, Carl," Ryan said.

Carl laughed. "Oh, yes, hours, I'm sure for you. But I've got a good meal here." He stepped inside the door and set the tray down on the floor. "Just be patient another few minutes," he said.

He left the room, the door stood open, and once again, Ryan could see out into the hall he had searched earlier. The bedroom and bathroom were to the right. The living room and then the kitchen were to the left.

Carl returned carrying a folding chair and a tv table. He set the tv table up in front of Ryan and then the folding chair next to Ryan. He picked the tray up from the floor and set it on the tv table.

"I need to explain some things to you. I'm going to feed you while I do that. It's important that you eat everything that's here." He sat in the chair and cut a piece of the chicken, and lifted it to Ryan's mouth.

"You're not trying to poison me, are you?"

Carl drew back in shock. "NO! Why would I do that?"

"You kidnapped me."

"I need you. I need you to save Eden and to save me. I would never hurt you."

They stared at each other a moment. Then Ryan took the chicken from the fork. Carl released a breath and continued to speak as he cut another piece of chicken.

"Eden is special. This is the true Eden, you know. My grandmother told me. She grew up here, and she said it was beautiful and perfect with wonderful people and that God loved and protected this place. That's why I came here. I knew this was my true home. I've known it since I was a child.

"When the fires came, I knew I had to do something. I couldn't let this place die. But I had to figure out why God had abandoned it, why He was letting it burn. I read my Bible every night, and I prayed that He would reveal to me what I had to do to save this place. One night my Bible fell open to the answer when I picked it up. "Behold, all souls are Mine; as the soul of the father, so also the soul of the son is Mine; the soul that sinneth, it shall die." Carl gathered up mashed potatoes and gravy on the fork and put it to Ryan's lips.

"Eden had to be cleansed of the sinners. They had to die. So I had to find the worst sinners in Eden County, and I had to kill them so that God would take Eden back into his arms and save it from the fires."

Ryan felt himself choking on the mashed potatoes, but Carl put his hand against his mouth. "You must eat all the offering, Dr. Edwards. It's important. I can't complete my work without your help. I need to be cleansed of my sins as well. You have to remove them from me so that I can continue God's work."

Ryan struggled not to heave. He heard Jim's voice in his head, 'We found the body of Reverend Hatcher, and he died from inhaling a meal he was throwing up.' He swallowed hard, and Carl offered him the glass of milk. He drank nearly half of it.

"You're a savior, Dr. Edwards. It takes a savior to cleanse my soul, and then I can go to heaven when this is all over. I won't be a sinner anymore."

Ryan looked at the meal and knew he would have to eat it. If he wanted to survive, he had to eat it. "Of course, I'll cleanse your soul, Carl. You're doing God's work."

Carl smiled, "I knew you'd understand! I knew you were the right one." He cut another piece of chicken. "It's a good meal. I went to the Magnolia to get it. I just had to warm it up a little. It's good, isn't it?"

Ryan smiled and nodded. "It's good, Carl." Okay, Jim, he thought, thanks for the warning. I'll eat the food. But dammit, you better be out there looking for me.

Carl continued to feed him, but stayed silent after his explanation. Ryan ate dutifully and tried to keep his eyes on Carl for any changes. Then he noticed the bandage peeking from the short sleeve of his shirt on his right arm.

"Are you hurt, Carl?"

Carl jerked back, "What?"

"Are you hurt? I see a bandage on your arm."

Carl pulled his sleeve down, but it still didn't cover the gauze. "It's fine, Dr. Edwards. Nothing you need to worry about."

"I could look at it for you. Make sure it's all right."

Carl shook his head. "No. I don't want you to touch it."

Ryan made himself smile, "I can't touch it, Carl. My hands aren't free. But I could look at it and tell you if it needed additional care."

Carl shrugged. "It doesn't matter. I must take what happens, then be cleansed of my sins so I can be sure to be with God."

Ryan thought that Carl might be planning to kill himself when he finished whatever plan he had. He realized that he didn't want Carl to die. Carl didn't deserve the peace of death. "Let me at least look at it, Carl? Please? I'm a doctor. It will worry me if I'm not able to help you."

Carl thought for just a moment, set down the fork, and rolled his sleeve up. Blood seeped through the gauze. He unrolled the gauze and revealed three deep, bleeding gouges, swelling with bruising. "Someone hurt you," Ryan said.

"I can take the pain," Carl responded.

"That's not the point, Carl. You need...medicine and...stitches. Those... marks are deep. I could do that for you, cleaning at least."

Carl shook his head. "No." He wrapped the wounds again. "I have antibiotic cream. I'll clean it again and put that on it. It doesn't matter."

"It does...you shouldn't...you need to finish...."

Carl picked up the fork and scooped up mashed potatoes and gravy. "I appreciate that you care, Dr. Edwards, but I'll take care of it. I promise. Now you must eat."

Ryan opened his mouth and accepted the food. It had been worth a try.

Chapter Forty-Eight

"Bobby Dale's on the phone for you!" Junior called out from the front desk. "You need to talk to him."

Jim sighed. Dee hadn't gotten back to the office, yet. Jim was anxious to hear the results of the deputies checking the white vans.

He picked up the receiver and heard muted coughing. "Bobby?"

The coughing stopped. "Sheriff, we need you out here at Libby's."

"You found blood?"

"No, sir, we found a body. In one of the vans."

Jim's stomach felt like it dropped to the floor. "Ryan Edwards?"

"No, sir. It's Richard Libby, and his head is twisted nigh on to backwards on his neck."

Jim nearly dropped the phone. He sat back in his chair. "Libby's dead?"

"Yes, sir. I asked Junior to call FDLE, and then to let me talk to you. We were going to check the vans with that Luminol stuff, but we pulled open the sliding door on one of them, and there he was. Looks like someone tried to take his head right off."

"I'll be out there. You keep everyone away from that van."

Jim hung up the phone and walked out and found Dee standing at Junior's desk, two other deputies with her.

"Bobby Dale found himself another body," Jim said to her.

"Damn," said Buck Neville. "That's his second one!"

Dee turned, "It's not a damned competition, Neville. But if you like, I'll make sure you find the next one first, 'cause it's going to be you."

Neville blushed.

216

"Out at Libby's?" Dee asked.

"Yeah, it's Richard Libby."

"Holy shit," muttered Manny Sota.

"Are you all finished?" asked Jim.

Buck shook his head. "The vans are spread out all over hell. We got the closest first. Manny radioed us he was running out of Luminol."

"I got shorted."

"You probably just sprayed too much," said Buck.

Jim rubbed his forehead. "Okay, Dee, give your bottle to Manny, and then you'll be with me. We're going to Libbby's."

"I already called for Bud. He's on his way back," said Junior softly.

"Thanks, Junior. You two, get back out there and check white vans, and stop spraying so much of the Liminol, Manny."

Manny ducked his head and smiled. "Yes, sir."

Jim went back to his office for his cap and his gun.

Dee pushed Manny Sota and Buck Neville towards the door. "Get going. We need to find the doctor."

When Jim came back from his office, Dee waited by the door. "I'm driving," she announced. Jim did not argue with her. Arguing with Dee didn't change what happened, it just annoyed her. Annoying Dee just led to making her angry and making Dee Jackson angry often led to people finding themselves on the floor clutching areas of their anatomy that should never be in that much pain. He'd rather keep himself intact.

He followed her out to her car and took the passenger seat. Dee backed out of her parking place and gunned the car down the road toward Libby's Diary. Neither of them said anything until they got there.

* * *

Bobby Dale and Andy Driscoll stood next to the van. Libby's son, Richard Libby III, stood away from the two deputies. His face was pale. Jim walked over to him and put his hand on his shoulder. "Richie, do you need to go somewhere and sit down?"

The young man shook his head. "I'll stay. I've already seen him."

Jim nodded, then he and Dee walked over to the van. Bobby Dale had pushed the side door to the van mostly closed, probably in deference to poor Richie. Now he pulled it open just slightly so that Jim and Dee could see the corpse.

"Damn," muttered Dee.

Jim shuddered. Richard Libby's body was lying on its back, and it was clear what had happened. Someone had snapped his neck. It had been violent. Jim was sorry that Richie had seen it.

"Bud's on his way, Bobby," Jim said. He turned back to Richie. "Is there somewhere we can talk?"

Richie nodded, and they headed up toward the office between the garage and the house. Dee followed Jim and pulled out her notebook. He knew she would take notes on what Richie said, and hopefully, it would help lead them to Libby's killer.

Richie led them into the office and took a seat in front of the desk. He lifted his hand toward the couch and chair in the same area. Richard Libby's office reflected the man. Deer and boar heads hung on the walls, the desk was huge, and the chair behind it, leather and regal. Jim noted that Richie didn't think about sitting in it.

"I'm sorry for your loss, Richie," Jim said. "I know you and your daddy were close."

Richie nodded.

"Did you see your dad today?"

"No. He said he had a meeting this morning in Alachua County, and he'd be gone most of the day. I didn't even think to look for him. He usually takes one of the vans when he goes out of town. I don't pay attention to how many vans are here anytime. The guys take them as they need them."

Richie looked at the desk. "I don't even know who he was meeting. He never told me. He'd do that. He'd just say he was going to Alachua or Levy County, and then he'd be gone all day, and I never knew what it was about. I pretty much run the place. I mean, I know the dairy side of things, but not…not what he did. I guess he figured I didn't need to know."

"Did he keep a calendar?"

Richie thought for a moment. "Yeah, yeah, there's one up at the house. It's in the kitchen. He used to write things on it so Mom knew where he'd be. He never got out of the habit even after they were divorced."

"Let's go look at it," Jim said.

Richie got up, and Jim and Dee followed him out of the office building and up the concrete path to the two-story cracker house. The porch creaked under their feet, but when they stepped into the house, everything was solid and in excellent repair. Richie headed straight into the kitchen, where he took a large paper calendar from a nail in the wall. He handed it to Jim, who tilted it so that Dee could read it as well.

In the white square for the day's date, someone had written in pencil, "Sheila Ward, 11 am, The Clock, Gainesville."

"Damn," sighed Dee. "I'll have Junior call Ronnie and see if he knows where Sheila is." She turned and left, and Richie looked at Jim.

"Did Sheila kill my dad?"

"No. I don't see any way Sheila Ward could have killed your father."

"But that's who my dad was supposed to meet."

Jim paused. "According to this, but I can't see how that's connected to your father being killed," he said. "We'll know more when we talk to her."

"You'll let me know?"

Jim reached out to Richie again, squeezing his thin shoulder. "I promise."

Richie nodded, and Jim thought how much like his mother he looked. Jim knew they were close, and that had been part of why Richard wasn't always open with his son. The divorce had been ugly, and Richie's mother lived in Levy County to put some distance between herself and her ex. Richie had lived with her until he'd graduated from high school, then he'd moved back to Eden and gone to work for his father. He'd learned the dairy business. One of the only nice things Jim had ever heard Libby say was that his son was a natural dairyman. Jim hoped that he'd said it to Richie at some point.

Richie let out a breath. "So, this doesn't have anything to do with my mother."

Jim nearly choked. It hadn't even occurred to him to think of Evelyn

Libby. "I can't say that for sure, Richie. Every angle will get looked at."

Richie nodded. "I can understand that. Is it all right if I call her and tell her what's happened?"

"Of course. That's fine."

"If she doesn't seem surprised, or says something that's...that's not right, I'll tell you, Sheriff. I know they hated each other, but I can't protect her if she had anything to do with this. Daddy didn't treat her right, but no one deserves what happened to him."

Jim gave his shoulder a couple of soft pats. "Thank you, Richie. I'll be sure to let you know what we find out."

Richie nodded, and the two of them walked back out of the house toward the office. Jim was glad they hadn't released the cause of death for either Buddy Bass or Michael Rountree. He'd hate to think how Richie was going to feel if it did turn out they'd all been murdered by the same man. That was not good company to be in, and the town was sure to make it the top subject of gossip for a long time. Richard Libby had never endeared himself to anyone except his son. The County Commission hated him, the environmentalists hated him, and pretty much every minority in town hated him. He hired the Mexicans, but paid them less than anyone white. He wouldn't hire anyone black at all. He'd been a bully and a racist and treated women like they were money-grubbing whores.

But he'd been Richie's daddy, and Richie had loved him, even if he didn't admire him. The Libby Dairy was very likely to do much better under Richie's supervision than it ever had for Richard. People liked Richie, and they respected him. He was known for being kind and treating the employees well. Lots of people speculated the only reason the place still had employees was because Richie had come to work there ten years ago and become the face of the company to the employees. Jim thought the company would probably thrive under Richie Libby in a way it never had under his father.

Jim left Richie at the door to the office and saw Dee coming from the car. He handed her the calendar. "Put that in an evidence bag."

Bud and two vans had arrived. Richard Libby would make a big corpse,

and there was no way they were going to get his body into the van with all
their gear. Jim could hear Bud calling out orders and directing his people
around the area. Bobby Dale and Andy had both moved away from the van.
He didn't doubt they felt relief at not having to stand anywhere near the
corpse anymore. Body duty was never pleasant.

"Richard the third have anything else to say after I left?"

Jim shrugged. "He was afraid his mother might have had something to do
with it."

Dee snorted. "Yeah, I can see that. Libby treated her as bad as everybody
else. Good thing his neck was broken. Three broken necks is not a
coincidence."

Jim nodded. "Any word on Sheila?"

"Ronnie says he hasn't heard from her, and he didn't know about the
meeting with Libby. You think Sheila's part of the murders?"

"God, I hope not. Much as I dislike the woman, I'd hate to think she'd get
herself involved in something this ugly."

Bud shouted Jim's name and motioned for him to come to the van. Bud
knelt over the corpse, and he had an evidence bag in his hand. Jim and Dee
walked over to see what Bud had found.

Bud gently manipulated something out of Libby's front shirt pocket. It
was thin paper, folded into a square. Bud unfolded it, holding it up so they
could all see the torn edge and the tiny printing on the page. "King James
version again." Bud moved it into the morning light, falling into the van.
"There's your verse."

Jim saw the words highlighted with blood. He could read the book of the
Bible at the top of the page Ezekiel.

"This is definitely your guy's work again. He must have had a fight on his
hands with Libby. There's already bruising showing up on the neck, and
he's got three broken fingers on his right hand. Going to be some deep claw
marks from those on the right arm. Your guy braces the right arm on the
throat and uses the left to pull the head around."

Jim's stomach lurched at the details. No matter how many bodies he'd
seen over the years, he never liked to hear the details. His father accused

him of having a weak stomach. He thought it more that he had a strong sense of how the dead had suffered.

Bud put the page into the plastic and handed it over. Dee reached out and took it. "How many Bibles does this guy have?" she muttered.

Bud laughed. "I've been wondering if he goes into one of the religious stores and rips that page out of the Bibles on display. That's what I'd do. Your man's old-fashioned, though. He may have a bunch of old King James versions."

Dee waited as Bud bagged Libby's hands and finally climbed out of the van. "I'll let the young'uns take over from here. That is one big dead guy." She handed him the evidence bag with the page from the Bible.

"Do you have an estimate on the time of death?" Jim asked.

Bud nodded, "The body being out here in the van is probably throwing it off a little, but I'd guess not more than an hour or so. The body's just starting to go into rigor mortis, and as hot as it is out here, that means it was not long ago at all."

Jim looked at Dee, "So he grabs Ryan before eight, and kills Libby sometime around 11:00."

"If he lives in the county, easy to get to Gainesville to meet Libby and then dump the body here in the last hour or so," Dee said.

Jim opened the front door of the van and checked the driver's seat. "Seat's still where Libby probably had it. Means whoever drove it back here had to be about the same size."

"Literally," said Dee. "But the guy kills Libby and then brings the body and the van back?"

Jim called over to Bobby Dale, who reluctantly jogged over from his position on the far side of the parking area. "Libby's got twenty vans. Are they all here?"

Bobby nodded. "Ronny said they were all here. We started checking the ones in the garage and then the five out here. This is the first one we looked at."

"And that's when you found Libby."

"Yes, sir."

"Where's your brother?"

Bobby shuffled his feet. "He's in the garage. Mr. Libby gave him this job when he dropped out of high school. Paid him decent enough that he could afford to get married and have children. He's pretty broken up about finding Mr. Libby dead."

"I need to talk to him. Should we go in?"

Bobby nodded. "Give me a couple of minutes and then come on in," he said.

Chapter Forty-Nine

Ryan had eaten the whole meal and drunk two glasses of milk, which seemed to assure Carl that he was now cleansed of his sins. Carl never said what sins he'd committed, and Ryan felt sure that knowing the specifics would not be good for him, so he'd asked nothing.

Carl had taken the tray away, and Ryan had listened to him moving around the house for at least an hour. At some point during all his movements, Carl had received a phone call. Ryan heard the phone ringing and recognized it as a cell. He and Danielle had both had cells in D.C., but when he'd looked at cell coverage for Eden County, he'd been told that his carrier didn't cover the area at all. He'd finally found one that covered the area, but he only used it for being on call. He'd had a landline put in for everything else. His parents had been shocked when he'd given them a landline number to reach him. They obviously felt he had moved into the dark ages by coming to Eden.

When the call finished, Carl had come into the room. "I'll be gone for a little while. Don't worry. I will be back, and if you've had to use the potty, I'll take care of it and get you cleaned up when I get back. I'm sorry that I can't let you go. I have to see if I've done enough. Once I know that I've satisfied God and Eden is safe, I'll be able to let you go. I promise."

"Thank you, Carl. I trust you," Ryan had said. Carl had smiled at that. He'd closed the door, and a short time later, Ryan heard the front door close and lock. He listened carefully and heard the sound of a car pulling away from the house.

He stood up, opened the door, and suddenly felt a wave of nausea. He realized the food he'd eaten was coming back up whether he wanted it to or not. He moved as quickly as he could with the chair to the bathroom. He did manage to raise the seat before he vomited. The force of it brought tears to his eyes and made his throat burn with stomach acid. He coughed and vomited again and again. Toward the end, he coughed up bile and nothing else. His throat felt as though it was on fire.

When he stopped, he sat back in the chair, gasping for air and feeling the soreness in his ribs and abdomen from heaving up the food he'd been fed.

"Guess you're fucked, Carl. Your sins all came back up," Ryan said out loud. His voice sounded raspy and raw. It served him right. Carl didn't deserve forgiveness for what he was doing.

Chapter Fifty

Ronny Dale looked very much like his brother Bobby, lanky and earnest. None of the Dale boys had much education, but Bobby was the over-achiever in the family with his graduation from both high school and the Santa Fe College of Public Safety in Alachua County. Ronny had married young and had four children already. His clean-shaven face showed the red eyes of someone who had been crying. He didn't seem to be embarrassed by that, though. He walked up to Jim and faced him squarely.

"You need to talk to me, Sheriff?" he asked in a voice so much like Bobby's that Jim wondered how their mother told them apart on the phone.

"I just need to know when Richard Libby left this morning and if he was driving the van he was found in," said Jim.

"Mr. Libby came down from the house around nine this morning. We talked about one of the vans I've been working on. It needs a new transmission 'cause it run over an alligator on some little road heading into Levy County, so we were talking about whether he wanted me to do the work and buy the parts, or just get it done. About nine-thirty, he said he had a meeting over in Gainesville with Sheila Ward and that he'd be back probably around one, and if Richie was looking for him, to let him know that. I saw him leave the yard in the van, but I didn't see it come back. I was in the garage ordering parts for an engine I'm rebuilding and pricing out transmissions when Bobby and the other Deputy showed up. I told him the vans weren't locked and to go on and check them for whatever they were looking for." Tears tracked down Ronny's face. "Bobby came and in and

226

told me Mr. Libby was dead in one of the vans in the yard. He used the phone in the office to call over to you guys."

"You didn't hear the van come back?"

Ronny shook his head. "I wish I had. I wish I'd been out there so I could stop what happened. Mr. Libby was always good to me, and I woulda killed whoever was out there trying to hurt him. He didn't deserve that."

Bobby stepped up behind his brother and put his arm across his shoulders. "It's okay, Ronny. He wouldn't have wanted you to get hurt on his account. He would have wanted you to be able to go home to your family."

Richie's voice came from behind Jim. "That's true, Ronny. Daddy liked you, and he told me more than once how he was a lucky man to have someone who worked as hard as you do. He thought the world of you, and he wouldn't have wanted anything to happen to you. Whoever did this was dangerous, and he might have killed you, too."

Jim turned around and Richie stood next to Dee. "Bobby, why don't you take your brother home. Driscoll can follow you and then bring you back to the station to file your report."

Bobby nodded, "Thank you, sir. We'll do that."

Chapter Fifty-One

Once again, Ryan managed to get the kitchen drawer open. He braced the drawer against his body and leaned over. He almost tilted face-first into the drawer, but managed to keep his balance. Finally, he got his face next to the knives. He was a little short of being able to reach one with either hand, so he had to stop and think about what to do.

He leaned forward as far as he could without losing his balance and falling against the drawer. His weight would either break it off or pull it out of its space, and neither would be good because he would land face-first into it. Some of the larger knives were stored blade up. If it didn't put out an eye, it would cut his face, and facial wounds bled like crazy. He stretched his neck and still could not get a grip on one of the handles with his lips. He swore and raised himself up, twisting his neck and shoulders, which felt strained from his position.

His lips just grazed the handles of the knives. There had to be a way to get a grip on one of them and lift it out of the drawer. He licked his lips and thought for a moment. He started to lick his lips again, and it hit him. His tongue. It would reach further than his lips. If he could lift one of the handles up he could probably get it close enough to get his lips and teeth on it.

He took a deep breath, twisted his shoulders and neck again, and then leaned back toward the drawer. Once his lips felt the handle, he stuck out his tongue and pushed it under the wood, lifting it slightly. He slowly pulled the handle toward his mouth, and finally, he felt it on his lips. He closed his eyes and concentrated.

He used his tongue and lips to pull the knife into his mouth so he could get his teeth on it. He breathed through his nose as he slowly rose up. He didn't let go. Not now. When his face was above the counter, he dropped the knife onto it.

He set the chair down again and allowed himself to sit and rest. He still had to manage to cut the tape, and that wouldn't be an easy task, but he had the knife. He had it, and he would use it.

After resting long enough for his breathing to get back to normal, he'd come to the moment of truth. He had the knife. Could he manipulate it enough to cut the duct tape that bound him to the chair?

He got his hand on the handle and nimbly moved the knife so that the blade ran back toward his wrist. Oh yeah, those hours of stitches, intubating, and using forceps to remove small objects from children's noses were really coming in handy. Muscle memory was a wonderful thing. Though he hadn't worked in the ER in over two years, his hands remembered how to flip something around in one hand as the other hand did something else. The necessity of doing that when stitching a wound or changing angles of tools when fishing for foreign objects in small spaces like noses and ears had been second nature to him for years. Grateful that the experience had stayed with him, he went to work.

He moved the blade up slightly into his fingers, then shifted the tip of the knife under the edge of the tape where it went from his wrist to the arm of the chair. When he felt it slip into the slot, he pushed the knife back until he had the handle in his hand again. He began to saw the tape gently with the blade.

It worked! He could feel the tape giving way under the gentle pressure of the blade. Yes, he could do this. By God, he would do this.

Once he had his right arm free from the chair, it was simple to cut himself free from the chair. He laughed as he sliced away at the last band of tape, keeping his right leg attached to the chair. He stepped away from it and took a deep breath. He'd done it.

He opened the drawer and put the knife back. Covering his tracks, making sure that the man wouldn't be able to figure out he'd gotten free felt important. He wanted to be sure that when he returned, he wouldn't immediately see that something had changed. The smear from the rubber on the potty chair legs was visible on the kitchen counter. Ryan grabbed a sponge from the sink and wiped at the mark. It disappeared. He grinned and carefully wiped the rest of the mark away. He rinsed the sponge and set it back in place.

Picking up the chair, Ryan carried it back to the room where he'd started. He set it exactly where it had been, but he peeled the tape off. He would take that with him, discard it elsewhere. He didn't want the cut marks to be seen. His escape needed to be as mysterious as possible. Give the photographer something to worry with when he found Ryan gone.

Chapter Fifty-Two

As Dee drove, Junior called in on the radio. Jim answered, and Junior relayed a message from Ronnie Weeks at the newspaper.

"You've been looking for white vans, right?"

"Yeah, why?"

"There's one in our parking lot."

"You know who it belongs to?"

"Carl Basinger."

Jim looked at Dee, "Do you have Luminol in your car?"

"Sure do."

The white Ford E-250's doors were locked. Dee took a slim jim out of her patrol car and popped the lock on the passenger door, and then got in and opened the side door of the van. Jim helped Dee tape up black plastic bags on the windows so the inside of the van was as dark as possible. Dee took the bottle of Luminol and sprayed it on the carpeted floor of the van. It glowed blue.

"Damn it," muttered Jim. He turned to Dee. "Let's go talk to Ronnie."

* * *

Ronnie's hand covered his mouth. "Oh my God, I can't believe this. You're sure, Jim?"

"Things are pointing that way. You haven't heard from Sheila today?"

Ronnie shook his head. "Not a word."

Jim pointed Dee toward the warehouse in the back where the printing was done. "You talk to everyone in there. I'll check the office."

In the main office, two people occupied desks, and the building was quiet. Doug Morgan wrote and edited the sports page. He recognized Jim and waved hello.

The older woman who sat nearby was thin and brittle looking. Jim knew her, too. Louise Mendenhall wrote social news and a religious column. She was notoriously bigoted and controlled the community page with an iron fist. It had only been in the last five years that she'd acknowledged any of the minority populations in Eden County.

She smiled at Ronnie, but ignored Jim. "Ronnie, is something wrong?"

Jim mentally bit his tongue to keep from being rude. The woman had adored his father, but only tolerated Jim. He didn't know why, and he didn't care. He didn't even tolerate her.

"Have you heard from Sheila today?" Ronnie asked.

"Sheila Ward and I do not speak," said Louise.

"What about Carl Basinger, the photographer? Any idea when he was here?"

Louise sniffed. "I have no idea. I prefer to take my own photographs and have never bothered to get to know him."

Doug called out to them from his desk. "I haven't seen Basinger today, but he and Sheila pretty much live in each other's pockets. He's got a place east of town. He rented a place through Rostrum's Realty. He asked me about finding a place, and I sent him to Rostrum."

Jim slapped Ronnie on the back. "Thanks!" Jim could see Dee coming back from the printing area. He went to meet her.

"Rostrum's Realty. We need to get someone over there and get Carl Basinger's address."

Dee smiled. "About damn time we got a break. I'll get on it."

Chapter Fifty-Three

Jim ran his hand over his face and realized that he was trembling. He thought back and counted how long it'd been since he'd eaten. Probably about nine hours ago. He'd had an endless series of cups of coffee, but nothing else.

Junior stepped into the doorway of his office. He set a sandwich and an apple down on Jim's desk. "Dee called and told me to get you something to eat."

"Thanks," Jim said. "Sometimes I think that woman is psychic."

Jim unwrapped the sandwich. It was tuna salad from the Magnolia House. It made his mouth water just looking at it. They made damn fine tuna salad. He bit into it, and the flavor exploded over his tongue. He sighed with pleasure.

"You screwing that sandwich or eating it?" asked Doc as he walked in and plopped down in the chair in front of Jim's desk.

"I may marry it," Jim said. "What are you doing here?"

"Just figured I'd come hang out over here."

Jim set his sandwich down.

"Go on, eat, Jim. I'm not here to make you feel guilty. I just couldn't stand to be in the office. We closed up early, and I sent Filly and Claire home. Though don't be surprised if Filly shows up here wanting to know if she can help."

Jim began eating his sandwich again. There was a tap at the door, and Jim looked up to see Filly and Claire both standing there. They looked over at Doc, and Filly said, "Guess we all had the same idea."

233

Jim set his sandwich down again, but Filly held up her hand, "Go on and eat. Junior told us the deputies are out looking for vans. You don't mind if we stay a bit?"

Jim shook his head, and went back to eating his sandwich.

* * *

Dee called and let Jim know Rostrum hadn't been in his office, and he had no secretary. She'd gotten Deputy Wills, and his lock picks meet her at the office. She'd let him know what they found.

Jim stood in the bullpen making notes when Michael came in the front door with Bonehead. Jim stopped what he was doing.

"I heard about Ryan," he said.

Jim motioned for him to come on in. "Might as well join the party. We're going to find him."

Michael sat down at a desk and nodded to Doc, Filly, and Claire, who also occupied chairs in the office. Bonehead planted himself across Michael's feet.

"It's all over town, Dad. I came here because some of the stuff people are saying is… well, stupid."

"What kind of stuff?"

"That there's a ring of organ thieves here, and they've been taking people for their kidneys, and that Ryan was taken because they're going to make him put them in other people."

"Good God Almighty!" said Doc.

"Yeah, that is pretty stupid," said Jim. "We don't have anyone stealing people's kidneys. And Ryan isn't a surgeon."

Doc snorted. "With stories like that running around, I'm surprised Sheila Ward hasn't been in here demanding an exclusive."

They all laughed a little, but Jim didn't laugh.

Doc looked at Jim. "If she knew, she'd be here, wouldn't she?"

Jim shrugged. "We don't know."

"Maybe she's been off on another story?" suggested Michael.

Jim shrugged again.

"What the hell is going on, James Franklin Sheppard? You know something you're not telling us. What is it?" demanded Filly.

"Carl Basinger has a white van. It's tenuous, but he and Sheila haven't been heard from all day. My guys are out looking for where Basinger lives. He never registered a home address with the paper, and he never changed the registration on his van to Eden County."

"Holy shit," said Michael.

The fact that Jim didn't have a fit at Michael's language told the people in the room far more about the seriousness of what was going on than anything else.

"That photographer," said Doc.

"Yeah."

Filly stood up. "You think that Sheila has something to do with Ryan going missing?"

"Don't know, Filly. But something's off about her and that photographer."

"Let me make a call. I know her mother," Filly said. She disappeared into Jim's office. He could hear the soft murmuring of her voice.

Doc shrugged. "I figured Sheila hatched," he said.

Michael laughed, and Jim swatted him gently.

"You delivered her," Jim said.

Doc shuddered. "Don't remind me. I've seen more of her and her mother than any man should ever be subjected to. I've never met a man I felt as sorry for as I did Mark Ward."

When Filly returned, her face did not look happy. "Sheila's mother hasn't been able to reach her, and she's seriously pissed off because Sheila was supposed to take her to get her hair done today. She no-showed. Which is not like Sheila. Her mother and her are attached at the hip. And if you think Sheila's bad, you haven't seen anything until you've seen her mama mad."

A collective shudder ran through the room.

"Junior," Jim called over to the desk. "Put out a missing person on Sheila Ward."

Junior looked at Jim. "You sure you want to do that? Seems like her getting kinda lost might be a good thing."

"Not in this case."

Junior nodded and went to work at his keyboard.

"Well, shit fire and save the matches," said Doc.

Claire snickered.

Filly swatted Doc.

"I maybe met a serial killer," said Doc.

"We can't say that," started Jim.

"I said maybe!"

"Can't say that either."

Filly looked at Jim and said, "You better find this guy. He kills Ryan, Doc will make sure your next prostate exam is done with a backhoe."

"Or a bulldozer," said Doc.

"Hell's bells, Doc!" said Jim.

The moment of joking helped. Jim felt like he could breathe again. These people, these friends and family, would help him get through this.

Chapter Fifty-Four

R yan searched the house as thoroughly as he could. Now that he was free of the chair, he needed to find a way out. He also wanted some clothes.

He found his own clothes in a trash bag near the back door. He thought he recognized the colors through the translucent white, and when he opened the bag, it contained his pants, shirt, underwear, socks, and shoes. It also smelled heavily of urine. Crap. Great. He'd wet himself, probably after he lost consciousness in the van. He rescued his shoes from the bag, then closed it back up. Pretty much everything just needed to be burned. He didn't want any of it. He'd certainly never be able to wear any of it.

Which also explained why he hadn't had to piss since he'd been awake.

He put everything back in the bag and then closed it back up. The photographer was close to his height, even if he was heavier. Ryan would take what he needed from the man.

He found clean sweatpants, socks, and a T-shirt in a drawer in the man's bedroom. A pair of tennis shoes laced tightly and with two pairs of socks fit enough for him to walk in them. Ryan then completed the second search looking for a phone. There wasn't one in the house, as far as he could tell. He'd seen a phone jack, but no phone anywhere.

The windows would have to be broken for him to get out. Paint sealed the edges so that they wouldn't open. He still didn't want to break out a window, because he wanted the guy confused and hunting for him close to the house. But, if necessary, he'd break a window before he stayed in the house for Carl's return.

The house was old and, from what he could see through the windows, isolated. He couldn't see any other houses from the windows, and a few windows had no view at all because of bushes growing next to the house. The small back yard enticed him. If he could get there, it looked as though he could move into the woods and keep hidden in the trees.

Of course, with the fires, staying deep in the trees had more than a little bit of danger attached. Fire moved fast through the dry landscape. Through the front windows, he could see that the driveway went a long way before it disappeared into the trees. If he stayed by the trees, but walked along the drive, he'd hear the car before he was in sight, which would allow him to duck into the tree line and hide.

First, he had to find a way out of the house.

He couldn't find a weapon other than the knives. He went back and got the butcher knife he'd used to cut himself free of the chair. He didn't want to get close enough to have to use it, but if the other option was giving up, he would use it. Using a knife couldn't be that different from a scalpel, and he definitely knew how to use a scalpel.

In the hallway, he looked up and saw a trap door to the attic. He reached up and grabbed the pull cord, and the door opened, and a ladder unfolded. Ryan climbed up and stuck his head up into the space above.

Dust and late afternoon light lit up the empty area. The joists above the ceiling were visible. There was a thin layer of insulation, and he could see that if he stepped between the joists he'd go straight through the ceiling to the room below. The roof and rafters were solid wood. The whole space was probably just over four feet tall and covered the entire area of the house.

In the distance, Ryan could see a vent at the front gable of the house. He wondered if he could kick that out. He could at least try. He had nothing to lose.

He climbed all the way up and pulled the ladder up behind him, closing the trap door. He'd rather have the guy searching for him if he did return, than just climbing up the ladder behind him.

He had to crawl across the joists on his hands and knees. He didn't have room to stand up, and it would be harder to walk on the joists crouched over than it was to crawl.

He got to the vent and examined it. He pushed on the edges of it. It seemed pretty firmly in place. He looked around and saw that there was an identical vent at the back of the house.

If he tried to kick the front one out and failed, it would be visible when the photographer pulled up in front of the house. The one at the back of the house couldn't be seen unless he went into the back yard.

"Yay, me," Ryan said sarcastically to himself. "Your brain is finally kicking in."

Dripping sweat, he turned around and crawled to the vent at the back of the house. It, too, seemed firmly in place, but Ryan felt no qualms about trying to kick this one out.

He set the knife down and sat back, bringing his legs up, folded against his body. He braced his arms on the joists beside him and kicked as hard as he could. The vent held. He kicked again, and this time one side moved out slightly. But it moved. It moved, so he kicked again and again and again.

Finally, the vent popped out of the gable wall and dropped to the ground below. The air from outside felt minimally cooler than the air in the attic, and he stuck his head out and took a breath. The opening was small, about two feet tall by a foot wide. He could get his head through it, but getting his body through it might not be possible.

Though he could only really see with his left eye, he got a good look at the back yard. He was maybe eight feet off the ground. An easy drop, if he could get through the space. Well, there was no time like the present.

Ryan pressed his right arm close to his body, curling his shoulders to make himself narrower, and shifted his head and shoulder out the window. He moved his arm up and out. He could reach the edge of the roof. He grabbed it, twisted his body and angled his left shoulder out through the opening. With both arms gripping the roof, Ryan scooted his butt to the edge of the joists and slowly moved his hips through the open space. He hung from the roof by his hands.

His only weapon sat inside on the ceiling insulation.

"You dumbshit!" he said out loud.

He curled up and got his feet back on the edge of the vent space. Braced with his feet just inside the attic, he let go of the roof with one hand and reached in past his legs. He fumbled around for a moment, and found the knife. He brought it out and tossed it out into the yard behind him.

Then he grabbed the edges of the roof again and brought his feet out. His feet were only about five feet off the ground. He let go and dropped straight down, letting his knees give as he hit the ground. He fell on his butt, but he was out. He was out of the damn house.

"YES!" he whisper-shouted again. He got up, brushed grass and debris off his butt, brushed his slightly raw hands, and then looked for his knife. He found it a couple of feet away in the thick grass. Carl must have been really occupied with his mission to save the county because the back yard sorely needed mowing.

Now he had to figure out where to go. He had no idea where this house was in relation to town. He'd been unconscious during the drive and the transfer into the house.

He was kind of glad he'd been unconscious during the whole undressing and being strapped to the potty chair thing. Granted, he might have been able to fight, but he had the feeling that injured as he was, he would have lost.

He walked around the house to the front. He hoped he would see a car or truck once he got to the road. If he could flag someone down, he might get a ride back into Warren. But if he saw a white van, he was heading straight into the woods. He'd take a chance on running into the fire before he'd let himself be captured again.

Ryan's surprise at the length of the driveway made the walk feel endless. Every time he thought the road must be just around this last bend, there would only be more drive. Without his watch, he realized he didn't have a sense of how long he'd been walking. He hadn't thought to check the bag of clothing for it. He'd been too focused on getting himself covered and out of the house.

Finally, the road came into sight. The dusty lime rock drive hadn't been pleasant to walk on, and he anxiously wanted to reach pavement to have some sense of approaching actual civilization. The macadam pavement didn't seem all that civilized. The heat made the tar sticky, and it felt hot under the soles of his shoes.

He moved over to the grass shoulder. The mowed grass gave softly under his shoes, even if it did crackle noisily. The sun beat down, making heat waves rise off the pavement ahead. He should have thought to grab a cap of some kind, but once again, his very narrow focus had let him down.

Ryan had turned left when he came out of the driveway. His reasoning had been simple. Most people went to the right when in an unfamiliar area. Or he thought it was right. He could be wrong. It'd been back in the days of his undergraduate degree when his mind retained information only as long as it took to get through the final, unless the class related directly to his potential medical studies.

Anyway, if most people turned right, he turned left. He liked doing the unexpected, being singular in a crowd of lemming-like humans. It had kept him at the top of his pre-med courses and led to an excellent medical school and falling in love with Emergency Medicine, much to his mother's horror. He loved the pace of it, the demands it made for thinking quickly, having a broad knowledge of different specialties so he could stabilize the patient before the specialist arrived.

He'd been a star in the emergency room.

Now he required the slower pace of the general practice. He used his wealth of experience in the emergency room every day in the practice that Doc Markham brought him into as a partner. These people needed him as much as the patients in the emergency room had needed him. With Filly at his side, he'd come to believe he could be a doctor again. That his brain still worked, even if his words didn't always come to him.

He focused on the road ahead, hoping he would see a vehicle soon and that it wouldn't be the white van that had brought him to that awful house where he was sure the young preacher had died.

Chapter Fifty-Five

Sheila's mother had given Filly a cell phone number. Jim's surprise must have shown on his face, because Doc grinned.

"Believe it or not, there's actually a tower now in Eden County."

"Where?"

"Libby's Dairy. I hear Richard Libby had it put up so he could give his people phones to use to communicate on the dairy. Personally, I think he did it so he could have one more thing that everyone else around here didn't have."

It would be like Libby to do that. The man had enjoyed being the richest man in the county, though in Eden, that wasn't saying much. Now he probably had already been laid out in a drawer in the coroner's office in Gainesville. Being rich ended up not being all that damn helpful when Libby faced a man determined to kill him.

Jim picked up the receiver and dialed the number that Filly had given him. The phone rang and rang, and then a recording told him that the owner of the cell number he had called was not available.

He hung up. "Either she's not answering, or she's too far away from the tower."

Dee radioed in. She'd gotten into Rostrom's office, found out he was meeting a prospective house buyer at the river, and was tracking him down. She had the address and Wills. They would not come back without him.

"Filly got a cell number for Sheila. I called it and got no answer."

There was a silence on the other end of the radio, then Dee said, "It could just be a stall."

That made sense. If Sheila was involved somehow in all that had been happening, she might just want time to get further away or hidden.

"I'll have Junior put out a 'be on the lookout.' If she shows up in another county, maybe she'll get spotted, and we'll get a call."

"Sounds good, sir. Once we have Rostrom, we'll be in."

"Thanks," Jim said.

Junior put out the BOLO for Sheila with the description of Sheila's car and tag number. A scant thirty minutes later, Dee walked into the office with Wills and a very frightened-looking man in a suit. She looked at the motley group that had taken up residence in the bullpen.

"You're having a party, and you didn't invite me?" Dee asked Jim. "Hey, Michael."

She brushed her hand through the mess of hair on his head. "Look at that. Didn't even move," she said. "This is Mr. Adam Rostrum. He knows where Basinger lives."

Jim smiled. If he didn't think Dee would punch him, he'd have hugged her. "We need to get everyone back here, and then we need to get to that place."

Rostrum spoke, his voice shaking, "Mr. Basinger was very particular about being away from town and off the road. It'd be easier to lead you there than to give you the address and have you find it."

"Sounds good to me, Mr. Rostrum. I appreciate your help," said Jim.

"Deputy Jackson made it very clear I was to cooperate," Rostrum said weakly.

Jim bit down on the laugh. He knew how Dee could strike fear into the heart of any man. He imagined Adam Rostrum was going to cooperate in any way he could think of, including facing Basinger himself if necessary. Anything to avoid pissing off Dee Jackson.

"Thank you, sir." Jim looked at Dee. "All right, Deputy Jackson, who do we call to go with us to this place to retrieve Dr. Edwards."

Dee smiled. "I can give you a list. You'll definitely want Wills in case we need to open locks. But be sure to get Manny Sota. He was a sniper in Iraq. Man's got mad skills. Wouldn't hurt to have Dinkem and Wooly, and then maybe Furner and Lockhart. And if you don't let Bobby Dale and Driscoll come along, Bobby Dale's never going to speak to you again. He might even quit."

Jim signaled Junior, "Start making calls. Where should we have them meet us, Mr. Rostrum?"

"I'd suggest the junction of 349 and 98. It's the closest intersection to the house."

"Excellent. Junior, get the word out to the Deputies Sargent Jackson listed and tell them to meet us there."

"Yes, sir, Sheriff."

Dee turned to Wills. "You take Rostrum, we'll be right behind you. We'll connect up with the other at 349 and 98 and decide how we're going to approach the property."

Dee looked over to Junior. "Be sure none of those knuckleheads you call use their sirens to get to the meeting point. Tell them to hurry but be silent. Sounds carries out there."

Jim grabbed his cap, and Dee led the way out to her car. As they got into the patrol car, Jim said, "Why won't you let me make you a captain?"

"Because I am not going to be in the office and attending fucking Commission meetings for you. I hate politics," Dee responded. "So, stop asking me that."

"You should be a captain."

"Talk to me in twenty years when I'm too old to be out on the road."

"You'll just retire on me then."

"Yep," she said and laughed. "Though I might let you promote me first so I get a better retirement rate."

The running argument they had going about promotion clearly wasn't going to get settled today. Dee Jackson should be a captain. She knew as much about the department as he did, and she kept up with the deputies and all their special skills. In fact, she often knew more about them because they talked to her when they didn't talk to him.

She frustrated the hell out of him. She liked being out on patrol. She loved the action, and she loved the adrenalin. The only thing that surprised him about her was that she hadn't yet taken up skydiving. But he'd give her until after she finished her masters to take up that hobby.

"You're going to be the most over-educated deputy in the history of the department," Jim said. Then a jolt of fear ran through him, "You're going to go somewhere else and get a better job!"

Dee laughed. "No, I'm going to be the first black woman sheriff in Florida, you jackass, and I'm going to do it in Eden County. Now, let's go get Doc Ryan."

Jim laughed as she pulled out of the parking lot. She was going to make a hell of a sheriff. He wasn't so sure she'd be able to do it in Eden County, but if any woman could, it would be her. He had made it clear to Michael that he would rather he not go into law enforcement, despite its long history in the family. So far, Michael had been non-committal about it, which made Jim fear he had the desire that Jim had always lacked.

Of course, it would be years before Michael could even become a deputy. All kinds of strange things could happen between now and then.

Chapter Fifty-Six

Ryan felt like he had walked forever. The sun was a little lower in the sky but still high enough to make it hotter than hell next to the road. He was tired and hungry, and he wished he'd grabbed a bottle of water or something before he left the house. At the time, the thought of even water made his stomach roil, but now he realized that, once again, he hadn't really been thinking clearly in his desperation to be out of the house.

He heard the car before he saw it. He stepped off the road, back to the edge of the woods. He waited to see if it was the white van.

A small gold sedan headed in his direction. Ryan took a risk. He moved back up next to the road and waved his arms above his head. He had the knife tucked into a pocket of the sweatpants.

The car rolled to a stop a short distance away, and the driver's door opened. It was the reporter, Sheila Ward. There was someone in the car with her.

Her voice trembled as she called out, "If you don't keep your hands in the air, he'll shoot me."

The photographer. That was the other person in the car. He kept his hands up. Sheila got back into the car and drove slowly until the back passenger door was even with Ryan. He could see the gun pointed right at Sheila's head. There were tears streaming down her face from underneath her big sunglasses.

The passenger window was rolled down. Carl looked at him and said, "Get in the back seat. Don't try anything. You do, and I shoot her first."

Ryan took a deep breath and went to the back door of the car.

"Open the door. Get in, and keep your hands on your head. You lower your hands, and I shoot her."

As much as Sheila Ward wasn't someone Ryan liked, he would do nothing to get her killed. He got into the car and closed the door, and put his hands on his head.

The knife in the pocket of the sweats pricked at his leg, but he just let it. It was his ace in the hole. As long as he had it, he had the possibility of defending himself. Though bringing a knife to a gunfight was a bad joke, it could be effective if he could catch the man off guard.

"Drive on, Sheila. The house is just a few miles from here."

"Carl, please don't do this. Please let me go. You can take the car and just leave me out here. I won't be able to get back to down for hours."

"Shut up, Sheila."

"I've done everything you wanted. I took you to Gainesville. I followed you back to the dairy. I've done everything you wanted, please just let me get out now."

"Shut up! If you don't shut up, I will put you in the trunk again and leave you there and you can just die!"

"I don't want to die, Carl. I've done everything you asked. I don't know what you're doing, and I don't care. You can take my car, and Dr. Edwards and I'll find my way back to Warren."

"You're not going anywhere. I have to feed Dr. Edwards, and then you have to give me another name. There have to be three. Once I feed him, we only need one more name."

"Why? Why do you want a name? What are you doing?"

"Stop asking me questions and drive!" Carl screamed.

Sheila was sobbing uncontrollably. Ryan felt sorry for her. No matter how difficult she'd been to deal with, she was terrified. Carl needed to feed him again. That meant someone else was dead. Ryan tried not to think about that. The idea of consuming another meal to wash away Carl's sins made him want to vomit, but he swallowed his nausea. He couldn't take a chance on making Carl any angrier than he already was, and he didn't want to become the target of Carl's anger.

Sheila continued mumbling why, why, why, and sobbing as she drove. Carl's face had turned a frightening color of red. Ryan wished Sheila would just calm down because if she kept this up, Carl might shoot her without even thinking about the fact that she was driving.

Ryan had no desire to die in an accident. In fact, he was determined that he was going to survive this if he had to kill someone to do it. He chanted inside his head, 'Not a victim. Never again. Not a victim. Never again.'

* * *

When they pulled up in front of the house, Carl took the keys out of the ignition and then got out of the car first. He motioned for both Ryan and Sheila to get out. Carl opened the door so that Ryan could get out with his hands still on his head.

He had Sheila put her hands on her head and then told them both to go to the front door ahead of him. He handed the front door key to Sheila and told her to unlock it, but then give him the key back before she opened the door.

He told Ryan to go in ahead of Sheila. Carl reminded him that if he did anything stupid, that he would shoot Sheila. Carl's voice was stern, and Ryan had no doubt that they would both end up dead if he tried anything now.

Ryan opened the door, put his hands back on his head, and stepped inside. He'd gotten out of this place. He'd made it to the road, and he was right back where he started.

Sheila sniffled a little behind him. He stepped forward enough for her to get inside, along with Carl. He heard the door close behind him, then the click of the deadbolt. Something inside him wanted to die a little at that sound. It had taken too much effort to get out. He'd worked so hard, and here he was again. Captured.

"You'll pardon me if I take care of Sheila first," Carl said. You move. Go back to your room."

Ryan walked down the hall to the room he'd been kept in before.

"Open the door. Go over to the far corner. Stay there. If I open the door and you're not there, I'll kill Sheila. Don't make me do that, Dr. Edwards."

Ryan opened the door, stepped inside, and made his way across the room to the far corner. He turned around and saw Carl standing at the door with the gun braced against Sheila's temple.

"Remember. I will kill her if you're not in that corner when I open the door."

"May I sit down, Carl?" Ryan asked.

Carl nodded. "Yes. Be comfortable, but stay there."

The door closed, and Ryan heard it lock. Ryan had promised himself he would never be helpless again. The anger he felt building inside his chest made him want to open the door and hunt Carl down, but he didn't have any doubt that Carl would shoot Sheila, and he would not let another woman die because he couldn't defend her. But when Carl came back into the room, gun or no gun, Ryan would use the knife. He'd fight Carl, and he would win, because he had to win. He wasn't about to die in this house with this crazy religious nutcase. He'd survived brain damage. He'd survived Danielle's death. He'd survived losing his career and having to start over. He would survive Carl.

As a doctor, he'd never done anything to deliberately end another life, but Carl made something dark fill him. He wanted Carl dead. He wanted to stand over his body and watch the light go out of his eyes. Maybe he desired justice for Danielle, or the minister, and everyone else who had died because of someone else's greed and desires. He didn't know, but he knew that if he had to, he could kill.

The feeling should have scared him, but instead, it filled him with adrenalin. This time would be different. This time he would be the one to walk away.

Chapter Fifty-Seven

At the intersection of 349 and 98, the two patrol cars pulled over to the side of the road. Five other patrol cars sat at the intersection, waiting for them. When Dee and Wills parked, The others walked toward Dee's car. They stood and waited for Jim to get out and let them know what they would be doing next.

Wills brought Rostrum up next to Dee's patrol car. Jim and Dee got out and faced everyone.

"We are going to Carl Basinger's house. There's evidence of blood in his van, which makes me believe there's a good chance that he's the person who took Ryan Edwards. I believe that Ryan's still alive, and I want to keep him alive, so we are going to approach carefully and quietly, and maybe we'll find him in the house."

All the Deputies stood up straighter.

"I want everyone wearing vests, and I want us prepared to defend ourselves. It's possible that Basinger is in the house, and he may have Sheila Ward in there as well."

Bobby Dale raised his hand.

"Yes, Deputy Dale?" Jim asked.

"Is Miss Ward involved?" he asked.

"No idea," Jim said. "We just know that she's not been seen in about the last 24 hours, and it's possible that she's with Basinger. We have to be prepared for her to be either a hostage or a co-conspirator with Basinger. That means we can't go in shooting. We've got to be careful and mindful that this situation is pretty much unknown. The only thing I think is a given is that Basinger is the one doing the killing. Sheila's not big enough or strong enough to kill the way it's been happening. Which means we need everyone alive. Sheila, Basinger, and especially Dr. Edwards. Are we clear on that?"

Everyone nodded. They all looked grim, but he knew that they would do their absolute best to make sure that no one died.

"Mr. Rostrum here rented the house to Basinger. He says it's hard to find because it's way off the road. He's going to lead us to the drive to the house. What else should we know, Mr. Rostrum?"

"It's up in the hardwood hammock on this side of the Suwannee River. It's heavily wooded on all sides, but there's a cleared front and back yard. I can get you to the entrance to the drive, but I think I'd be better left back with the cars."

Jim turned to Manny. "Put him in your car and take the lead. No sirens. Get in as close as you can without being seen from the house." He turned to Rostrum. "You make sure that's what happens."

Rostrum nodded.

"We'll come in behind you, but when you stop, we'll coordinate from there how to approach the house." Jim looked out at his deputies. "Let's be careful and be quiet. No one does anything until we figure out the best approach."

Everyone agreed, and they all moved to their vehicles. It wouldn't be dark for another three or four hours, which was the one blessing of summer. Jim hoped like hell it worked in their favor. Even if it didn't, they were going to get Ryan Edwards out of that house alive. Jim promised himself that no matter what it took, Ryan Edwards would not die today.

Chapter Fifty-Eight

When the door opened again, Ryan put his hands on his head and waited for Carl to come in. Carl stepped into the room, closed the door behind him. He had the gun pointed at Ryan. "I need you to get back into the chair." He held up a roll of duct tape.

"No."

Carl's eyebrows raised in surprise. "I can shoot you if you don't."

Ryan shrugged. "Then do it, but I'm not getting back in that chair."

Carl seemed intrigued by Ryan's attitude. He took a few steps closer. "I could go shoot Sheila."

"Go ahead. I don't care. I'm not getting back into that chair. I won't make this easy for you. You want me in that chair, you're going to have to put me there."

Carl smiled, obviously pleased. "Yes, yes, you're the one. I was wrong about Reverend Hatcher, but I'm right about you!"

Ryan didn't like the sound of that at all.

"That was the problem. Hatcher was a good man, but he wasn't a strong one. He just kept praying. He didn't understand that what I was doing was necessary. If we're going to save this world, we have to do this. It takes courage and drastic action, but sometimes that's what God requires. I mean, he has generals and soldiers, and the angels are warriors. They defeated Satan. God needs brave men. Men like us."

Carl kept his distance, his back against the door. He smiled at Ryan, but kept the gun pointed toward him.

"The fires. They're a taste of what is to come. But it can be stopped. I'm sure of it. We're being given a chance to prevent it. We've been entrusted with the opportunity to save this place. This special beautiful place is where it all began. This is Eden. My grandmother told me all about it. I came here, came home, and then the fires came. If I'm to make sure that Eden is saved, I had to find the way. So, I prayed, and I let my Bible fall open the way my grandmother taught me. And there was the answer."

Ryan kept his eyes on Carl and the gun. The man didn't move any closer. He stayed where he was. His face had taken on a radiance. The man was one highly delusional headcase.

Ryan felt his heart start to race, and he began to deliberately breathe slowly, to calm himself. He'd faced evil before, but this was something entirely new to him. Fanatic belief.

"It opened to Ezekiel. I read. I read and I tried to make sense of what I read. And it was made clear. This was a test. This was a trial. The fires were a taste of what was to come if we did not make the world better. And the way to make it better was to find that savior and have him, as Jesus did, consume the sins of the world. I was wrong the first time. I chose poorly, but God gave me a second chance. He led me to you. You have the strength. You can save Eden with me. We've had to start over, I realize that now. So, we've started with the first one. Then Sheila gave me the second one, and he's dead. I'll need you to cleanse me again. Once we've done that, Sheila will give me a third name, and I will kill him. You'll cleanse me, and then, then the fires will stop, and Eden will be saved. God will be pleased. We'll have shown him that we can and will do what is necessary.

Oh crap, Ryan thought. Crap, crap, crap. Consuming the sins of the world. That's why he fed Hatcher the food. He thought that sins could be removed by having a "savior" consume them, destroy them in their body.

"I needed to find the right savior. 'Behold, all souls are Mine; as the soul of the father, so also the soul of the son is Mine; the soul that sinneth, it shall die.' Once we've saved Eden, we'll see what God wants us to do. There may be a need for more cleansing. I'm sure you understand that if God shows us, it's necessary that we can do it together. Though I don't think Sheila will be able to help us with the others. She's weak. She pretends she's strong, but you saw. You saw that she isn't suitable to do what needs to be done. I have had to hide it from her."

"You killed a good man," Ryan said.

Carl shook his head. "No, no, I haven't killed any good men."

"You killed Hatcher. He was a good man."

"That wasn't my fault. He died because he wasn't strong enough to consume the sins."

"You chose him. You brought him here, and you fed him all the sins, and he choked on it and died. It's all on you, Carl. You can't be cleansed of that. You killed a good man, a man of God. Nothing will ever clean that off your soul."

Carl's face went red, and he gritted his teeth. He stretched out his arm as though to get the gun closer to Ryan, who sat across the room from him. "You shut up. You shut up and you get in the chair."

"Whose sins are worse than yours, Carl? Seems like the worst sinner around right now is you. You killed an innocent man, a good man. Is there a worse sin than that?"

"YOU SHUT UP!"

Ryan shrugged. "Whose sins, Carl? Sheila's? You say she's not suitable. So you're going to kill her, too?"

Carl shook his head. "She's the one God sent to show me the men who needed to be cleansed. She's a messenger. She's not evil. She's just weak. We'll have to leave her behind. It's more merciful to make sure she doesn't suffer."

"You're evil, Carl."

"I'M SAVING EDEN!" Carl screamed. "You'll eat the sins, and you'll see. The fires will stop."

Carl stepped out of the room, slamming the door behind him.

Ryan lowered his hands to his lap. He'd wait it out. The door only locked from the inside. He'd leave with Sheila, forcing her to pick someone for him to kill. Once they left, Ryan would get out of the room again, and he would escape again. He would not die in this house at the hands of some lunatic.

BANG! BANG! BANG!

Ryan jumped. That sounded like someone hammering on the door. BANG! BANG! BANG!

The end of a huge nail came through the door frame, splintering the wood. Ryan got up and went to the door. He put his hands on it and felt it vibrate with the hammering of each nail, Carl nailing the door shut. Ryan could hear him grunting with the effort of the hammering.

Ryan stepped back and looked at the door. Crap. Crap. He looked around the room. The boards over the windows would have to be pried off. Then he would have no choice but to break one of them to get out of the house. Unless he could maybe push the window unit air conditioner out of its window.

The banging stopped, and he could hear Carl stomping away.

Ryan turned back to the door. What could he do? He looked back to the window unit. Was it possible to push that so that he could crawl out of the window? How much did it weigh?

He looked back at the door, seeing the nails coming through the door frame so that it couldn't be opened.

Then he really saw the door. Ryan smiled. Carl had nailed the door on the side it opened. The hinges for the door were on the inside. Carl hadn't thought it through. He'd turned the door so that the lock was on the outside, but it was a bedroom door. That put the hinges on the inside where Ryan was standing. He might not be able to open the door with the doorknob, but the hinges meant he could open the door on the left side. He got the butcher knife and looked at the hinges. All he had to do was pry the pin out of each hinge. The knife would easily slip between the top of the pin and the rings of the hinge.

Ryan knelt down next to the lowest hinge. He would take out the bottom pin first, and the top pin second. He'd wait for his moment, sure there would be one when he could remove the center pin and pull the door in.

He needed sound to cover the noise of pulling the door against the nails, and he felt like there was a damn fine chance of Sheila Ward providing that. Even now, he could hear her voice. With Carl already angry, the probability of shouting between Carl and Sheila seemed quite high.

He just needed to be ready.

Chapter Fifty-Nine

The smoke in the trees got heavier as they headed north on 349. Jim had wanted Manny to take the lead because he drove better than anyone else in the department. He could drive both fast and safely. A caravan of patrol cars followed and Dee.

Manny slowed and took a turn off 349 that went east again for about eight miles. He called over the radio they should all stop. Manny pulled his car onto the shoulder, got out, and walked back to Jim's.

"Rostrum says the drive to the house is about fifty yards down. There's nothing between here and there except a lot of trees. I suggest that we park here, leave the cars and walk in."

"All right. Get Rostrum back to one of the last cars. We'll leave one deputy here with him."

Manny nodded. Jim pulled up on the shoulder of the road, far enough to be out of the way, but not too close to the tree line. He looked back, and everyone fell into place along the side of the road behind him.

Manny took Rostrum out of the passenger seat of his car and walked him back to the last car in line.

Quietly everyone got out of their vehicles and began to check their weapons. Shotguns were pulled from trunks, and duty armor put on. Dee made hand signals to everyone, and they made their way up to where Jim stood.

When Manny joined them, Jim looked to Dee. "You've got the most experience with this kind of thing. We'll follow your lead."

Dee nodded, her dark face thoughtful. Then she said, "Once we get to where the drive starts, we split up, go in on both sides of it. No one moves out of the woods until I give the signal. Is that understood?"

"Yes, ma'am," answered Bobby Dale.

Everyone nodded at that. Dee nodded to them and then motioned with her head and walked down the pavement. When they reached the dirt drive, they disappeared into the trees.

Chapter Sixty

Once the pins came out of the hinges, the door leaned dangerously toward Ryan. He put his ear to the crack to hear the sounds from the house. Sheila sobbed loudly from somewhere toward the front of the house. Carl ranted about her stupidity and that he needed her to point him to the next sinner. Sheila didn't answer, her cries turning into wailing as Carl became more and more enraged at her.

A loud bang, and Sheila screamed, and Carl shouted for her to stop it. A bang came again, and Sheila screamed louder. Then the banging became continuous, with Carl's voice raging above it.

Ryan quickly pulled on the door, and it creaked, the nails beginning to give way as the door pulled away from them. The banging and shouting didn't stop. As soon as the opening was large enough, Ryan slipped through it. He ran into the hallway and pulled down the ladder to the attic. He ascended it as fast and as quietly as he could, pulled the ladder and the door up, and closed behind him. He waited a moment, but the sounds below continued.

He crawled across the joists to the back of the house. The smell of burning wood was stronger than it had been when he'd climbed out earlier. When he reached the back vent, he looked outside and gasped when he saw the tops of the trees in flames. The smoke rolled out of the trees and across the small backyard. The yard, ill-kept and dry, would burn fast once the flames reached it. The question of whether or not he could outrun the flames flashed through Ryan's head. He didn't know how quickly it would move once it hit the dry grass.

"I will kill you if you don't help me!" Carl yelled. Ryan froze, waiting to see what would happen next.

Sheila screamed, babbling incoherently. Ryan could barely make out what he thought was Sheila begging for her life.

"SHUT UP!" Carl yelled. "You have to tell me who to get next! Who is next on the list, Sheila? Who do I need to kill next?"

Ryan could hear him banging on something. He roared with rage, and suddenly he fired the gun. The shot came up through the ceiling and exited through the roof from the living room area.

Ryan shrank back against the wall at the back of the house. He could hear Carl throwing things and slamming his fists into the walls.

Sheila screamed, and Ryan heard what sounded like a chair being dragged.

"I'll kill you! I'll kill you if you don't help me!" Carl yelled.

Ryan didn't think Carl would kill Sheila. He didn't want to hurt the woman. But his rage grew as the minutes passed, and he might hurt her, even just from dragging her around with her tied to a chair.

Ryan's instinct was to get out. He looked to the vent at the back of the house. Smoke was beginning to drift inside. That had to mean the fire was getting closer. He began to doubt that he'd be able to drop out the back without the fire catching him.

Carl shot through the ceiling again. Ryan watched the spray of torn insulation that followed the bullet up through the roof.

Cursing silently, Ryan stopped thinking about what he was going to do and tossed the butcher knife out of the vent into the grass and leaned out, and grabbed the eaves of the roof again. He had to get out. He could do nothing to save Sheila where he was. If he even moved toward the attic ladder, he'd be closer to the bullets that came through the ceiling. He had to chance it. He took a deep breath and then pulled himself out of the attic and dropped to the ground,

He found the butcher knife and moved around the house to the side, the furthest from the flames. When he ran around the corner, he stopped. If he walked out in front of the house, Carl might see him. The woods on this side were thick with smoke, but so far, nothing actually burned. He quietly made his way into the trees.

Chapter Sixty-One

The sound of a gunshot made everyone freeze. Dee turned to Jim, "That's a handgun."

Jim's radio clicked, and Manny Soto whispered, "Sheriff, we're getting more smoke over here. How is it on your side of the drive?"

"Getting heavier. You heard the shot?"

"Yes, sir."

Dee didn't hesitate, telling everyone quietly to move forward. A few moments later, a second shot and Dee made the call, "Move it, now!"

Stealth went by the wayside, and all of them began to jog through the trees, staying hidden but not worrying about noise.

"I'll kill you!" A voice yelled from inside the house. "We have to finish this to stop the fire! If you don't give me a name, I'll kill you and have him eat your sins! I know there are enough of them! I know you let criminals get away with things until you were sure you had the story! You don't care about anybody but yourself! You'd let Eden burn if it would make you famous!"

Dee almost growled. "That bastard has a hostage." Dee looked at Jim. "I'm going to move up to the side of the house and see if I can get close to those windows."

Jim nodded. He told everyone to hold their positions.

Carl pulled the drapes back and looked out at the yard. Jim found himself holding his breath, afraid that Basinger would see movement, or color or something in the trees. If he began shooting out at the trees, someone could easily be killed. Carl closed the drapes and began yelling again, "I will kill you! If we don't finish the plan, we'll all die!"

* * *

Jim could see smoke beginning to gather in the tree branches above the house. He told the deputies to keep an eye out for ash or sparks. The house was wood frame. It would go up like a tinder box if the fire got to it.

Carl fired again, but the bullet must have been aimed inside the house. The sound was muffled.

Jim watched as Dee edged out of the woods on the north side of the house. Dee stood and looked into one of the windows. Carl was mostly hidden behind a drape in the front of the house. Jim kept his eyes on Carl. If he saw the man make a move toward where Dee knelt, he would shoot to draw his attention away.

Dee's voice on the radio was soft, "He's got Sheila. She's tied to a chair, and he's hanging onto her. I've got the shot."

Jim held his breath. Time was running short. The smoke in the trees was getting heavier by the minute, and if they didn't all get out of there before the fire hit these woods, more than one of them might die.

"Not yet," Jim said into his radio. He holstered his gun and stepped out of the trees, walking toward the house.

"Carl Basinger, this is Sheriff Sheppard. I need you to put down the gun and come out here."

Carl screamed with inarticulate rage. "NO! You are messing everything up! You have to go away. I need to do this. If I don't, Eden will burn!"

"I don't understand what you need to do, Carl. If you'll come out and explain it to me, maybe I can help." Jim's heart raced, and he could feel a cold sweat running down his sides under his shirt. He had never been more scared in his life, but he had to try to stop this.

"No, no, you're messing it up. I need Dr. Edwards. I need him, and then I need bad people. He'll eat the sins and clean Eden. God will spare it."

"I'm the Sheriff, Carl. I can help you get the bad people. We've got lots of them." Jim waited for an answer, but only got silence.

"I can't," Carl finally called. "You won't let me come back."

"We'll go together. You come out of the house, and we'll go together."

There was movement, and then the door opened. "Ryan stays here. He and Sheila stay here."

"Of course. That's fine." Jim pulled out his handcuffs. Jim couldn't see Carl, but his voice was clearer through the slightly opened door. He could also hear Sheila sobbing. As much as he disliked her, he hated hearing that. He hated knowing she was terrified.

The door opened a little further, and Jim could see a bit of Carl's face. "How did you find me?"

"I talked to Rostrum. I drove out here to see if I could find you and Sheila. I was just going to talk to you, but now I know this is important."

"This is Eden. My grandmother told me."

"She was a Spiney. Married a Forrenberry in Pensacola, right?"

Carl stepped in the doorway, a smile bloomed across his face. "You know of her?"

"Of course. Who wouldn't know such a fine old family. They were related to Casey. He nearly succeeded in stopping the Seminole War through negotiation. It's an amazing history."

Carl laughed, "Yes! That's so great! You know. We have to stop the fires, Sheriff. We have to. And the only way to do it is to cleanse it."

"The soul that sinneth, it shall die. You need Ryan to eat the sins, and it will stop the fires."

"Yes."

Carl stepped out onto the front steps. "I should have known. I could tell you were a good man, Sheriff. Dr. Edwards is a warrior. You can see that. We need a good man who's a warrior."

"Makes perfect sense, Carl. You and I will go into town and pick two men."

"Three. We need three to be sure. Reverend Hatcher only managed two. I think that the last one counts as first for Ryan. He did eat the meal, but I'm not sure. We might need three. I need to be sure this time. Hatcher couldn't eat the second meal, that's why it didn't work."

"Of course, three. Like the Trinity. Got to do it in threes. Come on, let's get this done so we can stop the fires."

"Sparks," came a voice over the radio.

Jim looked above the house, and he could see ash and sparks in the air.

"I'll take Sheila back to the kitchen. I have Dr. Edwards locked in a room," Carl said. He stepped back into the house and closed the door slightly behind him.

"Hell's bells," Jim whispered.

Jim looked up and could see flames in the tops of the trees that backed up the house.

"Carl! Carl! We have a problem," Jim yelled.

The door opened again, and he could see just a bit of Carl's face. "What?"

"The fire, there's fire in the trees behind the house. We'll have to find another place to do this. If we leave them here, they'll die in the fire when the house burns."

Silence. Except for the crackling of the flames and the rush of hot air sweeping up behind the house, there was no sound.

"Fire? No, no, it can't come here." Carl slammed the door closed, and Jim glanced over to where he knew Dee stood at the side of the house.

"No shot. He's run into the back," she said over the radio.

Chapter Sixty-Two

T he sound of Jim's voice stopped Ryan in his tracks. Was he actually trying to talk that maniac out of the house? Ryan moved closer so that he could hear the conversation better. Their voices carried better once Ryan had gotten closer to the edge of the woods. He saw Dee standing next to the house, facing toward the drive. She crouched under a window, which she had probably used to try to get a fix on where Carl stood inside. She had her gun out and held it in both hands, her finger resting along the barrel above the trigger guard. Startling Dee would be a very bad idea.

Ryan moved through the woods quietly until he could see more of her face. He whistled softly. Dee's face and gun turned his way.

He held his hands up above shoulder height.

Dee spoke softly into her radio. "Sheriff, Dr. Edwards is outside the house."

Carl screamed from inside the house. "NO! NO!" A loud thumping sound echoed out into the yard, punctuated with Carl's screams of no. Gunfire boomed from inside the place, and Sheila began screaming along with Carl, but their voices came from different places.

Ryan heard Jim's voice softly over the radio. "I think Carl just realized he's gone."

Dee motioned for Ryan to come out of the trees and stand behind her. He thought to shake his head no, but it occurred to him it might not be his best move to piss off Dee Jackson. Everyone in town knew Dee put up with no shit from anyone. Jim called her his right hand in the department and said he'd put her up against any man when it came to self-defense or shooting.

Ryan had wondered if anyone had felt that strongly about him. He'd been a star, but he hadn't been anyone's right hand. He'd always been exceptional, but singular. The only time he'd been part of a team was with Danielle. And he'd failed her miserably.

Dee hissed at him, and he looked at her again. She emphatically motioned for him to come to her and stand behind her and quit fucking around. As much as it scared him to not follow her instructions, his fear for Jim was greater.

He moved deeper into the woods and headed toward the front of the house.

Chapter Sixty-Three

Doors slammed, and Carl raged. Sheila screamed in terror. The front door of the house slammed open, and a shot boomed out, and glass shattered, then there was a thunk as a bullet hit the metal of the car parked in front of the house. Carl fired two more times, stopping finally.

Jim had not moved. He stood completely still in the open in front of the house. He kept his hands out to his sides so that Carl could see that he didn't have his gun. He hoped Carl was a good enough shot to not hit him unless he actually meant to do it.

"What's going on, Carl?"

"Dr. Edwards is gone! Where did he go?"

Jim raised his hands, palms up. "I haven't seen him, Carl. Where could he go? How could he get out? You said you had him locked up."

"I nailed the door shut, but he got out."

"Is there somewhere in the house he could hide from you?"

Sheila was still screaming and sobbing. Carl turned and pointed the gun, "SHUT UP! I can't think!"

Sheila sobbed.

"I will kill you!"

"Carl, you can't kill Sheila. You need to calm down," said Jim.

Carl swung the gun back toward Jim. "Did you do this? Did you get him out?"

"Carl, I've been standing right here. You've been talking to me. How would I do that? It's just me. I'm alone."

"If I shoot you, he'll come out. He'll come out to save you."

"Carl, you don't want to do that. You need me. We have to save Eden. You can't do that without me."

"I can't do it without HIM!" Carl yelled. "He has to eat the sins! If he doesn't cleanse the county, it will all burn! Everything! We'll all die!"

"We're not going to die, Carl. We're going to find three bad men, and Dr. Edwards will eat the sins. He'll do it if I ask him to do it. He's my friend."

"Are you sure?" Carl's voice quavered. "We have to save Eden."

"We will. I love Eden, too. We'll save it together."

Carl stepped out on the porch. He still held the gun, but the barrel had dropped toward the floor. "I only meant for the bad people to die. I didn't want the preacher to die. He was a savior. Just like Dr. Edwards. He saved people, and that's why I chose him. I thought someone so good would have to be able to save Eden, too."

"Donald Hatcher was a good man. He had a wife he loved and who loved him."

"He wouldn't eat the meals. He got the first one down, but when I brought him the second one, he started vomiting, and I tried to stop it, and he died."

"You didn't mean to kill him."

"He just died. I didn't kill him. He just stopped breathing. I did right by him, as much as I could. I washed his body and sweetened his body with good smelling things. I wanted him to be clean for his family."

"Did you know he had a rare blood type?"

Carl looked at Jim in surprise. "He did?"

"He donated regularly because he knew he could save lives. If we'd had his body sooner, he could have saved more. His organs would have saved lives. I met a man whose life he could have saved."

Tears began to run down Carl's face. "I didn't know."

"I know you didn't, Carl," said Jim. "But I don't know if God would want Eden saved this way."

Carl drew himself up, "He told me. I asked Him, and He showed me the way to save Eden."

"That was before Donald Hatcher died."

Chapter Sixty-Four

Ryan thought seriously about walking out of the woods right then, but he couldn't. He wouldn't let that madman take him again. If Jim could talk him down…Ryan realized he was shaking. His entire body was shaking with fear. He couldn't let Jim die. He had a son. Michael needed his father, and the town needed its sheriff.

Dammit, he thought. He'd spent so much time building up his body, making himself stronger so he would never be a victim again. He was a victim. He'd never not be a victim.

Ryan walked out of the woods and into the front yard. He heard twin fucks, one from Dee and one from Jim.

Ryan looked at Carl. "I'll eat your damn food," he said. "I'll help you, but you have to let the Sheriff find you the bad men to kill. He'll be better at it than Sheila, and hell, maybe he'll bring them to you so you don't have to go and fight them."

Carl pointed the gun at him. "You promise?"

Ryan nodded. "Yes. But you have to let Sheila go, too. She's giving me a headache with all her screaming. And you put that damn gun up. You shoot anyone, and I will disappear again. I'm good at doing that."

"I nailed the door shut," Carl said.

"Yeah, you did. Didn't stop me, did it? I think maybe God wasn't too happy about the way things were going, because all of a sudden, I found myself outside again. I could hear you and Sheila screaming at each other and you shooting up the house."

Carl's mouth dropped open, and when he finally spoke, it was a whisper.

269

"You mean it was a miracle? Right here?"

Ryan nodded. He swallowed hard. "Yeah. It was a miracle. I think he's unhappy about the way you've been doing things."

"Did he give you a message?"

Ryan nearly laughed. He felt more than a little hysterical right at that moment. He'd stepped out of the woods and faced the man who'd kidnapped him and who had been shooting up everything around him.

"What is it? What does he want me to do?"

"He said you should listen to the Sheriff. He said to tell you that you needed to listen to Jim Sheppard."

Ryan heard twin whispered fucks again. "The only way I'll help you is if you do whatever Jim tells you to do. And you have to let Sheila go."

"Sheila isn't the right person."

"No, she isn't the right person. Jim Sheppard is."

Ryan tried not to hold his breath as he waited for Carl to make his decision. He half expected the madman to raise the gun and shoot him in the head. He would deserve it. This was the dumbest damn thing he'd ever done.

He felt his body start to tremble. Carl looked at him intently, but he didn't raise the gun. Ryan felt like he wanted to drop to the ground and maybe take a nap for a couple hundred years. His ears rang and he felt his stomach start to roil again. "Carl, if you don't agree to this, I think maybe God's going to.....make me gone again. I'm feeling like I'm...."

Jim's voice interrupted. "He's looking pretty insubstantial, Carl. I think maybe he's fading."

Carl's face turned to Jim. "No! He can't fade! We need him!"

"Tick-tock," said Ryan softly.

Carl nodded his head. "All right."

"Sheila...," Ryan said.

"I'll get her now."

Carl turned around and went back into the house.

"I should shoot both of you stupid fuckers," said Dee from the side of the house.

Ryan was pretty sure he heard Jim snort.

Carl came back, dragging the chair that Sheila was tied to, putting her on the porch in front of them.

"Good, Carl. Thank you," said Ryan. "Now go give yourself over to Jim. You need to do whatever he says." Carl walked past him. Ryan took the butcher knife out of the pocket of the sweatpants and went to the porch, where he cut Sheila from the chair.

Chapter Sixty-Five

Carl walked to Jim and handed him the gun. "I'm sorry I got so angry, but Sheila wasn't helping me. Thank you for helping me. With you and Dr. Edwards, we can make everything work. I've been trying so hard."

"I know you have, Carl. I've seen what you've done."

Jim put his hand on Carl's shoulder and turned him around. Then he grabbed one of his wrists and clicked a handcuff on it.

"What are you doing?" Carl asked.

"I have to arrest you, Carl."

"What? No, you said you were going to help me!"

"You killed four men, Carl."

"Three were bad men. That Bass man was a really bad man. He hurt people for fun. Sheila and I saw him. He beat a man until he was senseless, and then he pounded his face against the floor. All because the man didn't tip him good enough."

"Yeah, he was like that. But his mother loved him, and she grieved for him. No matter how bad someone is, there's often someone who loves him. Same with Rountree. His father loved him. He searched for him in those woods after he disappeared."

Jim finished handcuffing Carl's hands behind his back.

"Granny said Eden was a holy place. She told me all about it. I dreamed of coming here all my life."

The sound of roaring wind rose up, and ashes and sparks began to fall out of the air. Carl looked up, "We can still save it. If you let me, we can still save it. I'll let you can arrest me after we're done."

"No, I can't," said Jim. "You know I can't."

"Dr. Edwards! Dr. Edwards, you have to tell him to help me! God told him to help me!"

Deputies came out of the woods. Jim pushed him toward Manny Soto, who grabbed him and began to march him away from the house.

Carl pushed against Manny, trying to get back to Jim. "You said you were alone! You lied to me! You lied to God! You said you were going to help me!"

As deputies ran out of the woods into the yard to help Manny with the struggling Carl, he continued to scream at Jim.

"No, no! This is wrong! Help me! Help me!"

Chapter Sixty-Six

The crackling of the fire got louder, and Dee ran from the side of the house and grabbed Sheila, and pushed Ryan toward Jim.

"Let's get out of here!" Dee yelled.

They ran, straight out into a pack of deputies. The deputies took Sheila. Ryan started to wobble, and Jim and Dee grabbed him, pulling him along as they all began to run. They were almost back to the road when they heard the explosion.

Jim, Dee, and Ryan stopped and looked back. Flames rose into the sky taller than the trees, bright and hot. "Gas," said Jim.

They turned and began to run again. When they reached the road, they saw that Carl had been placed in the back of Manny Soto's car. Sheila, wrapped in a silver shock blanket, curled up in the back seat of another car.

Bobby Dale let Rostrum out of the car where he'd been sitting. "What the hell happened? That was an explosion!"

"Gas kitchen?"

Rostrum said, "Yes."

"Gas and forest fires are a bad mix. The house is gone," said Dee.

Rostrum's knees folded, and Bobby Dale had to grab him. "Oh my God, it's gone?"

"We're lucky we weren't closer. We'd be dead," said Jim.

"It's gone?" Rostrum said more softly.

Jim snorted and pointed to one of the cars. "Get him back to his office, Bobby."

As Bobby dragged Rostrum away, Ryan started shaking again. Jim and

Dee both grabbed him and held him up until they could get him to the passenger seat of Dee's car.

"Sorry," said Ryan softly.

Dee laughed. "Are you apologizing for being in shock?"

Ryan looked at her and said, "I think so."

Jim shook his head. "I'll take him to Doc. You mind going with Manny and helping him book Basinger?"

"It will be my pleasure, sir." Dee snapped off a salute and headed back to Manny's car.

Jim got into the driver's seat, and Ryan looked at him. "I…suck at…savior thing."

Jim reached over and put his hand on Ryan's trembling arm. "We all do, Ryan."

"I…can't stop…shaking," said Ryan.

"Some of us shake during it, others shake after it. No one is built for this. We're not meant to be saviors."

"Okay," Ryan said. Then he fell back in the seat unconscious.

Chapter Sixty-Seven

Jim used his radio to notify Dee that he was taking Ryan into Gainesville to the Emergency Room. If Ryan was unconscious, this was more than something simple for the Doc. Plus, he looked like warmed-over shit. His nose was bent and bruised, and his right eye swollen shut. He had cuts on his arms and legs.

For the first time Jim realized the clothes he was wearing were too large. What the hell had Carl done to him?

He flipped on his lights and siren and took off for Gainesville as quickly as he could.

Fire trucks zoomed past him, headed in the opposite direction. There wouldn't be anything to save, but maybe they could keep the fire from reaching the road.

The drive seemed too long, but suddenly he was pulling into the ambulance lane in front of Shands' emergency room. Two orderlies with a gurney and a nurse immediately came out of the building and to the car. They efficiently removed Ryan from the passenger seat.

"Where can I meet you?" asked Jim.

"Sheriff, you're not meeting anyone. Have you looked at yourself?" asked the nurse.

Jim glanced into the rear-view mirror and saw that his uniform had holes in it where hot sparks had fallen on him. His hair was singed, and he smelled like a forest fire, which made sense.

"Oh," he said.

"Get inside, sir. Leave your keys. We'll have someone move the vehicle into a safe area."

Jim got out and felt his knees start to give. "What the fuck," he muttered.

"We've got you," said two other orderlies who had appeared out of nowhere. They grabbed his arms and helped him inside. He and Ryan were both taken into the treatment area. Ryan disappeared behind one set of curtains, and he was helped onto a bed in another cubicle.

Before he could grasp what was happening, a nurse had a blood pressure cuff on him and clipped an oxygen monitor onto his finger.

It would be some time before he saw Ryan again.

* * *

Jim opened his eyes and saw Dee sitting in a chair near him. "Hey."

Dee looked up from the magazine she was flipping through. "You ever pull a dumbass stunt like you did back at that house, I'm going to shoot you," she said.

"Fair enough."

She tossed the magazine aside. "The doc's fine. He's in a room upstairs. They're going to discharge him tomorrow after they've got him pumped full of fluids. He was dehydrated as hell, not to mention in shock. Got a broken nose, too."

"I noticed that."

"You are both idiots. It's a miracle there's enough of you men around to procreate with the shit you pull. Sir."

Jim grinned. "Yes, ma'am.

"I've been told I can take you home tonight. That you were just exhausted. Figured you'd sleep a few hours and be all right. Oh, and you're going to need a new uniform. The one you had on was burned to shit. Michael gave me some clothes for you."

"He knows I'm okay?"

"I told him you were too fucking stupid to die."

"Thank you."

Jim sat up slowly. "Carl at the jail?"

277

"Yeah. Still calling you a liar, too. Which you are."

"I had to get him out of the house."

"You got him out of the house. Almost burned up both your butts doing it. You're damn lucky he didn't shoot you."

"Sheila?"

"Stormed out of the emergency room talking about suing the county for making her miss a deadline with the best story of the year."

They both rolled their eyes.

"You take your time getting into those clothes, and then I'm taking you home. You got a son that's not going to stop worrying until he sees your sorry hide." She patted the jeans and shirt that sat on the side table. "I'll be right outside."

"You're really mad at me," Jim said.

Dee gritted her teeth, and her eyes got wide. "You walked out in front of a fucking madman with a gun and told him you were going to help him murder people to keep Eden from burning up. That kind of asinine shit could have gotten you shot, and...and...and I would have had to shoot him, and dammit, if you were dead, who would they get to be Sheriff? Some asshole white guy who wouldn't want a black woman sergeant, much less be arguing with her about letting him promote her. He'd want some other white asshole as a sergeant, and I'd be looking for a damn job and having to take out a loan for school, and no matter what I'd, I'd...well, I'd just be screwed."

"I'm sorry, Dee. I'm sorry I scared you and that you might have had to kill someone. I didn't think...."

"No! You didn't think. You pull that shit again, you do it with someone else as your backup. You get Manny or somebody."

"I promise."

She was quiet for a moment, then she patted the sheet over his leg. She took a deep breath and shook her head. "Dammit. Manny's good, but he might not know you enough. You'd better make sure it's me."

"I'll try to not do anything that stupid again."

She nodded and walked out of the room, closing the door behind her.

Jim smiled and wiped at the tears that were threatening. Dee Jackson wasn't just his sergeant, he realized. She was his friend. He wouldn't want anyone else backing him up. Not ever. And he was going to kick Tim Mackey's ass if he ever hurt her. She was too good for any man.

He moved slowly as he dressed. Jim hadn't realized how tired he'd gotten in the past few days. Stepping out into that driveway had been terrifying. He'd seen it as the only real option. The man was behind a locked door with two potential victims. He had to take the chance. Jim knew he was lucky that it had worked. His only other hope had been that Basinger was a lousy shot. But Dee was right. Had Basinger shot him, or tried to shoot him, she'd have had no choice but to shoot the man. That was not fair to her, or to any of the other deputies that had followed him into the dangerous situation.

When he opened the door and stepped into the hallway, Dee was waiting for him. They nodded to each other, neither really wanting to speak right then, and headed down the hall to check him out and take him home.

Dee held onto his arm as though she were afraid he'd wander off and do something else stupid. Who was he to argue? It was damn possible she was right.

Chapter Sixty-Eight

The week moved surprisingly fast. Carl Basinger had been assigned a decent public defender who'd immediately demanded a psych evaluation. It took the psychiatrist less than two hours to decide he was dangerously disturbed and recommend he be sent to Mcclenny, where the State Hospital would hold him until such time as he was competent to stand trial.

Jim didn't see that would happen any time soon.

Hatcher's body had been released to his wife for burial, and Elvin Rountree had had Mike cremated. He's taken the urn to the Cypress, where Edna Bass had let him hold a memorial service. Basically, everyone got drunk, and Elvin had punched out two guys from Libby's Dairy who'd called Mike a drug-dealing scumbag. Jim had let him go with a warning.

The goddamn swamp was still burning. The smell of burning peat continued to fill the air. Jim stood in the back yard and threw the tennis ball to Bonehead. Sometimes he bounced it off the fence. Sometimes he lobbed it high into the air. No matter where it went, Bonehead caught it and brought it back, obediently dropping it at his feet and waiting for him to throw it again.

Ryan sat on the steps. His eyes were still swollen, and he'd had two teeth loosened on one side that the emergency dentist at Shands had needed to treat so he wouldn't lose them. But he was very much alive.

Sheila Ward had written a front-page story about surviving near death at the hands of a madman, and according to Ronnie Weeks, she was turning it into a book.

The house where Carl Basinger had lived and where at least Donald Hatcher had died burned to the ground. Rostrum found out the owner had the place insured, so he was out the rental money, but the owner was actually happy.

In a move that had surprised the hell out of Jim, the County Commission had approved overtime pay for the deputies who had worked their own time on the case that was now being called "The Armageddon Murders" by every newspaper in Florida. They'd even put a letter of commendation in Jim's record. No extra money for him, but he'd been fine with that.

Michael came out of the house. "The stir-fry is ready," he called.

Bonehead came back with his tennis ball, and Jim looked at him and said, "Sorry, boy, we're going inside to eat. The dog dropped the ball and headed for the back door of Jim's house, where Michael stood waiting.

Jim turned to Ryan. "Are you allowed to have a beer?"

"I'm going to drink it whether I'm allowed or not," Ryan answered. He got up slowly. He'd also broken two ribs jumping out of the attic.

Jim worried about how quiet Ryan had been since that day, but Doc told him to give it time, that he was tough. He reminded Jim that Ryan had come back from a brain injury to practice medicine again.

Michael beamed with pride as the two men dug into the meal he'd made. Apparently, he'd actually paid attention when Ryan showed him how to use the wok. He'd gotten Junior to take him over to Gainesville where he'd bought one and some kind of special oil to use in it.

Jim had to admit that the food was really good, and it had actual vegetables in it. Jim had never known Michael to willingly eat vegetables, much less cook them. So, this was a win in many ways.

After dinner, Jim and Ryan washed the dishes. Michael disappeared into his bedroom. When everything was dried and put away, Jim and Ryan sat at the table with newly opened beers. Bonehead snored beneath Ryan's feet. Ryan shook his head and laughed.

"Danielle used to love it when he snored. One time I fell asleep on the couch, and he was asleep next to the couch, and she said she heard stereo snoring for the next hour."

Jim laughed.

Ryan took a deep breath. "You do know you were crazy stepping out into that driveway the way you did."

Jim shrugged. "I just knew I had to do something, or someone would get killed. And it's not like you didn't share in the crazy. I mean, you walked out of those woods and told him you'd eat the damn meals after I helped him find three men to kill."

"Dee was swearing the whole time you were out there."

"Yeah, that doesn't surprise me. She was pretty pissed off at me. She wasn't exactly happy with you either. She told me that it just proved all men were dumbasses."

Ryan turned the beer bottle in his hands, "It was the second time I'd gotten out. I didn't want to let myself be a victim. Never again."

"That's why you have to be strong."

Ryan nodded. "If I'd been stronger, I might have been able to save Danielle. I've always been tall, but I was skinny, and when he swung that bat, it broke my arm like it was a twig and smashed into my skull. I was in a coma for months. She was dead minutes later. I never saw her again, and I can't even remember that last time."

Jim set his bottle on the table. "Annie and I had a huge fight. She wanted me to come back to Warren and take a job with my father. Be a deputy. I wanted to teach history, and she did not want to be married to a teacher. She'd had her heart set on being a sheriff's wife since the day we started dating in high school. I'd never known that. So, she took Michael, and she left. The last thing she said to me was that I was a coward. That I didn't have the balls to be a sheriff, and she wanted a man as the father to her son. Not some weak-assed high school teacher."

"Wow."

"Yeah."

"But the whole time you were in school?"

"She thought I'd come to my senses. Realize where I belonged."

"That would be worth forgetting."

Jim nodded. "Yeah. It would. But I can't. And with her dead and Michael needing someone to take care of him, I took the job my father offered. My mother took care of Michael. I couldn't finish my master's and take care of him."

"So, you became a deputy."

"If I'd just said I would do that—"

"You couldn't have known."

Jim grinned. "Neither could you."

"We're quite the pair, aren't we?" said Ryan.

"A matched set."

Ryan tapped Jim's beer bottle with his own. "You're a good sheriff."

Jim took a sip of beer. "You're a lousy victim."

Ryan smiled, and then he began to laugh. "He never did realize I was getting out through the attic."

Jim smiled. "Well, he was a madman, not a genius."

"That's true."

They drank their beers silently.

"You think they'll ever put Carl on trial?" Ryan asked.

Jim shook his head. "Man's crazy as a rabid dog. He'll die in Mcclenny."

Ryan sighed, "I hope you're right."

Chapter Sixty-Nine

The smoke was still thick enough that the sun looked like a hazy red ball just above the trees. Traffic moved normally, the line at the drive-through at Mcdonald's was full. Jim carefully made his way across the street to the office. Junior sat at the front desk, tapping away at his keyboard. His big shaved head reflected the fluorescent lights in the ceiling.

Two deputies in the bullpen two-finger typed their reports on the computers at the desks. Jim set a large Mountain Dew with no ice on the counter in front of Junior. Junior's broad smile greeted him.

Jim nodded toward the deputies at the desks. Junior took a long sip of his Mountain Dew then said, "Speeder on 27. He tried to run for the county line."

Jim shook his head. "Anybody hurt?

"Nah. Just his pride. Bobby Dale was waiting at the county line with stop strips. He's going to have to buy all new tires."

"Good."

Jim waved to the deputies as he headed for his office. The air conditioning blew hard from the vents along the ceiling. The heat hadn't improved in the new month, and the fires had gotten worse. About the only thing left to burn in Eden was the beach grass, and Jim was pretty sure it would go at some point.

He'd just sat down when Junior called out to him, "Call for you, Sheriff!"

Jim looked at the blinking light and sighed. He'd hoped to at least have a chance to look at his calendar before his day started full-on. That daydream wasn't happening today and probably wouldn't happen anytime in the near future.

He picked up the receiver. "Sheriff Sheppard speaking."

"Sheriff, I'm Dr. Specter. More specifically, I'm Carl Basinger's doctor."

Jim's first thought was that Basinger had died, but the doctor continued.

"He asked me to contact you. He said that he needs to speak with you. That there is something he must explain about what happened in Eden County."

One of the last things in the world that Jim ever wanted to do was to hear Basinger's voice again. His nightmares were still plagued with the sound of the man explaining what they had to do to save Eden from the fires. He hadn't told anyone. He'd thought about telling Ryan, but that seemed unfair. The man probably had nightmares of his own.

"I think that it's very important in his coming to understand the reality of his crimes that he speak with you. I wouldn't ask, but if he can truly grasp what he has done, then he will be able to face his peers in a trial and accept the justice that is meted out to him."

"I'm sorry, Dr. Specter. I can't do that."

The silence on the other end of the line was heavy. "He asked for you. He said it was important that he speak to you. That you would understand."

"I don't, and I won't." Jim hung up the phone.

He looked up, and Dee stood in his doorway. "You don't and won't what?"

Jim leaned back in his chair and looked at Dee's dark, serious face. If he didn't tell her himself, she would find a way to get the information. It made her both the good cop she was and a pain in his ass at the same time.

"Basinger wants to talk to me. His doctor thinks I should."

Dee's head bobbed a little as she thought about it. "I'm going with you."

"Who said I was going?" Jim asked.

Dee snorted and started to turn around to leave. "You act like I don't know you."

Jim ground his teeth as he watched her walk away. He didn't want to go. The last thing in the world he wanted was to hear that man's voice telling him how they were going to save Eden. Justifying the horrible things he'd done through some Biblical mumbo-jumbo.

On the other hand, if he didn't go, he'd spend God knows how many nights lying in bed staring into the dark and wondering what the hell the man had to say, and if he was making a horrible mistake by not finding out.

If Dee went with him, would Basinger talk? Jim smiled. He damn well would if he wanted to say anything to him. He would not be the only one to hear it. There'd be no denial of what had been said. No bullshit from a doctor that the delusional man could say things he didn't mean.

Basinger might be delusional, but he acted on every damn idea his head came up with, and he likely would do it again, given the opportunity. Better to know than to not know. If he was going to lie awake and worry, he sure as hell was going to know what it was that he was worrying about.

"Jackson!"

Dee appeared in the door as though she'd been standing just to the side of it. Probably had been, waiting for him to argue with himself and come to the same conclusion she had without ever having to think about it.

"Yes, Sheriff?"

"You want to ride to Mcclenny with me?"

Dee smiled. Bright white teeth in her dark face showed menacingly. "Yes, sir."

"Then let's go beard the lion in his den."

Chapter Seventy

Jim had Junior call and let Doctor Specter know he would be in Mcclenny in less than two hours. Jim let Dee drive. Her department-issued car would make the trip more easily, and it would allow him time to calm himself without having to focus on driving. Dee had already set her mind to what she would be doing, so he didn't even have to think about that.

When they reached the gate, Dr. Specter had already called in passes for both Sergeant Dee Jackson and Sheriff James Sheppard. Clearly, Junior made it clear that both individuals were to be allowed in to see Basinger, whether that was what he or anyone else wanted.

Dee parked, and they made their way into the main entrance, and Dr. Specter waited for them. A short, squat man with thinning dark hair, the doctor made no bones about not being pleased at Dee's presence. He did show enough sense not to try to stop her from accompanying Jim to the building and room where they would see Basinger.

"As I said to you on the phone, I believe this will be good for Carl's rehabilitation. To face you and tell you whatever it is he wants to say, will be a big step for him."

Dee's cough didn't quite cover the word bullshit, but it delivered every ounce of her doubt that anything the doctor or Basinger had to say would amount to anything anyone wanted to hear.

"I'm not sure that bringing the Sergeant with you into the interview room will make Carl feel comfortable."

Jim laughed. "I don't care if HE's comfortable."

Dr. Specter frowned but said nothing more.

Jim saw no reason to make Basinger comfortable. In fact, being uncomfortable would probably be to Jim's advantage. One thing about it, Dee would not present a friendly face to the man. He'd caused a lot of pain in Eden County, and neither of them would forget that. Ever.

The hallway to the room had that institutional smell, disinfectant, human sweat, and stale air. Behind each door existed an example of human misery, either within one tortured mind, or a combination of one tortured mind and the crimes it had committed. Jim thought there were ghosts in this building, and none of them were happy.

The room where they would talk to Basinger had a guard and a locked door. A small window only showed bare walls. When it was opened, Basinger was seated at a table. Another guard stood against the back wall.

Dr. Specter followed them in. He spoke softly to Carl, "Sheriff Sheppard is here to speak to you, Carl. Would you like me to stay?"

Carl's eyes never strayed from Jim. "No."

Dr. Specter seemed surprised, but he nodded and quickly exited. There was one chair across from Basinger. Jim sat down.

Dee took up a position directly to the right of Jim and one step behind.

"I don't want her here. I just want to talk to you."

"Then I guess we won't be talking." Jim began to rise, and Basinger waved his hand. "Fine, fine. Let her stay."

Jim sat back down.

"Sergeant, would you like me to get you a chair?" asked the guard against the back wall.

"Thank you, no. We won't be here that long," said Dee without ever taking her eyes off Basinger. She smiled. Jim almost smiled seeing her, but he managed to keep his face as expressionless as possible. He didn't want to give Basinger anything to work with.

The silence before Basinger finally sighed and spoke was short. "I was wrong, Sheriff. I realize that now. I had it all wrong about Eden County. I made a mistake. I misunderstood the message. I've done a lot of thinking and praying while I'm here, and I know that. If I'd taken more time, it would have been clearer to me. I wouldn't have hurt that preacher or the doctor. I had it all wrong."

Jim and Dee both remained silent.

Carl glanced at Dee, and then he turned his body and his focus onto Jim. "I've been studying the Bible. I've been trying hard to understand how I could have been so wrong, and it was because I hurried. I didn't give God time to make it clear to me. I did wrong, and I will pay for that. I know that, and I'm all right with that. I'll stand and take my judgment when it's time. I'm prepared for that.

"It wasn't about stopping the fire. That wasn't what was supposed to happen. I know that now. I found the answer, and I did terrible things that I will be punished for, but now I also know what was supposed to happen. I know what I need to do."

"What you need to do?" asked Jim.

"Awake, O sword, against my shepherd and against the man that is my fellow, saith the Lord of hosts: smite the shepherd, and the sheep shall be scattered: and I will turn mine hand upon the little ones. And it shall come to pass that to all the land, saith the Lord, two parts therein shall be cut off and die; but the third shall be left therein. And I will bring the third part through the fire and will refine them as silver is refined and will try them as gold is tried: they shall call on my name, and I will hear them: I will say, it is my people: and they shall say, The Lord is my God."

A black hand slammed down on the table between Basinger and Jim, making both of them start.

"You will not raise any damn sword against any damn Sheppard, because you are going to spend the rest of your sorry life rotting in this place. And if you try, I can promise you that you just think that judgment waits. 'Cause judgment is going to come from a bullet from my gun. Only I won't kill you, Carl. I'll just maim you. I will hurt you in a way that you can't imagine, and I will stand over you, and I will watch you suffer, but I won't let you die. No, I will make sure you live, and you will spend the rest of your life trying to figure out exactly where you fucked up. But I can tell you the answer right now. You fucked up the minute you drove across the line into Eden County.

You may think it's paradise, but I will ensure that hell rains down on you every day for the rest of your life, because you will never, ever recover from what I will do to you. Do you understand me?"

Basinger sat, eyes wide, mouth hanging open.

"I SAID, DO YOU UNDERSTAND ME?"

"Yes." Carl's voice was very soft.

"Good. I would hate for you to do anything without knowing what the consequences will be."

Dee stood up straight, touched the Sheriff on the shoulder, and motioned with her head. Jim stood up, and together they left the room.

Dr. Specter stood in the hall, his face pale. "I didn't know…" he started.

"Shut the fuck up," said Dee, and she walked Jim out of the building and back the way they came. They were in the car pulling out onto the County Road before Jim managed to say anything.

"Sheppard?"

"In the Bible, it's spelled like the sheep herd, but there's no doubt what that dumb bastard thinks it means."

"Fuck," whispered Jim.

"Don't worry, sir. I gave him a little something to think about." Dee looked over at him and grinned. "Black hell will rain down on him, sir. He's going to be afraid of that. And I damn well mean it. He won't know what the fuck hit him, and when I finish, he will suffer for the rest of his natural life. I will make damn sure of that. And you, sir, will survive. No Sheppards are dying on my watch."

Jim leaned back in his seat. He didn't fear Basinger. Should the man get out, he'd just warned Jim about what he had planned. Plus, if the man was stupid enough to not take Dee Jackson seriously, that would not be Jim's fault. Black hell, indeed.

A Note from the Author

Eden County is fictional. It is based on the landscape and the small populations of a number of counties in North Florida. The characters in the book are entirely invented and are not based on any individuals who live in this region.

Acknowledgements

First of all I want to thank Harriette Wasserman Sackler. She saw promise in the first three chapters, kept in touch, asked to read it when the book was finished, and then offered me a contract. I'm aware of how rare this is, and I'm grateful. Nick Byrd explained to me how County Sheriff's offices are set up in Florida and provided information on investigating crimes. Neil Plakcy told me I was writing a police procedural. Alan Orloff gave me advice on things that a writer should know to do with a first book's publication. Loretta Sue Ross educated me about reviewers. Pat Payne read everything I wrote, corrected my typos and told me that the work was good. Several members of Sisters In Crime offered advice about how to classify my police procedural, offered tips on cover text and showed me covers of their police procedurals—so thank you, Annette Dashofy, Marcy McCreary, and Cindy Pauwels! A special thank you to Dr. James Sunwall for being my friend and mentor.

About the Author

Sarah Bewley has been a freelance writer, a playwright, a licensed private investigator, a homeschool tutor, and held administrative positions in medical offices and nonprofits. She lives in Gainesville, Florida with Patrick Payne, a visual artist. Burning Eden is her first book in the Eden County Mysteries series.

SOCIAL MEDIA HANDLES:
  https://twitter.com/WPAdmirer
  https://www.facebook.com/sarah.bewley.50
  https://www.instagram.com/wpadmirer

AUTHOR WEBSITE:
  https://www.sarahbewley.com

Milton Keynes UK
Ingram Content Group UK Ltd.
UKHW010625100823
426647UK00001B/81

9 781685 123444